Some people say probing other planets for intelligent life is an exciting, romantic job. As far as I'm concerned, that only goes to show they've never done it. Me, I do it for a living, and I'm here to tell you it's nothing but a pain in the orifice. The air smells funny even when you can breathe it, the animals smell even worse (and taste worse than that, half the time), and even when we do find people, they're usually backward as all get-out. If they weren't, they would have found us, right? Right.

Down we went, into the atmosphere. Iffspay—he's my partner—and I rolled dice to find out who got stuck wearing the calm suit. I give you three guesses. The calm suit we needed for this planet is the most uncomfortable one in the whole masquerade cabinet. It's bifurcated at the bottom, it's got tendrils near the top, and then an awkward lump at the very top. Guess who got to put it on. I'll give you a hint: it wasn't Iffspay. I think he uses loaded dice. Before we could really start quarreling, the heat-seeker indicated a target. Three targets, in fact, grouped close together.

Trouble was, they were at the edge of a swamp. I worried that they might escape into the water or into the undergrowth, calm suit or no calm suit, before I could slap the paralyzer ray on them and we could antigravity them up into the ship. And if they did—if even one of them did—we'd have to go through this whole capture-and-release business somewhere else on the planet, too. Once was plenty. Once was more than plenty, as a matter of fact.

—From "Hi, Colonic" by Harry Turtledove

I, ALIEN

EDITED BY
MIKE RESNICK

DAW BOOKS, INC.
DONALD A. WOLLHEIM, FOUNDER
375 Hudson Street, New York, NY 10014

ELIZABETH R. WOLLHEIM
SHEILA E. GILBERT
PUBLISHERS
http://www.dawbooks.com

First Printing, April 2005
1 2 3 4 5 6 7 8 9

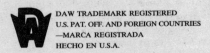

DAW TRADEMARK REGISTERED
U.S. PAT. OFF. AND FOREIGN COUNTRIES
—MARCA REGISTRADA
HECHO EN U.S.A.

PRINTED IN THE U.S.A.

ACKNOWLEDGMENTS

"Introduction" copyright © 2005 by Mike Resnick.

"Diary of a Galactic Émigré" copyright © 2005 by Laura Resnick.

"The Injustice Collector" copyright © 2005 by Kristine Kathryn Rusch.

"Creature for Hire" copyright © 2005 by Paul E. Martens.

"Pedagogy" copyright © 2005 by Michael A. Burstein.

"The Last Wave" copyright © 2005 by Kay Kenyon.

"The Eagle Has Landed" copyright © 2005 by Robert J. Sawyer.

"Correspondence with a Breeder" copyright © 2005 by Janis Ian.

"Resident Alien" copyright © 2005 by Barbara Delaplace.

"Xenoforming Earth" copyright © 2005 by Tom Gerencer.

"The Skeptic" copyright © 2005 by Jennifer Roberson.

"Natural Selection" copyright © 2005 by Laura Frankos.

"Aortic Insubordination" copyright © 2005 by Batya Swift Yasgur and Barry N. Malzberg.

"Harvesting" copyright © 2005 by Nina Kiriki Hoffman.

"What Must Be" copyright © 2005 by Josepha Sherman.

"And I Will Sing a Lullaby" copyright © 2005 by Paul Crilley.

"Aquarius" copyright © 2005 by Susan R. Matthews.

"First Contract" copyright © 2005 by Linda J. Dunn.

"Anakoinosis" copyright © 2005 by Tobias S. Buckell.

"Threshold" copyright © 2005 by Terry McGarry.

"Nobodies" copyright © 2005 by Adrienne Gormley.

"The Loaves and the Fishes" copyright © 2005 by John DeChancie.

"Alien Ground" copyright © 2005 by Anthony R. Lewis.

"Hi, Colonic" copyright © 2005 by Harry Turtledove.

"Acts" copyright © 2005 by William Sanders.

"Life Happens" copyright © 2005 by Ralph Roberts.

"You" copyright © 2005 by Stephen Leigh.

"Me" copyright © 2005 by Mike Resnick.

CONTENTS

INTRODUCTION

by Mike Resnick

SCIENCE FICTION LOVES aliens. We've had cute aliens, frightening aliens, brilliant aliens, stupid aliens, friendly aliens, hate-filled aliens, lustful aliens, aliens who think and sound just like us, and aliens whom we will never begin to understand.

The true alien is a cypher that doesn't serve much use in science fiction. If he exists—excuse me: if *it* exists—it probably breathes methane, excretes bricks, smells colors, reproduces by budding, and has totally different concepts (if it has any at all) of love, hate, fear, and pain.

So, very early on, science fiction writers learned to use aliens as metaphors for various aspects of the human condition—as a funhouse mirror they could hold up to humanity to examine whatever happens to be pleasing or annoying the writer that particular day.

The history of science fiction is filled with aliens, many of whom became more popular than the humans from the same stories. You can go all the way back to Tars Tarkas in the Martian stories of Edgar Rice Burroughs; the whole crew of Second Stage Lensmen in Doc Smith's Lensman saga; Tweel in Stanley G. Weinbaum's "A Martian Odyssey"; and on through memorable and beloved aliens created by Eric Frank

Russell, Roger Zelazny, Vonda McIntyre, and dozens of others, right up to Chewbacca in the *Star Wars* saga.

Every science fiction writer has created aliens at one time or another. Even Isaac Asimov, who populated his robotic and Foundation futures with nothing but humans, eventually got around to it in *The Gods Themselves*. And certainly every writer in this book has created aliens in previous stories.

But this time we asked them to do something different. Remember that I said aliens were incomprehensible? Well, not anymore—because each author was asked to write a story in the first person of an alien. The aliens in these stories are not just the main characters; they're the narrators.

Last year I edited *Men Writing Science Fiction as Women* and *Women Writing Science Fiction as Men* for DAW Books. Those were nice imaginative stretches, but nothing compared to the stretching the authors in this book were asked to do.

And, being science fiction writers, they succeeded in ways that surprised even the editor.

DIARY OF A GALACTIC ÉMIGRÉ

by Laura Resnick

GALATIC DATE: 17%.8*!0/MWUG PRETTY GIRL TUREEN

After a long and arduous journey during which I traveled five thousand light-years without a bathroom stop, I have arrived safely at my destination, code named "The Planet with Waffles" by the Interstellar Council on Covert Relocation (ICOCR). However, there were several mishaps during my voyage which made me fear I would not survive long enough to submit my application to the Bureau of Galactic Refugees, Escapees, and Synchronized Swimmers (BOGRESS) for my Relocated Interstellar Fugitive benefits.

The catastrophic explosion of my transport vehicle's sound system when I neglected to install proper safety devices before exposing it to With Wafflish music, code named "Britney Spears," caused my navigational system to malfunction. Consequently, I am not in the designated landing zone, code named "City of Angels." That destination was selected for me by ICOCR on the basis of a report in the seven hundred-fifty-third edition of *The Interdimensional Guide to Galactic Emigration* which cited experiential evidence indicating that my arrival would go unnoticed there. So I was very alarmed when I realized I had missed the target zone by quite some distance due to the technical malfunction which made my navigational system mistake virtually all landmarks for my former mother-in-law.

Fortunately, however, despite this problem, I seem to have landed in a zone as benign as the designated one, this one being code named, according to my observations, "Sin City." Despite causing some negligible destruction to indigenous machinery upon landing, my arrival attracted no serious attention and incited no comment beyond a few untranslatable exclamations from several natives making elaborate but incomprehensible gestures.

After emerging from my vehicle, I discovered that the transport pod's molecular-restructuring device was damaged during landing and no longer functioned. To quote the most sophisticated philosopher whom I have encountered in my background reading on the Planet with Waffles: It's always something. This mishap meant that I could not disguise the pod as a nuclear warhead, though I'd been informed that this was advisable in order to conceal evidence of my arrival and to protect the pod from discovery in the event of a laborious indigenous ritual, code named "UN weapons inspection."

Eager to avoid exposure as a newly-arrived interstellar fugitive from injustice, I immediately adopted the personal demeanor which ICOCR advised me is appropriate on the Planet with Waffles, which is to say that I began wriggling and drooling whenever encountering native inhabitants. Concerned about my inability to camouflage my transport pod as planned, I have spent the past three planetary solar cycles discreetly observing it from a nearby vantage point, code named "Caesar's Palace." I am now convinced that the pod arouses no curiosity, suspicion, or agitation in the indigenous life-forms of this hot, arid, rather garish locale. I believe I can safely abandon it.

Admittedly, I was alarmed at one point when a na-

tive armed with a club, a projectile weapon, and restraints approached the pod and spent some time
examining it. However, he merely made brief nota-
tions on a small piece of paper, which he then affixed
to the pod, and he walked away and has not returned.
Based on my information about With Wafflish customs, I believe he is offering me a written salutation
or else giving me a personal voucher for monetary
compensation.

With my demanding journey completed and my
anonymous arrival confirmed to my satisfaction, I now
turn my attention to fully assimilating myself into the
world of Waffles.

GALACTIC DATE: CORFU &^3>9?=*4$=9 VER-
VET MONKEY

I am, of course, merely guessing about the galactic
date, since I have yet to find a quasar-cycled time-
keeping matrix on this primitive planet. For the purpose of keeping an accurate record of my activities
here, I have attempted to reprogram an arcane but
readily-available informational system known as "Windows" to compute a galactic calendar by extracting
what logical reference points it can from the localized
sesquicentennial equinox balanced vertically against
the ratio of the adjusted theoretical galactic axis to
the mean acceleration of solar expansion.

To this end, I am encountering some technical
difficulties.

GALACTIC DATE: ABORT, RETRY, FAIL

My caseworker at the ICOCR recommended the
Planet with Waffles because of its obscurity in the galactic scheme of things. Her/his/its exact words were,
"No sentient being will ever find you in that remote
rear-liquid of a star system." (I believe he/she/it meant
"backwater," but universal translation devices are no-
toriously literal.)

My caseworker evidently gave me good advice, since

I have yet to spot a familiar race, let alone a seemingly intelligent one. Given the high price on my head back home, due to my fearless opposition of the Anti-Gravity Tax Penalty and my bold leadership of a rebellion which nearly brought down the government and all its hairdressers, I cannot risk coming into contact with any individuals who might recognize me, expose me, or send me back to the oppressive regime which has vowed to neuter me and take away my toys if I'm captured alive. (And what they've vowed to do to me if I'm captured dead is so cruel that I cannot bear to repeat it.)

Luckily, as my caseworker anticipated, my physiology ensures that I am so far passing as a native inhabitant of With Waffles. Unfortunately, however, With Wafflers seem to be a deeply suspicious race. Whenever I query individuals for information, they're alarmed to the point of hostility.

GALACTIC DATE: BATTLE OF HASTINGS, JULY 4, 1776

Yesterday, curious about the planet's code name, I entered an establishment where the natives consume waffles. I was shouted at, pointed at, kicked, and then chased back outside while being assaulted with sturdy objects.

Given the peculiar (even vulgar, if I may be so blunt) appearance of most With Wafflers, I find this treatment puzzling. It's clear that there is some manner in which I'm failing to assimilate. Unfortunately, my period of background reading and cultural instruction before coming here was limited, due to the haste with which I was obliged to flee my own planet—in my idealistic naiveté, I had never anticipated just how vindictive governmental hairdressers could be.

Anyhow, though I am speculating in an informational vacuum at the moment, observation has led me to wonder if I would encounter fewer difficulties among the With Wafflers if I covered my genitals, as so many of them do.

Of course, this notion may merely be a stress-response to my social and intellectual isolation on a primitive planet five thousand light-years from home.

Meanwhile, through further investigation, I discovered that partially used waffles are sometimes deposited in a receptacle code named "trash can." Using stealth and cunning, I managed to acquire one of these . . . and must now report my puzzled disappointment. It's rather like getting close enough to a spectacular nebula to discover that, in fact, it's just space rubble.

Still lingering in the vicinity of Caesar's Palace for the time being, I remain uncertain of my plans and increasingly confused about the actual date.

GALACTIC DATE: FILE 404, ERROR
Disaster! I have been seized by my enemies!

GALACTIC DATE: SLURP MURMTAG 17 MINUS Σ
According to the time-traveling Glamorgellian scientist in the cell next to mine, my captors are not, as I feared, mercenaries preparing to collect the bounty on my head by returning me to my home planet to face unspeakable punishment. Instead, it seems that my disguise has been *too* effective, in a manner of speaking, and I am now incarcerated as an indigent member of a native With Wafflish species, code named "man's best friend."

The victuals in this facility are tolerable, though far from exciting. My quarters are not uncomfortable, but the abundance of odors overwhelms my senses.

GALACTIC DATE: MOZART MOZZARELLA MUEZZIN MUZZLE
Captivity is proving to be surprisingly educational. The time-traveling Glamorgellian scientist, code named

"Spot," has been on the Planet with Waffles for seventeen centuries—or five minutes, or sixty-four metric tons, depending on which time-keeping system you use. In any event, an experienced veteran of this planet, he is a veritable font of information about it.

However, he's not sure of the galactic date either.

GALACTIC DATE: FOR A GOOD TIME, CALL STELLA 555-7413

According to Spot, I am physically identical in every way to a popular indigenous With Wafflish subspecies, code named "Golden Retriever." Spot assures me that I was given good advice about the wriggling and drooling, but someone at ICOCR should have cautioned me against questioning the natives. My repeated attempts to communicate, in search of information, appear to be what attracted suspicion to me and led to my being incarcerated here. According to Spot, my conversational overtures were almost certainly misinterpreted as hostile, or at least annoying.

Additionally, I now learn, I was not given the requisite accessories, talismans code named "collar and tags," which virtually all extraterrestrial species here need in order to move about without undue interference (and eventual incarceration).

ICOCR is going to receive a *very* angry communication from me about this idiotic oversight.

Moreover, I'm not the only one. By now, I've recognized nearly twenty other sentient races imprisoned in this facility, most of them having arrived on this planet without suitable talismans, either.

Spot assures me, however, that I am likely to be released soon, thanks to a bureaucratic loophole, code named "adoption," which is usually applied to members of my species. This is fortunate compared to his own situation. Spot tells me he resembles a Wafflish subspecies code named "bull terrier," and consequently encounters not only legal difficulties wherever he goes, but also projectile weapons. Given that Glamorgellians developed time travel, interdimensional travel, and chew toys, I find the With Wafflish attitude to Spot's race truly shocking. Spot, however, assures me that he's accustomed to it after five minutes or seventeen hundred years or sixty-four metric tons, and has even grown to enjoy his sojourn on this planet. His assignment here, which he is currently wrapping up, has been to study the effects of global warming on processed organ meats in a carbon-based planetary system. So far, his findings are staggering in their galactic implications.

GALACTIC DATE: PUCE

According to the Shirulian explorer code named "Lassie" in the cell on my other side, our situation is more precarious than Spot or I realized. If we aren't adopted within a specified number of solar cycles, we face execution.

This strikes me as a rather severe penalty for traveling without talismans.

When my caseworker at ICOCR warned me that the Planet with Waffles is a primitive, backward place, I should have taken her more seriously.

Fortunately, Lassie has a plan. There is a rebel group which she believes can be convinced to attack this facility and free us. Members of the current dominant species on this planet, they are sophisticated enough to oppose the execution policies which currently threaten our lives. Unfortunately, they are also too timid to act without sufficient influence from someone among us. However, Lassie, like all Shirulians, possesses telepathic abilities and—what luck!—has experience in astral projection. Under her influence, the rebels are expected to attack tonight.

GALACTIC DATE: THAT NIGHT
Success!

GALACTIC DATE: 42
Upon being set free by the rebels, Spot (depending on which time-keeping system you use) went home to

his own space and time, or will go home to it, or is gaining mass and weight there. He intends to publish his findings on global warming and processed organ meat so that an interstellar exploratory committee can be established to examine the ramifications of his research. Lassie, remarkably well assimilated into Wafflish culture, is on her way back to Hollywood to resume her career.

Meanwhile, I have been adopted by a member of the antiexecution rebel league, and she has provided me with the appropriate talismans to protect me from another episode of incarceration. I have filed a complaint against the ICOCR for their life-endangering negligence. For the time being, I am working on a comprehensive guide to With Wafflish customs so that other galactic fugitives may be better prepared than I was for the pitfalls of assimilating into this world.

THE INJUSTICE COLLECTOR

by Kristine Kathryn Rusch

R ECORD OF PROCEEDING
  Incident at Gray's Brook
Injustice Collector 0080 Presiding

Testimony of Requesting Party

They trusted us with their children.

Later, they claimed they trusted us because we resembled animals from their world. Canines. I have
seen representations of such things, and the resem-
blance is superficial.

We are thinner, taller, and we do not stand on all
fours. (Many of my people were insulted by this
implication—that we could not walk upright—but I
was more insulted by the look of the beasts: shaggy,
unkempt, and that appendage at the base of the spine—
the tail—looked vaguely ominous to me, as if the creatures were slapped together by a careless scientist.)

It is true that we do not have bald skin as the humans do; ours is dusted attractively with fine hairs,
making each of us distinctive. Our noses are larger
and our mouths open beneath them—perhaps the
most canine of our features—but we, as a people, have
come to resent the word *snout*.

As for the rest, we do not see ourselves as too dif-

11

ferent from the humans. We use our arms in much
the same way, we have hands, we wear clothing. It is
true that we do not wear shoes, but the bottoms of
our feet are tough and hair-covered. We do not injure
as easily as the humans do.

Which, I suppose, is the heart of the problem.

They came half a season ago. Their ships were shiny
and silver, made of materials we had not seen before.
Their leaders offered to teach us how to create such
materials, but the lessons never happened—one of
many such incidents. Among my tribe, the humans
have became known as the People of Broken
Promises.

The humans created a settlement on the ice plain,
not realizing, of course, that we were in summer, and
the plain was at its best. Trees flowered, insects buzzed,
and a thousand varieties of summer vegetation grew
across the expanse. The air, thick with humidity, was
nearly unbearable to us; to them, it spoke of
comfort—the "tropics," "paradise," and other words
that we did not then know.

We did know that soon the fall would come with
its rains, destroying all but the hardiest of plants.
Those would die in the cold, buried beneath the sheet
of ice that gave the plain its name.

We doubted the humans would survive the fall, let
alone the cold. We did not tell them of the cycle,
believing that such warning would reward ignorance.

That is why we did not contact the Injustice Collector at the theft of land.

We believed justice had taken care of itself.

Interruption in the Proceeding
*Two Cycles into the Requesting Party's Testimony,
A Breach of Protocol:*
    Breach of Protocol by the creatures known as
human require in-depth reporting methods not em-
ployed in two centuries of Injustice Collecting. The

humans, it seems, are unfamiliar with the concept of Justice/Injustice. They believe such decisions might be rendered on the small scale, and as a result, have appealed to me in unorthodox ways, which under rules 7,765 and 11,235 I am obligated to report.

As a result, my presence will intrude on the record of these proceedings. I beg the Review Board's indulgence.

—Injustice Collector 0080

Explanatory Note:

This meeting is taking place, as is customary in cases of cultural disputes, in the Great Hall of the Collecting Ship. Four members of the Requesting Party, both male and female, stand to the left. Twenty members of the Non-Requesting Party stand to the right.

Both sides have been instructed in the rules of the proceedings, although for the two days of rules' instructions, only two of the humans attended.

Since the number of humans has grown significantly, I can only assume the added eighteen were not briefed by their colleagues.

[*An Aside*: Working conditions are barely tolerable. The Great Hall barely accommodates all of these bodies. As is mentioned in the opening testimony, these human creatures are as large as the MugwL. The crowd presses against my Decision Desk. The temperature in the Great Hall has risen significantly. The Collecting Ship's systems are not designed to accommodate so many heat-giving sources in such a small area.

[To complicate matters, both the MugwL and the humans have distinctive—and competing—odors. The MugwL's fur stinks of rone spice—a sharp peppery scent that invades the nostrils—and the humans, beneath the coating odor of soap, give off a musk that burns the eyes. When I inquired, I was told that such an odor is called a "nervous sweat" and it cannot be controlled. Human suggestions to control the temperature were ignored as untenable. My suggestion that some of the human party leave was met with severe protests. However, if the stench worsens, I will be forced to cut the human presence in half.]

The Non-Requesting Party is inattentive and disrespectful. They speak without tone—in something called a "whisper"—and believe they cannot be heard.

They have obviously not met an Injustice Collector before. They seem to believe that because I am small and do not have features they can readily identify, I am somehow less than they are.

Already, I can see why the MugwL find them so intolerable.

The Breach of Protocol began when the MugwL Representative stated, "That is why we did not contact the Injustice Collector at the theft of land."

The "whispering" rose to an intolerable level, and one human, not one of the original two (I believe, since it is hard to tell—the bald skin is, as the MugwL implied, offensive), cried out, "We didn't steal! We asked permission to settle there!"

The MugwL Representative continued over the disturbance, adding his phrase, "We believed justice had taken care of itself."

At which another of the humans, one of the tallest, turned toward the MugwL so quickly that I feared violence.

"You fucking bastard," the human said—and judging by its tone, the words *fucking bastard* are an insult. "First you kill our children, now you tell us it's our fault! Judge, this is all wrong. You gotta hear our case—"

I clapped two of my hands for silence, and to my surprise, the human complied. Perhaps it was the spray of red light that flew from my fingertips. That seems to impress the lesser species.

As I clapped with two hands, I used the other three to set the collection bag beneath the Decision Desk. It became clear to me in that moment that the humans do not understand the proceedings.

I do not sit in Judgment, therefore I am not a Judge. I merely listen to the reports and determine to whom the Injustice has occurred. Then I collect it.

Or rather, the bag does. Most of my efforts go toward corralling the bag.

I try to explain this to the humans again (more confirmation that the initial human representatives did not report back to their colleagues), but the humans did not seem to understand.

More "whispering" occurred, and a common sentence wound its way through the Non-Requesting Party: *It's obvious that we have suffered the injustice. Our children are dead.*

If matters of Justice/Injustice were so easily determined, there would be no need for the Decision Desk. Again, I explain, but the humans seem confused.

They seem to believe that the decision is a judgment which I would therefore make. They do not seem to understand the distinctions required by the customs of the Alliance.

I call for a recess, insist that both Parties leave the Ship, and order scrubbers into the Great Hall to attempt to alleviate the stench.

Then I transmit my request for assistance to the Board of Governors.

I tell them I am concerned that I might commit an Injustice myself.

Excerpts from the 500-page Gubernatorial Response to Inquiry Presented by Injustice Collector 0080 in regard to Non-Requesting Party Involved in the Incident at Gray's Brook [Requesting Party Reference: MugwL Case 3345678221]:

The self-named Humans are an unknown, unstudied species. A careful search of the records reveals that they have never been a Requesting, Non-Requesting, Peripherally Involved, or Bystanding Party in any Justice/Injustice proceeding . . .

Cases involving unknown, unstudied species must proceed as if the species is sentient, according to Justice/Injustice standards . . .

. . . and so, to satisfy your request, we had to return to the earliest records of Justice/Injustice proceedings, in which species now known to us [but which were, at the time of the proceedings, unknown] established Justice/Injustice Precedent . . .

. . . what the early Injustice Collectors learned was that the bags did not accept as an Injustice cases presided over by an Injustice Collector in which a Party of Unknown Sentience did not understand the intricacies of the proceeding . . .

Therefore, certification continues in the Incident at Gray's Brook, also known as Requesting Party Reference: MugwL Case 3345678221.

Record of Proceeding
Incident at Gray's Brook
Injustice Collector 0080 Presiding

Testimony of Requesting Party [continued]
Human children are curious creatures. They share some traits with the adults of the species, but no one would intuitively understand that such a small creature, less than a meter in length at first appearance, would eventually become the towering figures now standing to my left.

In fact, we had no idea at the time of the incident that the creatures called "children" were also a type of "human." We believed them to be a related Earth species, rather like the Canine we had referred to in our previous remarks.

It is counterintuitive to believe these creatures would grow at such an astounding rate. It is also counterintuitive to believe that a group traveling the great distances that the humans traveled would bring the young of the species, carrying with it the very future of the species itself.

We therefore request that the surviving children join this proceeding as the Bystanding Party—

Interruption in the Proceeding
Eight Cycles into the Requesting Party's Testimony, A Breach of Protocol:
This protocol breach [and, I am certain, all others] are caused by the factors listed in the Second Cycle breach described above. I see no reason to repeat that finding here. In future breaches, I shall simply describe the breach, and continue with the Report of the Proceeding.

If any member of the Review Board has an objection, I refer him to the Board of Governors' Response to the Official Inquiry on the Humans [attached above].

—Injustice Collector 0080

"Your Honor," said the human who, before this morning's proceedings, introduced himself [they assure me that this creature is a male] as the one in charge. At my request, he wears a large red badge which lists his designation: John Graf. I do not know what these words stand for; I know only that I am to use them whenever I refer to the human with the red badge. "You can't let them do this."

The "them" in that sentence refers to the Requesting Party. The "this" refers to the introduction of the "children" as the Bystanding Party.

I cite regulations, as I have done for days now. The "humans" apparently have a short attention span. We discussed the rights of the Requesting Party in regard to the Bystanding Party on the first day of the explanatory proceedings.

"No, sir," the John Graf human said, "I'm afraid *you* don't understand. By our laws and customs, the only people who speak for our children are their parents."

I do not know this word "parents" and I tell the John Graf so.

His bald skin turns an alarming shade of red, nearly the color of his badge, and I am concerned that my words have harmed him physically. The "whispering" begins again, and I beg for silence.

Then I tell the John Graf that he may recess for medical treatment if he so desires.

His tiny features press together, as if he is trying to make them into a MugwL face. "I'm in perfect health, Your Honor."

He sounds—and I am merely guessing—offended. I look down at the bag which I have stored under the Decision Desk to see if it detects an Injustice that I may have inadvertently caused, but it hasn't even twitched.

"I just find it appalling that you don't know what parents are," the John Graf says. His voice has risen to an intolerable level. "I'm opposed to a legal proceeding when our cultures are so different that we have to explain something as basic as parenthood."

I hold up my middle hand. "We are discussing 'parents,' not 'parenthood.' Please do not confuse the issue."

He makes a blatting sound, like the wind through a malfunctioning weezer engine.

"I am not confusing any issue," he says. "You people are. We can't continue with this charade any longer."

Another concept I do not know. But I do not ask him to explain it, since I am beginning to agree with the MugwL's characterization of the humans as People of Broken Promises. I ask the John Graf to explain "parents" and instead, he confuses the issue by adding two more unknown words into the proceedings.

No explanation of "parents" appears to be forthcoming.

"We're leaving," the John Graf says.

The nineteen other humans nod in agreement. They all turn toward the Great Hall doors, but I do not open them.

"You cannot leave when the Proceedings are underway," I tell them. "The doors will only open in case of Recess or Final Determination."

[*An Aside*: I wish for nothing more than the opening of doors and the disappearance of the humans. The stench seems worse this day. My eyes have been burning since the presentation began.]

"We refuse to participate any longer," the John Graf says. "This is a joke!"

Joke. Another new word. I choose not to focus on it, but on the preceding sentence.

"You cannot refuse to participate," I remind him. "The time for that is past. You had from the moment the Request for a Justice/Injustice review was made to the Board of Governors to the moment the Collecting Ship arrived to demand a cancellation. You did not make such a demand. So the proceeding must continue."

"Another stupid law no one bothered to tell us about," the John Graf says, waving his arm downward, as if he is compacting a pile of snow.

"We should've just killed the fuckers," one of the other humans says, rather loudly. This is not a "whisper." I believe it was meant to be heard. "Blasted them all to hell and back for what they did to the kids."

Murmurs of agreement thread through the human crowd. The MugwLs look at me as if they expect me to stop it.

They should know better. If the humans take action, I can only observe. If the MugwLs or their survivors then believe that the human action was wrong, they can make yet another request for an Injustice Collector. I will become a Peripherally Involved Party, and will not sit on the Decision Desk.

[An Aside: I confess that such a change would please me. I find this case taxing, and would like as much as the humans for it to end.]

"It could've been an accident," says the John Graf. "It's pretty clear we don't understand these aliens any more than they understand us. I'm not going to be in charge of a genocide, even when—"

"Even when they kill our kids?" the other human asks.

The John Graf expels air, and shakes his head from side to side. He is clearly in charge, but the others do not agree with him. I fear trouble of a type I am not equipped to deal with.

I glance down. The bag has turned a light lavender. It is getting greedy. I slam its top closed with two of my hands, using the other two to twist the top into a knot. The bag fades, but I worry that this is just an act.

The John Graf is leaning close to his compatriots. "We've been here for fifty years," he says, as if this is important.

It sounds strange to me. The MugwL claimed in his opening testimony that the humans had only been here half a season, and I see no evidence to the contrary.

But the other humans do not disagree with that characterization. In fact, many of them nod which, as their representatives informed me on the first day, is a sign of assent.

"This is our home. Our children were born here," the John Graf is saying.

I am leaning toward the conversation, even though I hear it more clearly than the "whispering." The MugwL watch me as if they expect me to do something about this exchange.

At least the MugwL are smart enough to know that I will not interfere.

"Leaving is not an option," the John Graf says. "We must peacefully coexist."

"Even if they kill our kids," the vocal human states. Although the words sound like a question, they are not.

"That's what we're here to determine," the John Graf says. "Whether it was intentional or not. Right?"

At this last, he turns to me. He seems to be expecting a Judgment again, but I do not give it to him.

Instead, I do as I have done before. I recite the law and the history. "The MugwL have requested our presence because they believe an injustice may have occurred."

"Hell, yes, an injustice occurred," says the vocal human. "They murdered our children. That's an injustice."

"But you did not request the proceeding," I say. "They did."

The vocal human starts to answer, but the John Graf steps in front of it. [Him? The genders are difficult to determine. I shall cease trying until I am told with certainty which of the six known genders I am dealing with.]

"Because of us," the John Graf says. He looks over his shoulder at the MugwL.

The two of them stand, hands together, heads bowed, as is proper procedure. Emotion does not cross their faces. Only the slight change in their peppery odor tells me that they are reacting to this at all.

"We went to them," the John Graf is saying to me, "right after the deaths. My people wanted an arrest, some kind of charges, sanctions—a few, like Victor here, wanted to take matters into their own hands. But we want to peacefully coexist. So I want to handle this by the book. I go to MegrP, their leader, and I say just that, we need to handle this properly so that we stay allies. He listens, then asks if I think an injustice has occurred. And I say, 'Hell, yes. Our kids are dead.' He nods, and says he will contact you."

I let him speak, even though the history of the request is not relevant. That, too, was explained in the first two days, and apparently not conveyed to all of the humans.

"Nonetheless," I say when it becomes clear that the John Graf is done speaking. "They are the Requesting Party, and it is by their aegis that I am here."

"So?" the John Graf asks.

"So you must let the proceeding continue."

"What, so they can tell you their side of the story without us saying ours? How fair is that?" His voice has risen to nearly intolerable levels. "It's our kids that're dead, us that've suffered here, and it sounds like we'll suffer some more when fall—however you people define your seasons—eventually shows up and washes our homes away. *That's* Injustice, Mr. Collector. We haven't done anything wrong."

"This is not a Judgment," I say yet again. "This is a Justice/Injustice proceeding."

"Yeah," the John Graf says, "and I thought that meant a finding of fact. You know, the truth will out and all that. Some impartial person would investigate, maybe even go to the crime scene, interview some MugwLs and the surviving kids and find out what happened. But if I understand your

rules right, you're just going to let this guy talk—
and he wasn't even there. Then you'll make some
kind of judgment, and we're done. That's not Justice, Mr. Collector. That's just plain wrong."

The bag is a darker shade of purple. I use my
middle arm to check the knot. The knot is tight.
The bag will not get loose.

"This Proceeding was Requested," I say. "It must
continue. When it is finished, you may seek this
'investigation' and 'judgment,' perhaps from your
own people. This Proceeding is what it is, and I cannot make it anything else."

[*An Aside*: although, in some ways, the Proceeding has become something else. It resembles the
Proceedings of the early Alliance rather than modern Proceedings, partly because of these protocol
breaches.]

"We have spent more than Eight Cycles here," I
say. "If we continue at this pace, we will be here
until fall. The Requesting Party must complete his
testimony. If there are no further objections, I shall
send my staff for the Bystanding Party, and we
shall—"

"But there are objections," the John Graf says.
"The very objection that started me. Children can't
be here without their parents' permission. And no
parent is going to allow a child to take part in
this farce."

Again with the unexplained words. I chose to ignore them.

"What your people want now does not matter,"
I say. "All that matters now is the Proceeding itself.
These 'children' are, at the request of the Requesting Party, the Bystanding Party, and by our
regulations, required to be here. You cannot change
centuries of law simply because you do not agree
to it."

"What'll happen to the children?" the John Graf
asks.

I am at the end of my patience. "We discussed Bystanding Parties on the first day. Consult with your representatives. We shall indulge you no longer."

The John Graf clenches his hands into fists and does not step away from the Decision Desk. The vocal human moves its head from side to side.

"Told you we should've blasted them," it "whispers." Its gaze is on mine as it speaks, and I know the comment is somehow directed toward me.

"Proceed," I say to the MugwL representative, and he does, with obvious relief.

Record of Proceeding
Incident at Gray's Brook
Injustice Collector 0080 Presiding

Testimony of Requesting Party [continued]
As I said more than Eight Cycles ago now, the humans trusted us with their children. This was not a trust we asked for or even understood. We had no desire to interact with the humans, but their intrusiveness forced us into relations.

They asked questions; they tried our food (and complained when it made them ill); they even came into the village during Privacy Cycles, demanding attention. All of that, we accommodated. We listened, we spoke, we spent time with them at their request.

We did not ask them questions, knowing that our lack of interest would show them they were not wanted. Yet they seemed to ignore that message.

Part of the problem, we assumed, was that they always sent new representation. The early Elders vanished, replaced by other Elders, and now we are being introduced to yet a new set of Elders. Even though the shiny silver ships the humans arrived in seemed small, they carried a multitude of beings, so many that we often found ourselves confused.

We did not even note the presence of "children" until late in the days of the first set of Elders. Then the Elders brought small creatures to us, and showed us the "children" proudly. We believed they had been sent in another mission, that the humans, in their folly, thought they could add their native creatures to our environment.

We did not know that these creatures were the young or that they were somehow created without waterbaths and the freezings of six winters. We did not know that the young could be created off the world the humans call Earth.

Interruption in the Proceeding
Nine Cycles into the Requesting Party's Testimony, The Arrival of the Bystanding Party.

This interruption is one I had requested when I insisted the Requesting Party continue with its Testimony without all Requested members present. The "children"—some thirty of them of various sizes and shapes—have been brought in by two Collectors-in-Training and five robotic helpers.

Like the other humans, the "children" do not seem to understand the proceedings. Since explanation did not work with the older humans, I do not believe it will work with the younger, and chose not to take the two days to reiterate the rules and regulations.

If any member of the Review Board has an objection, I refer him to the Board of Governors' Response to the Official Inquiry on the Humans [attached above].

—Injustice Collector 0080

In the midst of the arrival of the Bystanding Party, the humans committed yet another protocol breach. I note this here, but do not place it into the record as a secondary interruption since this is an interruption of an interruption.

Nonetheless, I report it here:

"I object," says the John Graf. "These children

have no legal rights here. Their parents must be present."

[*An Aside*: there are now fifty humans, two MugwL, two Collectors-in-Training, five robotic helpers, and the bag in the Great Hall. Even if I complied with the John Graf's demands, the additional humans [if, indeed that's what these "parents" are] would not fit into the room. I do not mention this. I have ceased arguing with the humans.]

"The 'children' are the Bystanding Party," I say. "If the Bystanding Party does not understand its function here, I suggest it choose one representative member, and set the rest free. The representative member will listen to the testimony, will spend time with the Collectors-in-Training to gain an understanding of the rules session which was missed, and will, if need be, relay the Justice/Injustice to the remaining members of the Party."

"Your Honor," one of the "children" says. It has a high voice with many overtones, "Our parents don't want us here."

Again, I ignore this. "We shall recess for One Cycle while the Bystanding Party picks its representative."

And so we do.

[*An Aside*: After the Great Hall empties, and the Scrubbers enter, attempting to clean the vile stench from the air, I look down at the bag. It is a faint lavender.

[It senses my attention, and sends me this message: *There have been too many protocol breaches already. This proceeding will fail its Review. Let me take the Perceived Injustices now in the interest of time, and it will save us all more Cycles of this.*

[I note the communication here in an aside, since it is within the bag's rights to make such a communication. Each case I have administered has included such a communication.

[Only this time, I actually contemplate the bag's request. This procedure *is* unusual and will receive great attention from the Review Board. I am tempted to save all of us the trouble and allow the bag this one indulgence.

[Apparently, it senses my hesitation and turns a violent purple. The color change and the shimmering hatred that rises from the bag's porous exterior remind me that, no matter how logical a bag's argument, the bag is always concerned with its own power. Too many Injustices, even Perceived Ones, might overload the safety protocols, and the bag would be freed.

[There are fifty bags within traveling distance of this sector. One free bag could free the others—that's how the Attwne System dissolved.

[I reject the bag's request, but note my hesitation here, in case the Review Board would like to bring me up on charges for even considering it.

[By the time the Representatives return—two MugwL, two human [as I note with relief], and two "children" of the larger variety—the bag is again pale lavender, and I have made certain the knot and the imprisoning devices are fixed securely.]

Record of Proceeding
Incident at Gray's Brook
Injustice Collector 0080 Presiding

Testimony of Requesting Party [continued]
By the time of the Incident at Gray's Brook, we had already been to the human settlement six times with the express purpose of seeing the "children." The "children" gather every other Cycle in a building called the "school." There they sit while a full-sized human passes knowledge to them via three different means—vocal communication, printed communication, and written communication.

The system seems inefficient to us, and is part of

what led us to believe the "children" were another species. We now believe that the human young are not born with the knowledge of the community implanted in the brain. The knowledge must be transferred by these inefficient means.

Since we use these means only with inferior creatures, ones that we hope to domesticate, we place this assumption of ours before the Decision Desk as a simple Misunderstanding, not an Injustice.

Interruption in the Proceeding
Eleven Cycles into the Requesting Party's Testimony, A Breach of Protocol:
Cause of breach is, as noted above, human ignorance.

—Injustice Collector 0080

"I don't suppose anyone wants to explain that distinction," says the John Graf. I believe he is referring to the distinction between the "Misunderstanding" and the "Injustice."

We have explained this, taking days—not cycles—to do so. But I weary of reminding him of that, so say nothing.

After a moment of silence, the John Graf says, "I thought not. Why do I even try?"

Record of Proceeding
Incident at Gray's Brook
Injustice Collector 0080 Presiding

Testimony of Requesting Party [continued]
Just before the Incident at Gray's Brook, one of the human Elders came to our Village Council and requested a "field trip" in which their "children" would see how we tend our own young. This "field trip" as best we could understand it was an educational venture designed to exemplify the distinctions between our two species.

It took the humans several visits to explain the need for such an event to us. Even so, we are uncertain as to whether we sufficiently understand it, and believe on this point that the Non-Requesting Party might like a voice.

[*An Aside*: I offer the opportunity to the John Graf. He raises and lowers his shoulders.

["This isn't a proceeding, it's a joke, and we're here under protest," he says by way of explanation.

[The MugwL seem to find this response as unsatisfactory as I do. But that does not stop their testimony. Their representative continues.]

To understand what transpired next, we must explain a distinction that we have learned over this half-season of dealing with the humans. In their language, "day" means "cycle." Their concept of time is different from ours in significant ways, ways we do not yet completely understand.

We have come to realize that even though we speak the same accepted Alliance tongue, our understandings break down at even this most basic level. Some of our scientists postulate that the humans have a summer's lifespan, although others believe this to be impossible based on the humans' ability to learn Alliance languages and travel in space.

This digression stems from our attempt to understand the humans' extreme reaction to the Incident at Gray's Brook and our culpability, if any, in it.

Interruption in the Proceeding
Eleven Cycles into the Requesting Party's Testimony, A Breach of Protocol: Cause of breach is, as noted above, human ignorance.
—*Injustice Collector 0080*

"Culpability, hell," says the other human representative quite loudly. "We'll show them culpability."

Record of Proceeding
Incident at Gray's Brook
Injustice Collector 0080 Presiding

Testimony of Requesting Party [continued]

At the time of the incident, our young were in the water-bath. The waters are at their lowest this time in the season, and the fetal pods are clearly visible.

The waters are also quite warm and, in the words of one of the "children," "inviting" although, it must be noted for the record, the MugwL heard no such invitation.

The "children" asked if it was permissible to touch the pods. We apparently did not understand the nature of their question. We told them that, indeed, it is always permissible to touch the pods.

We did not, however, expand the answer, expecting more questions. Apparently, however, the "children" are unlike the humans in more ways than knowledge and size.

The "children" did ask one other question. They asked if the water was harmful.

The question was, on its surface, unnecessary. If the water was harmful, would we have put our fetal pods into it? Of course not. We answered the question we believed was asked. We answered according to our biology and our customs. We did not realize that the "children" could not frame their questions correctly.

Again, we plead Misunderstanding, not Injustice.

Interruption in the Proceeding
Eleven Cycles into the Requesting Party's Testimony, A Breach of Protocol: Cause of breach is, as noted above, human ignorance.
                              —*Injustice Collector 0080*

"Lying manipulative bastards," says the other human representative.

The John Graf puts his hand on the other representative's arm. The other representative moves away.

Record of Proceeding
Incident at Gray's Brook
Injustice Collector 0080 Presiding

Testimony of Requesting Party [continued]
The devastation was stunning and terrifying. The people who witnessed the deaths are not the same. They cannot go near the human settlement; they are appalled at the very mention of humans. This emotion grew worse when it became clear to all concerned that the "children" are also human young.

[*An Aside*: for the first time, the MugwL representative is having trouble controlling his voice. It breaks. This is the first obvious sign of emotion from the MugwL and it is quite moving.

[I do not look at the bag, waiting at my feet, below.]

The "children" shed their clothing with a rapidity that startled us. Then they plunged headfirst into the water. A few jumped feetfirst.

We had never seen anyone but registered tenders step into water, and even then, they followed distinct and important protocols.

These "children" followed no protocols at all. They drenched themselves and arose, laughing—a sound that is the same among both of our species (something we did not know and did not want to learn in this context).

Then the laughter turned to shrill, high-pitched sounds that the humans later identified as sounds of extreme fright. The "children" had rested their feet on the pods—a few "children" had gone underwater and touched the pods with their hands—and the pods—the pods—

The pods absorb food through the exterior shell. It

supplies the fetal material and maintains the growth necessary for development. Anything that touches the pod becomes food, unless certain protocols are followed.

Even the tenders do not touch the pods without wearing special equipment, equipment that we did not bring on our "field trip" with the "children."

We managed to save five of the children, but ten of them—ten of them—

We learned, to our dismay, that human blood is red. When combined with water and flailing limbs, bubbles are created, making a pinkish foam.

Many of us still see this foam in our dreams.

Record of Proceeding
Incident at Gray's Brook
Injustice Collector 0080 Presiding

Citing of the Injustice[s]
According to custom, I place the bag on the Decision Desk. The bag maintains its composure above the desk; the bag's porous outer layer is now a creamy white.

Then I state the interrogatory: What do you believe are the Injustices in this Incident?

The Non-Requesting Party attempts to respond, but is silenced. The Bystanding Party simply shifts from foot-to-foot as if the proceedings do not concern either representative. The Requesting Party looks at the bag with great fear before replying:

"The Injustices are, as we see them, as follows: One Injustice occurring against the Requesting Party, and one Injustice occurring against the Bystanding Party."

Interruption in the Proceeding
Eleven Cycles into the Requesting Party's Testimony, A Breach of Protocol: Cause of breach is, as noted above, human ignorance.
—*Injustice Collector 0080*

The John Graf steps forward. "What the—?"
He does not finish his own sentence.

Record of Proceeding
Incident at Gray's Brook
Injustice Collector 0080 Presiding

Citing of the Injustice[s] [continued]
   "The Injustice against the Requesting Party is this:
The humans should have explained to us the nature
and vulnerability of their young. In this, they should
have explained the purpose of "children" and the car-
ing of them. We should not have been responsible for
beings we know nothing about.

> Interruption in the Proceeding
> *Eleven Cycles into the Requesting Party's Testi-*
> *mony, A Breach of Protocol: Cause of breach is,*
> *as noted above, human ignorance.*
> —*Injustice Collector 0080*

   "Right," the other human representative says,
surprising me with his agreement. "Go ahead.
Blame the victim."

Record of Proceeding
Incident at Gray's Brook
Injustice Collector 0080 Presiding

Citing of the Injustice[s] [continued]
   "The Injustice against the Bystanding Party is more
severe. It is this: Although these human young, these
"children," are adaptable enough to survive their
youth away from their home world, they are not
strong enough to face challenges inherent in space exploration. It took less than a season to wipe out ten
of these youth. One can only surmise how many more
will die before the fall comes and the floods—"

Interruption in the Proceeding
Eleven Cycles into the Requesting Party's Testimony, A Breach of Protocol: Cause of breach is, as noted above, human ignorance.
                    —*Injustice Collector 0080*

"For Crissake," the John Graf says, using yet another unknown phrase. "We did not bring the children here. We gave birth to them here. We're colonists, for God's sake. We're building a life here. Can't you people understand that? My father explained it all when the ships landed. He told you what we were doing, and you agreed to let us have the land. You agreed to let us live here. And all our studies said it was safe. There's no injustice in that. Don't you get it? We're just living—"

Record of Proceeding
Incident at Gray's Brook
Injustice Collector 0080 Presiding

Citing of the Injustice[s][continued]
According to custom, I place another hand on the bag, and ask: Does the Bystanding Party accept the Injustice claimed in its behalf?

The representative of the Bystanding Party has to be prodded by the John Graf. The representative of the Bystanding Party appears startled, then says, "I dunno."

Again, faced with the ignorance of the humans, I cite the Gubernatorial Decision, accepting that response as an affirmative, and continue with the procedure.

"In this case," I intone, "as in all cases of this nature, the final decision on the Injustices will be made by the Wiwendian." I add for the humans, "the Wiwendian is what you have casually heard us refer to as 'the bag.' It is, instead, the true Injustice Collector, in that it feeds on such violations, needing them to survive. We feed the Collector, so that it and its people will not create new Injustices, simply for the sake of devouring them. In stating this old truth, I remind us all of the oaths we have taken to maintain Justice in our universe."

I place my remaining hands on the bag, and undo the knot I tied in its opening. "Do you accept these Injustices?"

There is a whooshing, and the bag turns a light lavender. The Injustices white and blue, swirl away from the Requesting Party and the Bystanding Party. For a moment, I believe I see something red near the Non-Requesting Party, but the redness vanishes.

The bag accepts the Injustices and then fades to its normal color. I place the bag beneath the Decision Desk once more, and declare the proceedings complete.

But the proceedings do not exactly end. I add these events as an addendum to my report:

"That's it?" the John Graf asks. "You ask a silly question of a *bag* and then it changes color and we get to go? That's all that happens? We spent months of our lives here for that?"

The time reference confirms yet again the MugwL's impression of time differences between the humans and our various species. More study will be needed to ascertain if this is, indeed, a fact.

"Yes," I tell the human. "The Proceeding has ended."

"But nothing has changed," the John Graf says.

"On the contrary. The Wiwendian—we—have taken the known Injustices from this world. The slate is clean. You may begin again."

"Begin what?" the other human asks. "Our children are gone. We've gotten no satisfaction here. You let those people—those murderers get away with feeding our kids to their pod thingies."

I signal my Collectors-in-Training. "I have done

my work according to the laws and customs of our Alliance. I have responded to the Requesting Party, brought the Wiwendian, and collected Injustices. If you perceive any violations, you may bring them up with the Review Board."

I have, of course, added this for the humans' benefit. It is more explanation than I usually offer after a decision has been rendered.

I feel the humans' displeasure and empathize with it, but even they must realize that nothing brings back lost lives.

That, perhaps, is the ultimate Injustice, but one so common that the bag usually rejects it.

"My assistants will explain how to file your petitions with the Review Board," I say as I open the doors to the Great Hall. The rush of cool air is marvelous. "But not in here."

The Collectors-in-Training usher the humans out, but they are not the ones that stop at the doors. The MugwL do, and as they do, they let out their own sounds of fear and displeasure.

I rise, peering over their heads.

In the distance, smoke rises from the MugwL village. Too much smoke, accompanied by leaping flames.

The John Graf looks upset. He puts his arms around the "children" and leads them outside.

But the other human, the vocal one, stops, turns, and looks at me, not the MugwL. I do not know human expressions, but this one seems, in some way frightening—the raised eyebrows, the half-contained amusement.

"On my world," he says, "when systems break down, only one kind of justice remains. We call it street justice."

And then he leaves.

The MugwL cry and wail, claiming their village is gone. My Collectors-in-Training still usher them out, and finally close the door.

I am alone, except for the bag. The bag that wants to collect these Injustices, in a Preliminary fashion, to save us a trip.

If my bag is any indication, the Wiwendians are becoming dissatisfied with our agreement to feed and house them in exchange for controlling their somewhat destructive talents. But that is an aside.

I would have refused its request on principle—one finished Proceeding is enough for any Collector—but principle is not my real reason for saying no.

I say no because I do not want to preside over another Proceeding involving humans. Too messy, too many chances for mistakes.

The red floating above them as the bag collected the Injustices disturbs me. Red is usually the color of violation. The Injustices from the MugwL and the "children" were not red.

The humans have a rawer, more passionate sense of Injustice than we do.

There is already so much Injustice in the Alliance that we barely maintain our hold on the Wiwendians. My Wiwendian already finds the human sense of Injustice attractive. Other Wiwendians will as well.

The humans will give the Wiwendians too much power.

Together, they will destroy everything.

And I fear that, after this Proceeding, they have already started.

CREATURE FOR HIRE

by Paul E. Martens

I WAS ALONE. And if you've never been the only one of your kind on a world of billions, then you don't know what being alone is. I was a monster, shunned and unwanted, with no place in the universe.

Morty was on the phone, confirming that assessment. "I'm sorry, E, I just can't get you another movie." Morty was my agent. "I mean, face it, you can't act."

"But, Morty, I'm an alien. Christ, I'm The Alien, the only one on the whole damned planet. There's got to be something." It occurred to me that my apartment was too big. It seemed to be getting bigger every day. And when I considered the rent vis-a-vis my bank account balance, the place was huge.

"The novelty's worn off, kiddo. I'm surprised it lasted for four movies. And that last one didn't really count, just a walk-on in a dream sequence. The point is, people aren't going to keep paying to see something they've already seen, even if he is an alien. I mean, it's not like you do anything. You're just there, you know?"

I looked around at the plush carpets, the antique furniture, the paintings that hadn't been painted by starving artists, things my next place would be lacking.

I caught sight of myself in the gilded mirror across from the couch. My Celtics T-shirt hung loosely from my spindly frame. My head, which I used to think was a perfectly normal head, seemed too big. I blinked silvery lids over my enormous black eyes.

"What about TV?" I asked, knowing that my voice was too high and thin for any hope to live in it.

There was a sigh. "Maybe. The producers of *Intergalactic Battlecruiser* have dropped some hints about a guest-villain spot. But they want to pay bupkes. And besides, people know you too well, they won't buy you as a bad guy."

"Couldn't we work on my image a little? You know, play up the Menace-from-Outer-Space angle?"

He didn't bother to say anything. It was my turn to sigh. What kind of world was this if you couldn't even depend on xenophobia to make a living?

"How about the lecture tour?"

"Ah, jeez, E, I just can't sell it. You've got nothing to say that people haven't heard already. You don't know how your spaceship worked. You don't know how anything worked. You were a cook's assistant. You don't even know where Tethys is."

Sure, I did. It was somewhere out there, far, far, far away. And I would probably never see it again.

"And anything you did have to say, you gave away for free when you spilled your guts to the Feds and let them record your interrogation. You remember what that did to the sales of your autobiography, don't you?"

"Morty, I told you, I didn't know . . ."

"Okay, okay. Water under the bridge. I'm just trying to tell you why I can't get you a gig."

"All right, Morty. Thanks, anyway. Let me know if anything comes up." I hung up and wondered if this was one of those times when a human would cry. I can't do it myself, but I was willing to bet that if I could have, I would have.

I didn't really mind moving. The apartment had

been Morty's idea. The other tenants were writers, accountants, lawyers, and so on. I'd never belonged there, and soon I wouldn't have enough money to make up for not belonging.

I sat and scratched the place where my nose would have been if I was human as I considered my options. What I needed was a secret hideaway, an inaccessible lair buried deep inside a mountain from which I could hold the governments of the world hostage with the threat of annihilation by my alien death-ray. That would make people notice me. Unfortunately, not only did I not have a secret hideaway, I was completely death-rayless, and there was no way I could persuade anyone otherwise. The only reason the government had let me go was because they were convinced I had nothing useful to tell them. If they had even suspected that I knew how to build an alien death-ray, or even an alien give-you-a-slight-headache-ray, I would have still been locked up tight in an NSA laboratory somewhere.

All right, then, how about this? I have a hidden receiver implanted in my head, and I just got a message from home that they were prepared to wipe out the Earth if I wasn't given a billion dollars and my own sitcom. No. The first thing they would do is grab me and start digging around for the receiver. My head might seem freakishly large on this planet, but I was still pretty attached to it.

I wasn't getting anywhere alone in my apartment thinking soberly and rationally about my problems. I decided I needed a drink.

I took the elevator down to the lobby and went out into the LA afternoon. I stopped to take a breath when I reached the sidewalk. As always, the air seemed to be missing something to me, even with all of the extras provided by the smog. It's breathable, but not exactly what my lungs are looking for. Like everything else, though, whatever is missing is a mystery to me. And there's something wrong with the sun. Some sci-

entist told me it had to do with the color of the light
and rods and cones or something, but I really couldn't
follow what she was saying. I was still learning English
back then, but I doubt I would understand it any better now either.

I did, and do, understand alcohol, though, and I
knew where to get it. I walked a couple of blocks to
Prof's, a dark little place owned by Doc Siegel, who
described himself as a defrocked teacher of Fantastic
Literature. I kept hoping someone would notice me,
maybe ask for an autograph, but all I got was a few
brief glances, a halfhearted gawk. Someone in a passing car did throw an empty coffee cup at me, but
that was probably just a coincidence. Morty was right,
nobody cared about me anymore. He'd told me about
something called a nine-days' wonder. I guess, after
five years, it was finally the tenth day for me.

Doc was sitting behind the bar, soaking up his
profits in the form of a glass of bourbon, probably not
his first. The sun refused to follow me into the place,
the only light came from a couple of three-watt bulbs
and some fizzling, red-and-blue neon beer signs over
the bar. There were a few customers scattered around
at tables in the murk. Prof's was a good place to
drink alone.

"Eyul, my alien friend and the word made flesh,
welcome." He bowed his bald head to me.

"Hi, Doc. A beer, please. A cheap one." I climbed
onto a stool.

He poured me a draft and asked, "How's the
alien biz?"

I swallowed some beer and said, "It stinks. A few
more weeks and a dollar draft will be out of my
price range."

"That's too bad, brother. What are you going to do
about it?"

"What can I do? I'm unique; a genuine, one-of-a-
kind, out-of-this-world alien, but no one cares. You'd
think all I'd have to do is sit in a room someplace and

charge people five bucks a pop just to look at me and I'd be rich. But, no, I'm old news. I'm last year's Christmas present, just another guy from out of town who couldn't make it in the big city. It's not fair!"

Doc squinted at me, aiming his blue eyes along his hawk-sharp nose. "Fair? It's not fair? What are you telling me, that life is fair where you come from? If that's the case, you don't just come from another world, you're from a whole different universe that operates under its own set of rules. Was it fair that I had to become a school teacher because no one would buy my books? Was it fair that I had to give that up because I had a slight drinking problem?" He took a guzzle of bourbon.

I blinked at him. "I didn't know you wrote."

"Yeah, well, it was a long time ago," he kind of mumbled it, as if he were embarrassed by his outburst. "But let me ask you this, would you be special if you were home?"

I hesitated, then finally admitted, "Okay, no. But I'm not home."

"Are you sure? What are the chances that you'll ever see Tethys again? Maybe you ought to get used to the fact that Earth is home, at least for now, and ask yourself what you can do to fit in."

"But that's the problem, I don't fit in. My agent's right, I don't do anything, I don't know anything, I don't have anything that anyone would want. What can I do to myself that would change that?"

Doc took a long gulp of bourbon, smacked his lips with every evidence of relish, and said, "Well, why not do what I do when I come up against an insurmountable problem? If you can't rise to the occasion, drink yourself under the table." He poured a glass of Kentucky's finest and slid it across the bar to me. "On the house."

Sometime and some bourbon later, it hit me. Actually, first, the bar hit me, or, rather, I hit the bar. I had been thinking that it would be really nice if the bar would elevate itself a few inches to help me hold my head up. After a little while, I figured that wasn't going to happen, and decided that if the mountain wouldn't come to Mohammed . . . and I let my head fall.

"Ow," I said. "I mean, eureka."

Doc peered at me and waited.

"It's a matter of pershpec . . . prospect . . . perspective. If I don't have anything they want, then I have to make them want what I have."

"Right!"

"Damned right I'm right. What I have to do is make people think there are aliens, other aliens, sneaking around, secretly doing alien things. Then people will want to know, who are they? What do they want? What should we do? And who will they ask?"

Doc thought about it.

"Me!" I told him.

"Okay."

"And I'll tell 'em, but it'll cost 'em."

"You bet."

"So, how do I make 'em think there are aliens?"

"Cows."

"What?"

"You know. Cows." He held fingers up next to his head. "Moo. Cows. Cattle mutilations. That's what aliens do."

"We do?"

He shrugged. "Some people think so."

And so, at three-thirty in the morning, after the bar closed, we found ourselves in Doc's ancient and mammoth purple Cadillac, on our way out of town, looking for cows. We knew they would be "in the country," but beyond that we were going on guesswork and bourbon. Eventually, though, the bourbon wore off, and our guesswork wasn't looking too good.

"Hey, over there!" I shouted.

Doc slammed on the brakes, fishtailing and almost missing a tree with his fender.

"Jesus, E! You want to give me a heart attack? What are you yelling about?"

I pointed.

"Those aren't cattle. Those are llamas."

"But," I said, "I haven't seen any cattle in the last couple of hundred miles, have you?"

"Well, no. Hell, it works for me if it works for you." He turned off the car. "You go ahead. I'll wait here."

"What?"

"Go ahead. You know, mutilate them." He made stabbing motions.

I stared at him. "How?"

"I don't know. You're the alien."

"But I've never mutilated anything in my whole life."

He shrugged.

"Fine." I got out of the car, slamming the door behind me. I went around to his side and looked in the window. "What do you have in the way of mutilating devices?"

He rummaged around in the glove compartment, finally pulling out a pen, a plastic spork, and an ice scraper. "Take your pick."

"What am I supposed to do with this stuff?" I asked. "And what are you doing with an ice scraper?" I grabbed the pen without waiting for his explanation and started for the field. There were six llamas munching grass and watching me with placid disinterest. They were mostly a shaggy, dirty white, but a couple of them had brown bits as well. As I climbed the faux-rustic wooden fence at the edge of the field, Doc yelled out, "Hey!"

"What?"

"I think some of them might be alpacas, or vicunas or something."

I looked at him. "Does it matter?"

"No, I guess not."

I shook my head and continued on my way. I held out my hands and called, "Here, llama, llama, llama."

They didn't come prancing up to me, but they didn't run away either.

Eventually, I was able to work my way up to about a foot away from the largest of them. It stared at me with soft brown eyes and kept chewing. It looked gentle and trusting. I stared at the pen in my hand, then back at the llama. What was I supposed to do, write antihuman slogans on the side of the llama? I supposed I could stab it in the eye. Would that count as a mutilation? It would certainly count as disgusting. I imagined the pen meeting the firm but spongy eyeball, finally piercing it and sending some kind of eyeball fluid squirting out all over the place. I let the pen drop into the grass. I couldn't do it.

"Okay, llama, you're off the hook. Live long and prosper."

It spit at me, filling my mouth with llama saliva. "AAAAHH!" I yelled. I spit and spit again. I ran across the field to the car, leaping over the fence. "Give me a drink! Anything!"

Doc got a fresh bottle of bourbon from under the seat, opened it and handed it to me. "I take it cattle and or llama mutilations are out, huh?"

I would have answered him, but I was busy rinsing my mouth and spitting out the window.

"Well, if mutilations are out, maybe you ought to consider a couple of abductions, with some anal probes thrown in for the sake of verisimilitude."

I looked at him. "Are you crazy?"

He shrugged. "You got a better idea?"

I thought frantically. "Not immediately, but it seems like there would have to be at least a billion ideas that are better than kidnapping people and shoving things up their rectums."

"Okay. I'll drive us back to town, you come up with alternatives. I don't think we need a full billion, just whatever sounds good to you."

*   *   *

"How about Tiffany?" Doc indicated our waitress with his chin. "I could see myself probing her a few times."

"Jeez, Doc, she could be your granddaughter."

"I don't know, I think she's interested in me." He smirked in my direction. "More interested in me than you, anyway."

"Oh, that's hilarious, isn't it?" I had to admit it rankled that no one had made a fuss over me when we'd entered the small-town diner to get some breakfast. It was the kind of place where the regulars sat in their regular seats every morning and ate their regular breakfasts and drank their regular coffees on their way to work at the local bank or feed store or whatever. A guy in a John Deere cap and red suspenders over his flannel shirt looked up from his fried eggs and wrinkled his forehead as he tried to recollect where he might have seen me before, then went back to sopping up his yolk with a piece of toast. We sat at the counter and the blonde waitress, Tiffany, according to the name stitched on her powder-blue nylon uniform, handed us menus and said, "Morning, boys, what'll it be?" She waited a second or two, then added, "Hey, aren't you that alien fellow?"

Well, I suppose I could have been a horribly misshapen, mutant human, but I wondered what kind of person needed to ask that question. "Why, yes, I am," I said, ready to sign an autograph.

"Thought so." She nodded. "So, you want coffee?"

As I ate my English muffin and Doc plowed through his scrambled eggs and hash browns, we discussed alien abductions.

"We can't just hold a spork or an ice scraper to someone's head and force them into your car and drive away, you know. There's nothing mysterious about that," I said. "Don't we need bright lights, and cars stalling, and watches stopping and things like that?"

Doc chewed for a bit. "Yeah, I suppose we do. How do we go about it?"

"How am I supposed to know?"

"Well, damn it, E, what *do* you know? You can't mutilate livestock, you can't handle a simple abduction. Sometimes I wonder if you really are an alien."

I held my grotesquely gigantic head in my long, skinny, insubstantial hands. "You're right, Doc. Morty's right. Everybody's right. I'm useless. I don't belong here and I never will. I wish I had been killed with everybody else when our spaceship crashed."

Doc's mouth dropped open. "Oh, man, E, I'm sorry. I didn't mean it." He sounded like he was worried I was going to commit suicide all over his breakfast. "You're . . . You're the stuff which dreams are made of. You're a thousand books that once made my existence almost bearable, brought to life. Your very presence on this planet fills me with awe and wonder. And for myself, and for everyone else who has failed to let you know just how special you are, I apologize."

I raised my head and blinked at him. "Gee, Doc, you sure can talk pretty when you want to. You ever think of writing that stuff down?"

He looked at me for an instant, then we both burst out laughing.

"You're an asshole, you know that?" he said.

"Yeah, you, too," I told him. It's what Earth guys say when they care about each other. "But, you know what, I think you may have your uses."

"Morty," I told the telephone, "I want a book deal."

"E, we've been there, done that. You can buy remaindered copies of your autobiography for a nickel."

"I'm not talking about that, I'm talking about fiction. Science fiction."

Loud cheers did not burst from the phone. "Eyul," Morty said eventually, then more silence, then a sigh. "E. I love you like a son. You know that, right?"

"Sure, Morty."

"So when I say this, you know I only have your best interests at heart, right?"

"Sure, Morty."

"E, you can't write. You don't know the first thing about writing.

"There are people who write hundreds of thousand of words, who take classes, who study, who never get anything in print. And you want me to go to some publisher, someone who may have at least tried to read your autobiography until he couldn't take anymore, and ask him to pay money for your fiction?

"Science fiction, no less?"

"Morty, listen. This isn't some wild scheme, I've given it some thought. You ever hear of a guy named Brian Aldiss?"

"No."

"Oh. Well, apparently he writes science fiction, and he's supposed to be pretty good. Anyway, you know why he said he became a writer? He said, 'Because I wasn't fit for society; I didn't fit into the system.' Who does that remind you of, huh? Me, that's who. Who do you know that is less fit for society?"

"E, it's not that easy. It takes more than just not fitting into the system. You've got to have talent."

"Morty, do me a favor, okay? Just try to sell the idea. An alien writing science fiction. It's a great concept. A one-book deal, that's all I'm asking. If it doesn't work, it doesn't work. But, Morty, it's going to work."

"All right. One book. I'll see what I can do. But don't get your hopes up."

I hung up and looked at Doc. "Okay, now it's your turn. Can you write something that I could have written?"

"Well, I'm not sure if I can rein in my abilities to that extent, but I'm willing to take a stab at it."

"You have to let people see the pain, the inner torment, of being a bug-eyed monster, a freak, cut off from everything and everyone he's ever known."

"Okay," he said, in an entirely too off-handed manner for my taste.

"I'm serious, Doc."

"Relax, E. You're going to be famous again."

And so I am. In a few minutes, a limo is picking me up to take me to the television studio to tape another talk show. This afternoon, I'm giving a lecture to some college kids. We're on our fifth book, all bestsellers.

We've got money. Doc is happy because he feels like he's screwing the publishers that wouldn't buy his manuscripts when he used his own name. He loves the way the critics and the academics gush over the books. His favorite was, "Eyul gives voice to that inchoate longing, that ineffable desire to belong in each of us. He reminds us that, whatever planet we are from, we are all aliens." Sooner or later, we'll "collaborate" on a couple of books to get his name out, then he can have his own writing career, too.

As for me, I finally found my calling. I still don't do anything, not really. I'm just there. But it turns out, if you do it right, sometimes that's all you have to be.

PEDAGOGY

by Michael A. Burstein

THE MOMENT I WALKED into the classroom, the first thing I noticed were all the differences. To begin with, I had to duck to keep my head from hitting the top of the doorway. The classroom itself felt much smaller than the classrooms I was used to back home, and not just because I towered over humans. This classroom was packed with students; I counted twenty of them, sitting at individual desks, each with its own terminal.

The students had been talking just before I entered the room, but as I walked over to the screenboard, they quieted down quickly.

I walked over to the front desk, which sat right next to the screenboard. I took the stylus out of the top drawer and turned to the students.

"Greetings, Earth children," I said.

Before I had a chance to say anything else, one of the students spoke. "You look like a lizard," he said.

The other students made an odd sound which I recognized as their version of laughter. I tried not to look disconcerted, as I had heard this sort of thing from other Earth people, even adults. But the interruption did surprise me. I looked at the boy who had spoken and checked the name on the display screen; it read John Palmer.

51

"John," I said. "It is rude to interrupt when your teacher is speaking."

"You're the teacher? Who are you?"

"My name is Xerpers Fromlilo." I paused, taking a moment to remember the teacher-student protocols I had been taught. "You may call me Mr. Fromlilo."

The students laughed again, which puzzled me.

"Why do your words come out of your neck?" John asked.

"I am wearing a translator pendant. As my ability to speak your Earth languages is limited, I speak softly in my own language and the pendant renders it into yours."

I waited a moment. There were no more interruptions, so I said, "Let us begin."

I turned around to start writing on the screenboard. "Everyone please turn on your machines—"

Something hit me on the back, and I turned around. I found a piece of paper sitting on the floor, folded into the shape of a glider.

I bent over to pick it up, and I examined it.

"What is the meaning of this?" I asked, holding the glider aloft and looking from student to student.

"You're the teacher," John replied. "Don't you know?"

I turned one of my eyes directly at him, while the other continued to look around at the other students. "I do know. I am asking what its purpose was."

"You're our science teacher, aren't you?" He pointed at the glider. "This is science."

"It does not matter if the glider illustrates principles of science, young man. It is inappropriate to throw it at your teacher. I would suggest—"

Suddenly, John stood up and began walking toward the back wall, where there was a cabinet containing school supplies.

"John, what are you doing? I was talking to you."

He stopped short and looked back at me. "I get distracted. All the teachers know that."

Some of the other students giggled. I walked over to John and looked down at him.

"Please return to your seat."

John laughed, but walked back to his desk and sat down. I returned to the front of the room and tried to start my lesson again. However, I could never get more than a few minutes into the material before John Palmer would either interrupt me, begin wandering around the room, or start fiddling with a pair of scissors and some paper.

Somehow, I managed to make it through the remaining forty-five minutes of the class.

That afternoon, Robby Greenberger, the principal of the school, called me into his office to discuss my first day.

He sat at his desk and at first I stood at attention. But then, when he looked up at me, the corners of his mouth turned down, and he pulled at his beard.

"I can barely see your face from here," he said. "Sit on the floor."

All of the Tenjant had dealt with this issue before, given the fact that our average height was approximately one and a half times that of the average human. I reluctantly lowered myself onto my knees so that Greenberger and I faced each other comfortably.

"I don't know if you realize this, but I was majorly opposed to this Interspecies Teacher Training program."

I had not expected Mr. Greenberger to start from there. I tried to formulate a response. Finally, I asked, "What made you change your mind?"

He snorted, an odd sound to my ears. "I didn't. But what with the shortage of teachers, it was the only way to get someone qualified to handle science." He paused and looked over my shoulder. "Although I have no idea how we're going to handle the sex education part of the curriculum."

My mind focused on the first comment. "You could

not find a human teacher qualified to teach your science classes?"

He shook his head, the human way of signifying negation. "Nope."

Although I did not want to appear judgmental of my host race, I gently said, "It is not rational for a race to neglect the education of their children."

He expelled air from his lungs. "Tell me something I don't know."

"I would be happy to do so, but I thought I was here to educate your young."

"No, no, I meant—never mind." He looked around the room, then back at me. "Tell me about what happened today."

"I wish I understood. But your students are not like ours."

"Back up, Xerpers. Start from the beginning."

He had mispronounced my name, but I ignored that. Instead, I said, "From the beginning."

"Yes."

"From the beginning, I had prepared my lesson in detail." I took out my handheld computer and showed it to him. "As you can see, my preparation was more than adequate."

Greenberger took my computer from me and scanned through my lesson plan. Again, as before, he expelled air from his lungs. "Did you expect the children to just sit there while you read aloud from your computer?"

"Of course," I said. "But they would also be able to read along as I wrote the words on the screenboard."

"You see, this is why I was opposed to this program." Greenberger leaned forward. "Look, Xerpers. Human children are not like Tenjant children. You can't just read aloud to them. You have to reach out to them, to engage them with your teaching."

"Does that include John Palmer?"

The corners of his mouth turned up. "Ah, yes, John Palmer."

"He seems reticent to learn."

"More like a pain in the ass."

I pulled my head back. "We do not refer to our race's offspring in that manner."

"Yeah, well, you won't hear me say something like that in public either." He clasped his hands together. "Look. John Palmer is a troublesome kid. He's a lot to handle."

"Perhaps it would be best to give me a class without 'troublesome' kids."

Greenberger barked out a grating laugh. "You've got to be kidding."

His comment puzzled me. "I am an educator of my race, Mr. Greenberger. I do not make jokes about my profession."

He leaned back. "Yeah, well. We don't have that sort of choice around here. If I do that for you, I'd have to do that for everyone."

"Would it not be rational to give me a class without 'troublesome' students, given my new status at your school, combined with the fact that I am Tenjant and not human?"

He expelled air. "Yes, it would be rational. But it's not going to work that way." He plugged my computer into his desk, tapped a few keys, then unplugged it and handed it back. "I've just given you a booklet of tips on how to deal with kids with special needs. See if that helps."

My brief training had dealt with the generalities of Earth children, but never once had our readings indicated the existence of "troublesome" kids. Perhaps this indicated just how desperate the humans were for good science teachers. I thanked Mr. Greenberger for the document and left the room.

I soon found out that teaching science meant running an occasional laboratory session. Tenjant children, of course, did all their practical work in virtual environments, but the humans had not yet developed that technology.

Before the class began, I set up the lab tables with beakers of water, digital scales, small plastic canisters with caps, and round tablets of sodium bicarbonate. As the children filed in, some of them started playing with the equipment on their desks. I requested that they stop doing so, and with the exception of John Palmer, they all did.

"Children, I have sent instructions to each of your computers regarding how to perform this activity, along with the name of your partner for today. You will see how sodium bicarbonate, when placed in water, releases carbon dioxide gas. The scales will allow you to measure the mass of the gas released. Please read your directions and let me know if you have any questions. Only then should you begin working with the materials."

I began to walk around the room, checking on the progress of the students with the instructions. Most of them understood what to do, and I told them to begin work.

Then I got to John Palmer, who was assigned to work with Eileen. Instead of reading the screen on his computer, John was standing on his desk.

"John? What are you doing?"

John began to jump up and down and swing his arms. "Ook ook ook!"

"John? This is not the proper behavior for a human child."

"I'm not a child! I'm a gorilla!"

"A gorilla?" I asked.

A student named Gerald who sat two desks over answered my question. "It's an animal, a primate. John's pretending to be one of them."

I recalled my basic studies of Earth. "Ah, yes. Gorillas." I grabbed John by the waist and gently lowered him to the floor. "Please work."

"You know about gorillas?" Gerald asked.

I walked over to his desk. "Yes. Humans evolved from them."

Gerald frowned. "I don't think so," he said, but I was already rushing back to stop John from pouring a beaker of water over Eileen's head.

I grabbed his arm before he had a chance to spill a drop of water. "John, this behavior is inappropriate. Please go to Mr. Greenberger's office."

He stuck out his tongue at me. "No."

I was unprepared for this disobedience. "No?"

He stuck out his tongue again and crossed his eyes. The room fell silent; I could tell that all of the other students were wondering what I would do next.

I was wondering that myself. Finally, I made a decision. "Class," I said, "please do not continue with the experiment until I return." I placed my hands under John's arms, lifted him up, and carried him out of the room to the principal's office. All the while, he made sounds such as "Wooo!"

When I got to the office, I dropped him off with Greenberger's assistant, whose mouth opened up as I brought the child in and remained open as I left. I returned to the classroom to see the students still in the position in which I had left them.

Mr. Greenberger had not been pleased at my attempt to control John Palmer's behavior. So, at his strong suggestion, I had arranged for a phone conference among John's parents and myself. At the scheduled time, a split image appeared on the screenboard in my classroom. John's parents were in two different locations, and I recalled that Mr. Greenberger had said something about a "divorce," in which the parents no longer resided in the same domicile.

I began by detailing the specific behaviors that I had witnessed. I began by telling them about John interrupting me and wandering around, and I finished by telling them about his pretense of being a gorilla and his defiance of my authority.

When I finished, the two of them sat there, staring. Finally, Mrs. Palmer said, "So?"

Unsure that I had heard her correctly, I said, "Excuse me?"

"What gives you the right to pick up my son? Do you know the humiliation you caused him?"

Flummoxed, I said, "Actually, he seemed to enjoy the ride."

"That's not the point," Mr. Palmer interjected. "The point is that you had no right to do what you did."

I tried to recast my argument. "Mr. and Mrs. Palmer, I do not think you understand. Your child is disruptive. He is unable to focus his attention long enough to learn properly." I paused, thinking of a phrase I had been taught to use in these situations. "Perhaps," I said, "he needs to be tested."

The Palmers recoiled, and the corners of Mrs. Palmer's mouth turned down. "How dare you even suggest such a thing! You're not a licensed psychologist! Hell, you're not even human!"

"I do not think that my race has anything to do with your son and his issues."

Mr. Palmer spoke. "This has nothing to do with our son and his 'issues,' as you put it. This has to do with your ability to teach our child."

"It is hard to get him to learn," I admitted.

"Well," Mrs. Palmer said, "get him to learn. That's your job, isn't it?"

"My job," I said as evenly as I could, "is to get all of the students to learn."

Mr. Palmer expelled air and rolled his eyes. "I don't even know why they hired an alien to be the teacher. You better watch yourself, Mr. Fromlilo, or I'll tell Earth to send you back where you came from."

That would be the greatest favor you could do for me, I thought.

But aloud, I said, "I will endeavor to be more careful in the future."

*   *   *

The next day, Mr. Greenberger called me back into his office. The Palmers had left him a rather irate e-mail.

"They tell me that you're not doing your job," he said.

"They told me that it was my job was to teach their child."

"Well, isn't it?" Mr. Greenberger asked.

"I don't understand. Among the Tenjant, education is a joint effort, among all the people."

"Look, some parents are more involved than others. Some take an active interest in their child's education, every step of the way. And some—"

"And some just expect the teacher to do everything?"

He pulled his shoulders up and then let them fall again. "It's their way."

"I do not understand. Perhaps it is because among my people, we don't even have parents."

"You don't?"

"Not in the way you define them. Yes, every child is born of a genetic father and a genetic mother. But the children of every community are pooled together, and cared for by one particular caste. It is the caste of which I am a part."

He leaned back and stared at me. "Xerpers, may I ask you a personal question?"

"That is why I am here."

"Are you male or female?"

"I am currently male. I will become female again in approximately three of your planet's years."

He nodded. "That may explain why you Tenjant have a different perspective on teaching and parenting than we do."

"Perhaps. But it does not help me deal with John."

He expelled air. "Look. Any teacher will tell you that in every class, there's always one kid who makes teaching the class almost impossible. He's disruptive, annoying, difficult to control—"

"That describes John perfectly."

He nodded. "Well, take out that kid, and poof! Guess what? The class runs much better." He shook his head. "The only problem, of course, is that we can't do that."

"Why not?"

"We're a public school, Xerpers. We have to instruct all children, for the public good."

"But what if the public good is served in a different way?"

"It just doesn't work that way among humans, Xerpers. Sorry."

"Mr. Greenberger, please listen. I have read over your materials on what you call discipline. None of the techniques have proven to be effective."

He rubbed his eyes. "Then use your own techniques, damn it."

Instinctively, I bared my teeth, then I relaxed. "Pardon?"

"Sorry; I forgot that you guys don't like cursing." He paused, apparently waiting for something. Finally, I figured it out.

"It is all right," I said.

"Thanks," he replied. "But my main point is still valid."

"I should use my own techniques to maintain discipline."

He nodded. "You know why the program was created, don't you? Cultural exchange. It's a two-way street. The idea is for you to apply your culture's techniques to teaching our children, as well as learning our techniques so you can bring them back to your home world."

"Let me just confirm this. I am expected to use Tenjant teaching techniques?"

"Expected?" He barked a laugh. "Heck, you're encouraged! Whatever works, man, whatever works."

I pondered this new information for a moment. "I understand."

"Good. Let me know how it turns out."

* * *

"Good morning, children."

Almost in unison, the class replied, "Good morning, Mr. Fromlilo." The only one who did not was John, who sat in his seat, with his right index finger digging into his left nostril. He removed some of the dried mucous from his nose and placed it in a small ball on his desk.

"I have been told to teach you more of my race, of our customs. For example, how many of you have parents?"

Every child's hand went up.

"How many of you would like to get rid of your parents?"

The children giggled now, John loudest of all.

"Well, among the Tenjant, we do not have parents."

"You don't?" asked Gabriel.

"Not in the same way as among you humans. My people do have children, but the children are given over to a specific caste for rearing and education. I am a member of that caste."

Gerald raised his hand. "Yes, Gerald?"

"Is that why you're our teacher?"

"Yes, it is. But I am more than just a teacher. I am a *Nor-Shant*."

The children laughed, and Gerald asked, "What does that mean?"

"It means that I am more than what you Earth people call a teacher. The members of my caste and I raise the children and improve our race by practicing a form of culling the herd."

Another hand went up. "Yes, Jennifer?"

"What does culling mean?"

"Allow me to demonstrate. May I have a volunteer?"

Quite a few hands went up, including that of John's. I called John to the front of the room.

"Watch carefully," I said, "and you will learn of one of the many differences between the humans and the Tenjant."

As I had done countless times in the past, I loosened my jaw, stretching my face as wide as I could. I grabbed John by his waist and shoved him into my mouth.

"Hey!" he shouted.

He squirmed as he went in, but of course the strength of the human child was no match for my own. I pushed him down my throat and swallowed him in one gulp.

With John eliminated, I expelled excess gas from my digestion chamber. "That is culling. It is the way my race improves itself. And now I share it with you."

Silence.

"Are there any questions?"

The silence continued; the blissful, beautiful silence.

I grabbed my stylus and began writing on the screenboard.

"Then," I said, "let us learn."

THE LAST WAVE

by Kay Kenyon

HERE'S THE OLD woman again. She peers over the side of the rowboat, her white hair framing a face wrinkled by years and the rippling water. She calls me by that name, the one I detest. *Nessie*, she whispers. She knows that I can easily hear quiet sounds, and that the loud ones hurt.

That awful name is the same one that the tourists use, as they stand on the viewing platform, or slog along the shore, with their tour buses fuming in the parking lot. So, even though the old woman leaves a gift behind, I begin my plunge into the deep trench of Loch Ness, ignoring her.

At the last minute, I have to admit I'm curious about what she's brought this time. In a slow-motion fall through the water is a wooden machine with a round face, and numbers around the perimeter. As it sinks past me, it is still ticking. Just before it hits bottom, I snatch it with my jaws. It will make a fine addition to my collection, which includes coffee pots, beer bottles, fishing rods, old shoes, a nine metal vase, and various items that remain unidentified. After so long among these creatures, I have their names for most things, but not always their purposes. For example, the iron tray with a handle is a frying pan (what-

ever *frying* means). The shoes are obvious. I've seen
them on tourists. Once I found an oval white chair
with a hole in it. Since it was too big to lift with my
jaws, I left it where it lay. I wonder what they'd make
of *that* at Home.

But this ticking machine . . . as I swim home with
it, I conclude that it is a device for marking the passage of time. The creatures are haunted by time. They
bemoan its swift passage, but are surrounded by instruments to remind them of what is being lost. For
myself, I have no need of reminding. It has been a
long age since my exile. To be more accurate, it has
been 10^{12} picoseconds. I am rounding the numbers for
simplicity, so as not to be obsessed with counting.

I deposit the time passage device next to the metal
vase the old woman gave me last year. And near the
representation (under glass) of her and the old man,
in a nicely wrought silver frame. Nearby is my nautical
collection including a mooring swivel, belaying pin,
lanyard, an old deck lantern, and various anchors (not
all of which I came by fairly, I'll admit). There is also
a ship's mast, from the old days when I was stronger
and could carry such things. I used to sort the entire
collection by what I was planning to bring Home and
what could be left behind. Back when I thought I was
going Home.

The time passage device has stopped ticking now.
Just as well. The smallest unit of time it counts is
seconds—to my taste, far too gross an interval. A surprising lapse for such a semi-intelligent species.

Resuming my swim up the lake, I note that the old
woman is already rowing home. The oars dip so slowly
that I can tell she's disappointed I didn't do *it*. Well,
I don't perform on command. Monsters aren't predictable; it's part of their appeal. I make rare and random
appearances—nothing too tasteless, just a curve of my
neck or a flash of tail—but enough to give the locals
a scare. It's become a matter of pride. But sightings

bring the inevitable rash of loud boats and oglers, and then I hate myself.

From what I gather, there are two competing theories about me. The ones who come with binoculars and cameras believe in the monster theory. I consider myself as siding with this group. The scientists, on the other hand, with their annoying echolocation devices, hold that I'm a prehistoric Earth creature, the last of my kind, cut off from my fellows. Sentimental drivel, of course. Drifting along under their hulls at night, I eavesdrop. They think I'm some kind of *fish*. But if they ever caught me, the DNA analysis would give them a bit of a jolt.

Inevitably, I find myself swimming up the fjord to the Going Home Place. Murk and silence greet me here, where it all began. When the chute is active, it glows. I've grown old waiting for it to glow once more. But even should it spring to life, there's no getting through, because of the hillside slump 10^9 picoseconds ago, when the world tremor sent a slurry of rock and boulders off the cliff, sealing off my route Home.

Coming here is an old habit, rather like the visits of the lady in the rowboat. She used to come out here with an old man. He was a busybody, always clanging his sonar echoes at the lake bottom, and marking things down in his notebook. I had him pegged for a retired engineer. She packed the sandwiches. Now, rowing out on the water alone, she dispenses with the sonar. Lately, she hasn't bothered with sandwiches either. Yet she's out here almost every day, dropping things into the lake, each gift more lavish than the last. I assume they're meant for me—perhaps as bribes to show myself—or perhaps just acts of charity toward an old monster who no longer horrifies.

A flash comes to my peripheral vision. A watery pulse of gold. No doubt it's just the sun penetrating the depths, reflecting off a copper lid, a gilt frame, a . . .

But I am swimming closer now. The jumble of mud

and stones blocks my view. Yet as I make sweeps past
the debris, a stuttering light escapes from beneath the
pile. Nudging my face as close as I can, I manage to
spy through a tiny gap. There, a strip of gold—is glowing. In my excitement, I thrust my jaws so far into the
crevice that I nick my skin, clouding my vision with
blood. But now I'm certain.

The chute is active.

I stare at it a long while. Then I turn away, my
ventral fin digging a furrow in the soft bottom sand. I
swim all the way to the western end of my prison.
There, taking a deep drought of minnows and trout,
I try to settle my stomach.

I can't get past the stony slump. It has been many
picoseconds since I had the strength to move rocks
that size. Not, mind you, that I'm counting the passage
of time.

The mast serves as a lever. Dragging it all the way
from my home cave has left a sharp ache in my jaws,
and carved up a plume of muck where its nether end
dug into the lake bottom. Now I have wedged one
end into a niche between boulders and, holding myself
down by wrapping my tail around a rock, I use my
neck and one of my pectoral flippers to pull down
with all my strength upon the skyward end. It groans
in its work—or is that me? The stone coughs up from
its hole for a moment, then falls back. Finally it tilts
and falls off the stack, but lodges close by, still imped-
ing my goal.

Repositioning the mast, I begin on another stone in
the pile. I am so far from the chute that I can't see it
glow, a reminder of how far I have to go. My under-
side is bruised from the labor, but still I pull down on
the mast, bending it with my effort. This stone,
though, will not budge.

I select another position on the rock slide, guiding
the mast into a gap, and grasping one end of the lever
with my flipper to keep it stable. Then, anchored by

my tail once more, I pull down, down with my full
strength.

In the exertion, memories escape from confinement,
from the prison I've built for them to keep from going
mad. I remember Itiia, and Ebiaria. They were so young!
As were we all. We must have been foolish young
pups to try such pranks as we did. To commandeer
the chute for the purposes of mayhem. Some of my
friends came back with fine monster stories. We
snorted with happiness at the images of creatures running from grotesque freaks: ourselves! To our delight,
many sentient life-forms were terrified of such as we.
At the time, it seemed amusing. My courage was slow
to kindle, so that I was one of the last to use the
chute. I selected Earth, because the creatures there
were known xenophobes, all the more hilarious. That
must have been around the time they caught my companions and shut down the interstellar chute. Then, it
seems, they went on with their lives, forgetting about
me.

Until now.

When I go Home, who will remain among the old
crowd? Itiia, I hope, and Ebiaria. Though we'll have
to act ashamed of what we did, I still plan on hearing
their monster stories. We might be old by now, but I
hope we can still laugh. Truthfully, my own stories
will be a bit tame. The creatures aren't really afraid
of me, not like they used to be. You can't keep a
good horror story fresh forever. Because over time,
people start to love their monsters.

That's something I've learned.

I've also learned that the lever idea is a bust.

Something dangles in the water from the sunny top
of the lake. Linked together are many small white
globules.

I'm interested, but don't like to admit it, because
they've come—whoever they are—in a power craft.
The propeller hangs in the water, churning it, scaring

fish away, and worse, growling at a painful decibel
level. I swim closer, to look at the item draped into
the water. Strung together are many lovely white
stones. The hand that grasps this item is wrinkled and
spotted. It is the old woman, having forsaken the fine
quiet boat for an obnoxious loud one. My spirits are
low. I think about seeking out the quiet depths of the
Loch. But instead, I move into the twilight realm,
where just above me, I can see the hull rocking on a
moderate chop of waves.

She turns off the engine. *Sorry about the loud
motor,* she says. She leans over the side, sending her
voice down to me, although this isn't really necessary.
Water carries sound all too well.

I don't row as well I used to. Did you like the clock?
Ah. Clock.

*It belonged to Jack's mother, and sat on her mantle
for sixty years and then on ours for, oh, decades.
There's no one now to appreciate it, really. Except you.*
She shakes the little white stones. *This is a pearl necklace, a rather good one, actually.* Her grip tightens. *But
you'll have to come get it.*

Her face scrunches up, and she emits a little gasp.
Disappearing into the boat, she takes the white stones
with her. She's playing a new game, one I don't much
care for.

I circle under the boat, waiting her out.

After a few trillion picoseconds, she peers over the
side again. *About the motor. I do apologize. Ugly,
stinky things, I quite agree. But I'm past my rowing
days, and since I'd like to die on the lake, this kind of
boat will have to do. If there was anything more you
wanted from the house, I would have brought it for
you, but I assume there's no way you can let me know.
You can't talk to me, of course. Maybe you can't even
understand me—though I used to tell Jack that you had
picked up our language. He scoffed, of course. Jack
was all for empirical evidence, but his eyes sparkled at
me, and I knew he'd love to believe it. I hope you liked*

the funeral urn. He asked me to commit it to the lake, and so I've given it to you. I like to think you're taking good care of him.

She leans farther over the boat. *Of course, if you insist on circling under this boat, I'll never know, will I?*

Her mouth purses up, her eyes closing. *Oh dear, that was a bad one. Gave up the little pills last week; they made me dizzy. Did you get them?*

I hadn't. Were they in a nice bottle, I wonder?

She isn't leaning over the side anymore, and by her voice, I judge that she is lying down. The old woman is sick. Now that I am paying attention, I notice by the quaver in her voice that she is very sick indeed. The creatures' inadequate medicine can't help her. No wonder. They still burn fossil fuels and use disposable diapers. (Yes, I've seen a few of *those*, as well.)

I glance into the deep. So I've got the old man's ashes. Well, as I say, people grow to like their monsters. In fact, she implied that—in my little stack at the bottom of the lake—I have everything she owns of value. It is startling to think that she has no one else to give them to, while for me, they're just trinkets and collectibles. It shames me.

I am hovering now, some distance out from the boat, where it's easier to see what she's up to. She's just sitting there, watching the water, no binoculars, no frenzy of anticipation. That's when the decision comes to do *it*.

The sun is setting behind the crags, dragging a mist over the water. Anyone out for an evening stroll won't see past the shoreline. I rise up, breaking the surface, unfolding my neck with considerable effort, and at the same time, extruding my tail in a matching curve above the water. The cool breeze wicks heat from my skin. I turn to regard her as she sits in the little boat. She is so small, her skin a pale pink like a turtle's tongue, her head sprouting white hairs as delicate as dandelion pollen.

Normally, I would immediately plunge back down, but something keeps me frozen in place. For one thing, she hardly reacts to my appearance, giving me a surprise of my own. She just sits and watches me, nodding to herself over and over. I swim a little closer, despite the strain of holding my head up. I have my pride, after all. Monsters aren't weaklings.

Her face has taken on an expression that I've learned is a smile.

You're just as I always thought you would be. Quite wonderful. She nods again. *Thank you.*

I let myself sink slowly, so as not to splash her. As I descend, I note that she has a long rope coiled in the bottom of the boat.

It hasn't been easy to teach her. At first she tried to give me the entire rope, and there was no end of misunderstandings. At last we got her end securely tied and a noose rigged on my end.

Half the night is gone now, and we must hurry in order to finish before daylight attracts unwelcome attention. Sometimes my helper rests, and I think she may not last until morning, but if she's in pain, she doesn't show it. She keeps herself entertained by guessing what we're dragging around down here. She has quite an imagination. Yet I feel sorry that I can't tell her, sorry that at least one Earth creature won't know the story of how I came here and how I went Home.

Above me, the motor screams under the strain of hauling the rocks, and the cacophony has shattered my tympanic membrane. Despite the pain, I reattach the noose, and give a tug on the rope. The old woman guns the engine, while I push with my nose. Somehow, the rock comes loose.

And so on, through the long night, moving enough rocks to allow my passage into the chute.

Now, dawn strains down through the depths, faintly,

like the memory of a memory. I know that our time is gone.

But we are ready.

Swimming to the surface, I find her lying in the bottom of the boat. I arch over her, worried.

She says, *Did we finish the work? Did you find what you were looking for?* She opens her eyes, but they are cloudy.

I lay my head on the gunwale, resting, past all pride in front of her.

She nods. *Good. It feels so good to finish something worthwhile.*

The mist on the water is rising, creating a thin white curtain, not like a lake at all, but some region of half-water, half-sun. Behind this scrim, I can perform the feat she's asked of me. Not that I care anymore, what people see. They'd see a monster wresting an old woman down to a watery death. A lurid tale. One I've fostered, I suppose.

She has managed to sit on the side of the boat, legs dangling over, rubber boots filling with water.

I'm ready, she says.

I open my mouth, and gently take her in my jaws. The thick coat she's wearing protects her skin from my teeth. She has folded her arms around my upper head, holding on tight. Then she pats me on the forehead. By this I know I have her permission to take her under.

And so I sink down. It's difficult to see where I'm going, her arms being in the way, but I send out pulses, and the path is clear. Her hair streams behind like bright grasses, growing dim as I leave the upper regions.

All night I've been thinking how needless it is for her to die of simple physiological malfunctioning. My kind don't live forever, but creatures like her have pitifully short lives. So I think of taking her through the chute, which, if done quickly, she might survive. Perhaps she could heal under our ministrations.

But I am not heading toward the chute. Instead, the old woman and I are approaching my lair. Her grip is loosening, but mine is steady. Now that we have arrived, I settle on the sandy floor, and wait with her. She has stopped breathing, but I sense her thoughts may still flow, and I would be ashamed to hurry this part.

It is a good time to reflect that during my imprisonment here not all things have been bad. I've formed a relationship with the local creatures. A twisted one, and built on lies, but still, it was better than being alone. Frankly, some years the tourists kept me alive, though it is a difficult thing to admit. And now, on the last day of my sojourn, I have made a friend. I feel that I know her, and her husband, too. Through the night she talked about their life together, and I listened well. So it is hard to bring her here instead of the chute.

But I think she wanted to be near the old man. She said so, though she didn't know all the options. I have had to figure out, from what I know of her, what to do.

I carefully tuck her body into a crevice, amid my collected treasures. Then I find the vase and wedge it next to her, securing it with a good stone.

A strange feeling comes over me, like deep waters trying to flow through my tissues, trying to pass through my body in hidden channels. I let the feeling surge and ebb.

Then I carefully nip the strand of pearls from her outstretched hand.

It's the only thing I'm taking Home.

Yet there is one more thing I have to do. As I rise to the surface, the sun is fully up, and the day's warmth has brought a crowd to the overlook.

I wait until the last of the mist has evaporated. Then I arch steeply up, sliding out of the water, and raise my pectoral flipper at the astonished onlookers. Before they can loose their boats on the water, I speed downward, laughing, toward the still-glowing chute.

THE EAGLE HAS LANDED

by Robert J. Sawyer

I'VE SPENT A LOT of time watching Earth—more than forty of that planet's years. My arrival was in response to the signal from our automated probe, which had detected that the paper-skinned bipedal beings of that world had split the atom. The probe had served well, but there were some things only a living being could do properly, and assessing whether a lifeform should be contacted by the Planetary Commonwealth was one.

It would have been fascinating to have been present for that first fission explosion: it's always a fabulous thing when a new species learns to cleave the atom, the dawn for them of a new and wondrous age. Of course, fission is messy, but one must glide before one can fly; all known species that developed fission soon moved on to the clean energy of controlled fusion, putting an end to need and want, to poverty, to scarcity.

I arrived in the vicinity of Earth some dozen Earth-years after that first fission explosion—but I could not set down upon Earth, for its gravity was five times that of our homeworld. But its moon had a congenial mass; there I would weigh slightly less than I did at home. And, just like our homeworld, which, of course,

is itself the moon of a gas giant world orbiting a double star, Earth's moon was tidally locked, constantly
showing the same face to its primary. It was a perfect
place for me to land my starbird and observe the
goings-on on the blue-and-white-and-infrared world
below.

This moon, the sole natural satellite, was devoid of
atmosphere, bereft of water. I imagined our homeworld
would be similar if its volatiles weren't constantly re-
plenished by material from Chirp-*cluck*-CHIRP-chirp,
the gas giant planet that so dominated our skies; a
naturally occurring, permanent magnetic-flux tube
passed a gentle rain of gases onto our world.

The moon that the inhabitants of Earth called "*the*
moon" (and "*La* Lune," and a hundred other things)
was depressingly desolate. Still, from it I could easily
intercept the tens of thousands of audio and audiovisual transmissions spewing out from Earth—and
with a time delay of only four wingbeats. My starbird's
computer separated the signals one from another, and
I watched and listened.

It took that computer most of a smallyear to deci-
pher all the different languages this species used, but,
by the year—being a planet, not a moon, Earth had
only one kind of year—the Earth people called 1958,
I was able to follow everything that was happening
there.

I was at once delighted and disgusted. Delighted,
because I'd learned that in the years since that initial
atomic test explosion had triggered our probe, the natives of this world had launched their first satellite.
And disgusted, because almost immediately after developing fission, they had used those phenomenal energies as weapons against their own kind. Two cities
had been destroyed, and bigger and more devastating
bombs were still being developed.

Were they insane, I wondered? It had never occurred
to me that a whole species could be unbalanced, but
the initial fatal bombings, and the endless series of

subsequent test explosions of bigger and bigger weapons, were the work not of crazed individuals but of the governments of this world's most powerful nations.

I watched for two more Earth years, and was about to file my report—quarantine this world; avoid all contact—when my computer alerted me to an interesting signal coming from the planet. The leader of the most populous of the nations on the western shore of the world's largest ocean was making a speech: "Now it is time," he was saying, "to take longer strides"— apparently significant imagery for a walking species— "time for a great new American enterprise; time for this nation to take a clearly leading role in space achievement, which in many ways may hold the key to our future on Earth . . ."

Yes, I thought. *Yes.* I listened on, fascinated.

"I believe this nation should commit itself to achieving the goal, before this decade"—a cluster of ten Earth years—"is out, of landing a man on the moon and returning him safely to the Earth . . ."

Finally, some real progress for this species! I tapped the ERASE node with a talon, deleting my still-unsent report.

At home, these "Americans," as their leader had called them, were struggling with the notion of equality for all citizens, regardless of the color of their skin. I know, I know—to beings such as us, with frayed scales ranging from gold to green to purple to ultraviolet, the idea of one's coloration having any significance seems ridiculous, but for them it had been a major concern. I listened to hateful rhetoric: "Segregation now, segregation tomorrow, segregation forever!" And I listened to wonderful rhetoric: "I have a dream that one day this nation will rise up and live out the true meaning of its creed: 'We hold these truths to be self-evident: that all men are created equal.'" And I watched as public sentiment shifted from supporting the former to supporting the latter, and I confess that my dorsal spines fluttered with emotion as I did so.

Meanwhile, Earth's fledgling space program continued: single-person ships, double-person ships, the first dockings in space, a planned triple-person ship, and then . . .

And then there was a fire at the liftoff facility. Three "humans"—one of the countless names this species gave itself—were dead. A tragic mistake: pressurized space vehicles have a tendency to explode in vacuum, of course, so someone had landed on the idea of pressurizing the habitat (the "command module," they called it) at only one-fifth of normal, by eliminating all the gases except oxygen, normally a fifth-part of Earth's atmosphere . . .

Still, despite the horrible accident, the humans went on. How could they not?

And, soon, they came here, to the moon.

I was present at that first landing, but remained hidden. I watched as a figure in a white suit hopped off the last rung of a ladder and fell at what must have seemed to it a slow rate. The words the human spoke echo with me still: "That's one small step for man, one giant leap for mankind."

And, indeed, it truly was. I could not approach closely, not until they'd departed, but after they had, I walked over—even in my environmental sack, it was easy to walk here on my wingclaws. I examined the lower, foil-wrapped stage of their landing craft, which had been abandoned here. My computer could read the principal languages of this world, having learned to do so with aid of educational broadcasts it had intercepted. It informed me that the plaque on the lander said, "Here men from the planet Earth first set foot upon the moon, July 1969. We came in peace for all mankind."

My spines rippled. There *was* hope for this race. Indeed, during the time since that speech about longer strides, public opinion had turned overwhelmingly against what seemed to be a long, pointless conflict

being fought in a tropical nation. They didn't need quar-
antining; all they needed, surely, was a little time . . .

Fickle, fickle species! Their world made only three
and a half orbits around its solitary sun before what
was announced to be the *last* journey here, to the
moon, was completed. I was stunned. Never before
had I known a race to turn its back on space travel
once it had begun; one might as well try to crawl back
into the shards of one's egg . . .

But, incredibly, these humans did just that. Oh,
there were some perfunctory missions to low orbit,
but that was all.

Yes, there had been other accidents—one on the
way to the moon, although there were no casualties;
another, during which three people died when their
vessel depressurized on reentry. But those three were
from another nation, called "Russia," and that nation
continued its space efforts without missing a wingbeat.
But soon Russia's economy collapsed—of course! This
race *still* hadn't developed controlled fusion; indeed,
there was a terrible, terrible accident at a fission
power-generating station in that nation shortly before
it fell apart.

Still, perhaps the failure of Russia had been a good
thing. Not that there was anything inherently evil
about it, from what I could tell—indeed, in principle,
it espoused the values that all other known civilized
races share—but it was the rivalry between it and the
nation that had launched the inhabited ships to the
moon that had caused an incredible escalation of
nuclear-weapons production. Finally, it seemed, they
would abandon that madness . . . and perhaps if abandoning space exploration was the price to pay for that,
maybe, just maybe, it was worth it.

I was in a quandary. I had spent much longer here
than I'd planned to—and I'd as yet filed no report.
It's not that I was eager to get home—my brood had

long since grown up—but I was getting old; my frayed scales were losing their flexibility, and they were tinged now with blue. But I still didn't know what to tell our homeworld.

And so I crawled back into my cryostasis nest. I decided to have the computer awaken me in one of our bigyears, a time approximately equal to a dozen Earth years. I wondered what I would find when I awoke . . .

What I found was absolute madness. Two neighboring countries threatening each other with nuclear weapons; a third having announced that it, too, had developed such things; a fourth being scrutinized to see if it possessed them; and a fifth—the one that had come to the moon for all mankind—saying it would not rule out first strikes with its nuclear weapons.

No one was using controlled fusion. No one had returned to the moon.

Shortly after I awoke, tragedy struck again: seven humans were aboard an orbital vehicle called *Columbia*—a reused name, a name I'd heard before, the name of the command module that had orbited the moon while the first lander had come down to the surface. *Columbia* broke apart during reentry, scattering debris over a wide area of Earth. My dorsal spines fell flat, and my wing claws curled tightly. I hadn't been so sad since one of my own brood had died falling out of the sky.

Of course, my computer continued to monitor the broadcasts from the planet, and it provided me with digests of the human response.

I was appalled.

The humans were saying that putting people into space was too dangerous, that the cost in lives was too high, that there was nothing of value to be done in space that couldn't be done better by machines.

This from a race that had spread from its equatorial birthplace by walking—*walking!*—to cover most of their world; only recently had mechanical devices given them the ability to fly.

But now they *could* fly. They could soar. They could go to other worlds!

But there was no need, they said, for intelligent judgment out in space, no need to have thinking beings on hand to make decisions, to exalt, to experience directly.

They would continue to build nuclear weapons. But they wouldn't leave their nest. Perhaps because of their messy, wet mode of reproduction, they'd never developed the notion of the stupidity of keeping all one's eggs in a single container . . .

So, what should I have done? The easiest thing would have been to just fly away, heading back to our homeworld. Indeed, that's what the protocols said: do an evaluation, send in a report, depart.

Yes, that's what I should have done.

That's what a machine *would* have done. A robot probe would have just followed its programming.

But I am not a robot.

This was unprecedented.

It required judgment.

I could have done it at any point when the side of the moon facing the planet was in darkness, but I decided to wait until the most dramatic possible moment. With a single sun, and being Earth's sole natural satellite, this world called *the* moon was frequently eclipsed. I decided to wait until the next such event was to occur—a trifling matter to calculate. I hoped that a disproportionately large number of them would be looking up at their moon during such an occurrence.

And so, as the shadow of Earth—the shadow of that crazy planet, with its frustrating people, beings timid when it came to exploration but endlessly belligerent toward each other—moved across the moon's land-

scape, I prepared. And once the computer told me
that the whole of the side of the moon facing Earth
was in darkness, I activated my starbird's laser bea-
cons, flashing a ruby light that the humans couldn't
possibly miss, on and off, over and over, through the
entire period of totality.

They had to wait eight of Earth's days before the
part of the moon's face I had signaled them from was
naturally in darkness again, but when it was, they
flashed a replying beacon up at me. They'd clearly
held off until the nearside's night in hopes that I
would shine my lasers against the blackness in
acknowledgment.

And I did—just that once, so there would be no
doubt that I was really there. But although they tried
flashing various patterns of laser light back at me—
prime numbers, pictograms made of grids of dots—I
refused to respond further.

There was no point in making it easy for them. If
they wanted to talk further, they would have to come
back up here.

Maybe they'd use the same name once again for
their ship: *Columbia.*

I crawled back into my cryostasis nest, and told the
computer to wake me when humans landed.

"That's not really prudent," said the computer.
"You should also specify a date on which I should
wake you regardless. After all, they may never come."

"They'll come," I said.

"Perhaps," said the computer. "Still . . ."

I lifted my wings, conceding the point. "Very well.
Give them . . ." And then it came to me, the perfect
figure . . . "until this decade is out."

After all, that's all it took the last time.

CORRESPONDENCE WITH A BREEDER

by Janis Ian

1624.12 ABR, MESKLIN
Dear Mister Mike Resnick——
Greetings from the future!?"

You may be appalled to learn that I am writing to you through judicious use of the MicroMac, a privilege rarely granted and more rarely accepted in my universe, and that we will be good friends soon*&!

My name is Torthan Volbiss, and as part of my Natural History science project I have elected to do research into the lives of great canine breeders of the nineteenth century. I have selected you for my project!*&!

I am hoping we can communicate via satelnet *<trans: Internet transmission>* regarding this project, as I am pressed for sunturns *<trans: time>* and must get this in quickly or my lectern will be degrading me.

Please advise as soon as possible:

1. How many canines have you bred in your past centurns *<trans: centuries>*?%$

2. Of the ones you have bred, which is your best-beloved canine *<trans: favorite dog>*@#?

3. Have you obtained superiority propagation certificates *<trans: best-of-breed>* from extra-Sol *<trans:*

any other galaxies> and if so, which planet did you like best?)(
  4. If not, why not?!*
  5. Are you accepting applications for lecterns?.#
Sincerely&*(
Torthan Volbiss

1624.17 ABR, Walpurgis III
Dear Mr. Resnick:
Thank you for correcting my punctuation? I did not realize only one character was needed at the end of each sentence@ I will enterprise with more awareness in future# [That is a joke, *future,* do you acquire it"]

Not being a transtemporality *<trans: time travel>* major, I cannot explain how the transmissions are effected. I only know that Woz Volbiss III, my great[3]-paternost *<trans: male ancestor>* invented a new way to take advantage of the SLF *<trans: speed of light factor>,* and somehow we are able to scratch heads *<trans: communicate>* this way*

Not many students are afforded the ability to use the MicroMac, and I must be brief or it will fire electrical charges into my system *<trans: shock me>*+

I did not realize you are in the twenty-first century* My how instants wing *<trans: time flies>* is I believe the correct term from your era:

Yes, the word I meant was INTERN* Of course I could not fulfill the mission *<trans: job>* in soft tissue *<trans: in the flesh>,* but I could certainly handle your datamail *<trans: correspondence>* from here$ To be less-than-sharply-honed *<trans: blunt>* it would also gain me extra scores, and as the Unicollege program is very competitive this would be of great aid to myself and my domestic unit *<trans: family>.*

If you have only sixty years how have you managed to attain your Q-factorization *<trans: pre-eminence>* in the field% Also are you speaking from the side of your mouth *<trans: lying>* when you say travel to other planets is not possible for the ordinary man=

Surely you are anything but ordinary, you are a breeder of some repute even in your era&

Thank you for your attenuation.

Genuinely,

Torthan Volbiss

1624.22 ABR, Herovit's World

Dear Mike,

Thank you for tolerating my use of your first name! Also thank you for the language lesson, I will confine myself to ! ? and . .

Are you always so polite to your data-friends. I am impressed that you have answered all sixteen of my packets within one sunturn *<trans: day>*? You must have a great deal of time on your maniples *<trans: hands>*, my elucidator says you will be a wonderful mentor for this study. I agree, I can feel it in my skeletal structure *<trans: bones>*? It is very kind of you to answer my questions?

I am sorry to hear you are no longer breeding canines, although I agree that the invention of dentistry has probably made this unnecessary. My misunderstanding due to lingual problems, I am sure. Sometimes the convertor *<trans: translator>* does not decode to perfection.

I am sorry I do not share your tongue, but the Micro-Mac will have to do as yours is a dead tongue. Perhaps eventually we can share tongues and become closer.

What is your habitat *<trans: home>* like, do you have wives! If so, where are they kept when their mouthpieces *<trans: motors/alt trans: lawyers>* are turned off. Do you regularly apneate *<trans: sleep soundly>* in a cama *<trans: bed>* or a Landsend *<trans: hammock>*!

I must penitate *<trans: confess>* that this project did not seem like much fun when it was assigned to me, but I am beginning to enjoy it.

Your new friend,

Friendily,

Torthan V.

* * *

1624.29 ABR, Darkover

Hi! Mike! How! are! you!

This was a joke as I have been wrestling your era.
You said to use only one punctuate! . or ? This was
only one for each word.

Are you laughing now. I am?

It is hard to translate humor, for instance I did not
understand that your earlier reference to canines and
dentistry was a joke. I will endeavor to be more atten-
tive in future/past/present.

It is also difficult for me to understand what you
mean by many of your references, since I do not have
the scaffolding *<trans: framework>* to compare. Perhaps you could hurl at me *<trans: throw, send>* a story
to scan *<trans: read>*! I promise to regard it with open
eyes *<trans: an open mind>*?

I am sorry for rushing but I am overdue at ergball
<trans: no possible translation> and must soar *<trans:
fly>*.

Rapidly,
Torthan V.

1624.39 ABR, Rama III

Dear Mike,

Thank you for your many answers, and the lesson on
punctuation. I have reported your educational efforts to
my elucidator, who has invited you to give a sermon
<trans: lecture> here when science permits. This is a very
great honor, I am pleased to present it to you!

I did not realize a sentient of your standing was
permitted only one wife. Is this by custom or by
chance? Also, what do you do when she is worn out?
Are there many replacements available?

I am afraid I have not read any of your fiction, it
is not encouraged in my family as we are reproduced
for science. I am familiar with a writer of your era
called Connie Willis, however, as we have elucidated

<trans: studied> her works in our econosociobiology class. They are not fiction, is that correct!

ABR is standing in for *<trans: short for>* After Bush Resigning or After Bioengineering Replacement or something of the sort. I am not an ancient history major and do not know the answers to many of your questions, including also whether your fiction has survived and where the last Worldcon was. I do remember from early studying that the concept of World was outlawed after the inhabitation *<trans: colonization>* of Hominid II and its subsequent stubborn insistence on taking over its galaxy.

Sincerely,
Torthan V.

1624.41 ABR, Trantor
Dear Mike,
I am sorry I cannot check the bookstores as we do not have any. Or libraries.

Perhaps I am vocalizing inadequately. Information is transferred directly from RNA before birth. Those who are unable to retain information are culled. That is why the MicroMac is so important! Much information was lost in the aevum *<trans: aeons>* since your time, and you are helping to replace it in me! Because of you I am confident that my progeny will not be culled!

I anxiously await one of your chronicles, as I am also going through pubertization and hoping there will be some "pointers" in it because you seem to be very wise. Particularly in your commentary about wives and their replacements.

I anxiously await your box *<trans: package>*.
Frankly,
Torthan V.

1624.48 ABR, Pern
Dear Mike,
I am having great enjoyment in slinging your story

words at my allies *<trans: using your slang with my friends>*. I'll be damned! that is correct yes?

Thank you for sending a most interesting chronicle, however you of all must know there are no elephants on Neptune. They were evacuated many universes ago.

I have gained credit nonetheless, as my former science elucidator was quite surprised that you are only a canine breeder who is a writer on the fringe *<trans: on the side>*, yet you know things from studies he thought were done many-mega later. He asks how did you realize the psychic bond elephants have, are there elephant genetics in your background?

Are you by chance the pen-alias of Dr. Asimov, and involved in this research?

Also thank you for sending me the list of "awards" you have received, though I was not familiar with the word. In researching your communications stream I see it means you were given a pat on the head *<trans: award>* for excellence. We do not have "awards" for excellence as it is assumed if you are not culled you will be excellent.

I am thinking of changing my majority field *<trans: field of study>* to one which will help me understand you better. There is an ancient history course available on Asimov V which refers to the little-known genus called "science fiction," the fiction of science. Since you are as you say a "science fiction writer," this will enable us to tongue more efficiently. And as it will also work with my science course, I am moving there in 3 parsecs and will not be available for the duration. I would appreciate any chronicles you could send in the interim turns.

Yours in excitement,
Excitedly,
Torthan

1625.12 ABR, Asimov V
Dear Mike,
My new elucidator *<trans: teacher>* of science fiction

was quite engulfed that I am in correspondence with you! She says my enthusiasm rating is high enough to qualify for a complete major change! This would enable me to enter the higher academicia and perhaps even graduate at some point in future! Please send more "stories," *The Return of Santiago* was very interesting even though there are no known planets of any description you use.

I am thinking of naming my initial progeny Peacemaker Angel One-Note MacDougal Volbiss in your honor. In fact, I am thinking of changing my majority report completely because of the effect you have had on me.

I am wondering if you have an opinion, should I become a breeder of canines or a science fiction writer? Both fields are, as you would say, broadly ajar *<trans: wide open>* here.

Please answer soon as I will get extra credit for your haste.

Earnestly,
Torthan

1625.13 ABR, Asimov V
Dear Mike,
Thank you for your answer. It does seem that since canines are only permitted on Stapledon I, II, and III, and they appear to breed themselves adequately without anyone's help, the profession of science fiction writer would be best.

There are no other science fiction writers on the known planets, although this does not infer that they do not exist in other dimensions. I would be the first here, which will also give me much esteem and will once and for always restore my family name.

I have been reading the advice you sent me in *I've Got This Nifty Idea* and have what I believe to be a Nifty Idea. When I am finished may I submit it to you?

Wonderingly,
Torthan

*   *   *

1625.18 ABR, Asimov V
Dear Mr. Resnick,
In the mannerism of formal speaking as you suggest
when a new author (myself, Torthan Volbiss!) is making submissions, below you will find my "story" *How
the Slime Gods Conquered Terra I*. I am very excited
because I have (I believe for the first time in science
fiction history!) managed to combine true science and
true storytelling!
In keeping with the sample submission you sent,
my submission is not simultaneous with anyone in this
system. The story length is only 34,295 words. I believe
the pace fits with your current system of ideology.
Should you decide to publish it, I will be glad to give
you the publishing rights, as your mode of monetary
exchange is not useful to me here.
My elucidator and I eagerly await your acceptance.
Eagerly,
Torthan Volbiss

1625.22 ABR, Asimov IV
Dear Mike,
As you can see I have been demoted an entire
planet because of your criticisms! I did not know the
science fiction world could be so harsh! You are not
equipped to judge my story on a scientific basis, because you have obviously not read Benford II's *History of the Terran Interdiction*, or Baxter IV's *Once
Slimed, Always Slimed*. If you had, you would realize
that I have been accurate to the n'teenth degree!
Terra I has been under interdiction for cents! <trans:
centuries!> and is considered uninhabitable by all civilized systems!
I realize now that all your questions about your phy-
sique <trans: stature> in the "science fiction" field
today were only a pathetic attempt to insert yourself
and your arrogant galaxy-view into this timeframe
<trans: era>! To what end! Perhaps you had visions

of starring in holovision commercials! It will never happen, you are not educated enough to wipe the footgear of our bots!

If you do not know your own history I cannot explain it to you!

You have used me shamefully and I will explain all of this to the board of reparations before they cull me!

Sincerely (still!),

Torthan Volbiss

1625.48 ABR, Asimov III

Dear Mike,

I am in very big trouble because of your continued refusal to make a promotion of my story. As you can see, I have been further demoted because of your insistence that my writing "does not exhibit a deep understanding of human culture." Now there is talk of demoting me to feline studies. It is impossible, everyone knows felines do not bond in family groups as do canines and sapients. You of all esteemed personages should know this.

I am sorry to tell you that I have filed a brief with the board of castigation which lays the blame for my present position entirely at your lower appendages *<trans: feet>*.

Your ignorance of Elkhorn's thesis on the demise of Terra I shows a lack of study habits that was probably inherited from your ancestors. There is no doubt that alligators throve *<trans: thrived>* in the sewers of New York City on Terra I! Or that they mutated into gigantic cold-blooded creatures that infected everything they touched with revolting diseases, the smallest of which was the flaking off of giant patches of derma and their replacement with hardened scales! Or the havoc that was created when the infected race molted while attempting procreation! Or that the giant alligators are still in complete habitation of Terra I, and are disgusting reptilian creatures with no sense of civilized behavior!

(Forgive me if I thumb my nasal passages at your ancestors with this intolerant remark, but we have not shared genus and I do not know your chromatic history.)

This is all well-known to any civilized culture!

If you cannot publish the story yourself, at least you could submit it to *Analog the Magazine of Science Fiction and Fact!* Once it is accepted, I can return to Asimov V and continue my studies!

I am disappointed in you, Mike. I thought we were allies.

Disappointingly,
Torthan V.

1625.5 ABR, Ender I
Dear Mike,
I have decided to terminate interaction for the mean-time while I prepare for my judgment *<trans: trial>*.

I am still hoping you will publish my story in any anthology, or will at least present a datamail I may take to the board which will admit your complete responsibility for this situation. The lack of adequate training I received from you is obviously largely to blame in this humiliation. Although such remedies are rarely considered, my castigants *<trans: lawyers, judges, fellow prisoners>* believe it might be of some help.

Please provide me with a clear, concise description of why you cannot present my chronicle, also explain how you could have prepared me better, and save me!

Mike, I come to you on curled *<trans: bended>* knee with this request.

Your old friend,
Sincerely,
Tor

1625.96 ABR, Penitence II
Dear Mike,
Well, thanks for nothing as you would say, though

why anyone would thank another sentient for the absence of anything is nontranslatable to me.

I have not been harvested, obviously, since the reviewers determined that I had been led astray by your false promises. It did not hurt that, being totally unfamiliar with your own history, and unwilling to believe a truthful account of that history, you were judged mentally unfit.

Do not ever think of visiting me, as you will be culled the moment you set chroma on any civilized planet. It is in the records now!

Instead, I am sent to Penitence II, which is one pace <trans: step> up from Penitence I. It is hoped that after many years of study, I may redeem myself enough to return to my Natural History classes, although gratitudes to you, propogation will be out of the question.

Further use of the MicroMac is, of course, not part of the inquiry <trans: out of the question> any longer. Unfortunately, this means I will not get to read your later work, which I hope is not devastating to your pride.

Of course, I assume that anyone who treats a fellow sapient in the manner you have treated me will embezzle my ideas for his own use, but there is nothing I can do about it from here.

Please do not attempt to contact me as we have nothing to speak about.

Torthan Volbiss

1628.93 ABR, Penitence IV
Dear Mike,

I am permitted to hurl this final datamail in order to complete my penitence.

As a portion of my reeducation, I am ordered to forge amendments <trans: make amends> with those I have behaved uncharitably toward. Unfortunately, since the lectern here has access to all of my datamail records, this includes you. I am therefore remorsing *<trans: apologizing>* with willing chambers *<trans: heart>* to the best of my ability.

I apologize for my remarks about your reptilian ancestry. It was uncalled for, and prejudicial toward the inhabitants of Campbell II.

I am also apologetic for any reference I may have made to the apneate habits of your wive(s). I did not realize that in your backward culture, discussing another being's bedroom habits might give offense.

I am sorry for stating that you could never star in a holivision commercial. It may be that someday they will be looking for a being of your genotype, whose RNA is not culturally recommended but who is capable of destroying entire lives with his shoddy, unwarranted criticisms. If that is the case, it will certainly star you.

Finally, I am apologetic for thumbing my nasal passages at you. I should have merely expelled my nose in your direction and hoped for the best.

As a last comment, in response to the datamail you kindly provided the court, which stated that I was "about as aware of human emotions as a bullfrog," and accusing me of "a complete inability to understand human nature, human behavior, or human passion"—Mike, what in galaxies made you think I was human?

Sincerely,
Torthan Volbiss

RESIDENT ALIEN

by Barbara Delaplace

I DREAMED OF HOME again last night. I was swimming with my family. It was so vivid I could almost taste the tang of the ocean, feel the blood-warm water against my skin, hear the surging of the waves against the rocky beach of the cove, where my clan has lived for generation upon generation. We swim against the lithe currents, lithe as the water ourselves.

It was a happy occasion, the celebration of the birth of new life. After we swam, we feasted, and then as it grew dark, we kindled the flames and danced for joy. I remember hearing the voices of the clan seniors, the laughter of my siblings, as we teased the new parents. They had done well—twins! Multiple births are extremely rare, and the Mother Supreme was very pleased with them. As were we all—they have brought honor to the clan.

My disappointment was bitter when I awoke and realized where I truly was. I envy the natives here their ability to release unhappiness in what they call "crying."

Perhaps my scholarship advisers were correct about me. They felt I was too full of myself, particularly

when I tried to turn down this assignment. It was unheard of, they told me sternly, for a candidate at my
scholarship level to turn down two possible planet assignments, let alone *three*. My Supervisor was blunt:
"May I remind you, Student Candidate, that you've
already turned down the first two species offered to
you for study? I would certainly have serious reserva-
tions about continuing as your Supervisor if you were
to turn this down for reasons as frivolous as your previous excuses."

Frivolous! I had gritted my teeth, raging inwardly at
that. Spending the next tenth of my life in a protective
atmospheric suit to study a *possibly* emergent intelligent life-form at the bottom of an ammonia sea had
not struck me as worthwhile, no matter how many
hardships those in my chosen profession have endured
over the slow eons of accumulation of knowledge. I
had exercised my option and turned down the first
assignment.

The second offering was even worse. Granted, the
species lived in an oxygen atmosphere, though the
overall planetary climate was uncomfortably warm to
my people. But the Tsaavii had been studied to death
already. While I could undoubtedly contribute to the
already large scholarly literature written about the
race, it wouldn't be the ground-breaking work I knew
I was capable of, that was expected of me. I wanted—
indeed, needed—to make a splash, capture scholarly
awards for advancing the understanding of the development of technological society. Justify my parents'
faith in me, my clan's financial investment in my education, the expectations of my sibs and cohort.

Refusing a third planet without an excellent reason—
by which they meant a sun-about-to-go-nova type of
reason—and I'd have a serious problem continuing my
work in cultural anthropology; indeed, I might even
be expelled.

They didn't consider my reason excellent enough.

"A survey was performed there eight hundred primary rotations ago. No civilization is going to change drastically in so short a time. There is no evidence whatsoever to indicate that this species is developing technologically at a greater rate than any previously known technology-using species."

Just who did I think I was, questioning the accepted wisdom of my field—me, a mere student, of limited experience. What made me think that *this* new species was so different from the dozens of other known, thoroughly-studied species?

Somehow, "gut instinct" hadn't seemed a particularly politic answer at that moment.

It's cold comfort to me now to know that my fears were absolutely justified—the preliminary survey was even more out of date than I had feared. The rate of change of this society is staggering. It's grim satisfaction to know that, in learning this, I've already made a significant discovery—and I haven't even begun my initial research. I plan on saying a very loud (and most scientifically phrased) "I told you so" when I face my final exam board.

I am woefully unprepared. The trinkets and toys I'm equipped with, suitable for a premechanized society, are totally unsuitable for a culture at this level of development. Instead of early explorations into metal smelting, these people are essaying their first steps into molecular-level manipulation of biotechnology. My gadgets are useless—simple devices intended to startle and amaze a hostile group just long enough to allow me to escape, or to lure a timid folk from hiding, nothing more. Such things are as out of place here as a medicine woman with her healing broths and spirit chants would be in one of this city's hospitals.

And I don't like my body. It's weak and clumsy now. I have to be so careful when I move in this awkward, heavy gravity. And only two hands! It amazes me the natives were able to develop any sort of technology at all. At least they have opposable digits on *both* hands.

My Supervisor isn't particularly sympathetic to my situation. "I would think you'd be delighted, Student Candidate. This is the opportunity you said you were waiting for, a chance to make a significant contribution to our field. You have an entire world's worth of development at your feet. A tenth-span certainly will not be long enough"—I clench the communication Link in my hand—"but it will serve as a beginning. You had best make the very most of your every moment there. Communication ending."

Communication is expensive and must be kept brief. Perhaps it's just as well. One does not gain honor by being disrespectful to one's Supervisor. And I must not forget, I am representing my species at the prestigious institute of learning I attend. The Mother Supreme pointed this out to me during my audience with her just before I left.

"Very few of us have ventured off-planet. Do not forget that you are an ambassador, even though you do not bear the formal title. For many—indeed, perhaps most—of the species you come into contact with, you will be the first of our kind they have ever met. Conduct yourself with dignity and bring us honor."

I bowed before her and backed out of her presence, grateful that protocol did not permit me to speak.

My Supervisor is of the school of thought that believes in interaction with a species, provided there is no interference with the society. Thus, I underwent extensive—though reversible—surgery to adapt my body to the conditions on this world, so that I may breathe and move unassisted. Surgery that also changes my appearance so that I blend in with the species I'm studying.

Of course such surgery is costly—as will be the procedure to restore my natural form. Be sure my parents made this clear to me.

"We're having to borrow heavily against our Family

shares to pay for this," grumbled my father. "I don't see why you need to be operated on in the first place. Don't most cultural anthropologists use skin projectors?"

I patiently explain, yet again. "My Supervisor feels it's vital to her technique of close study of other peoples. 'There's no substitute for real interaction,' she keeps saying."

"Sounds like a typical scholar to me. No head for finance . . . no experience of the real world . . ." His grumbles die away.

"She's one of the foremost experts in the field," I say. "I'm extremely lucky that she agreed to accept me." My parents, concerned but supportive after my first refusal—my clan is known for its indulgence of its young—had been gravely displeased after my second refusal, so there really was no choice left for me.

"Yes, and an extremely high Supervisor's Fee she charges, too. You'd damned well better win some of those academic awards you talk about and bring us honor."

"Of course he will," says my mother soothingly. "He's our son. He's always lived up to our expectations and beyond." She beams proudly. "And he will again."

Yes, I will. I will be a dutiful child and do well. My father complains about expense but it's pure ritual. I'm expected eventually to make good on all the loans and fees that are paid out on my behalf. Duty and obligation, over and over, the watch-words of my culture.

Maybe that's why I went into this field of study—to learn about other societies and see if they're any freer. The crushing burden I owe my parents and my clan . . .

These are unworthy thoughts and I'm glad my family is not privy to them. I should not be having such selfish feelings. A mature individual is able to school his feelings, focus on his duties, and take satisfaction from fulfilling his obligations.

Obviously I have a long way to go to reach maturity.

This culture is as unlike my own as any storyteller could imagine. Chaotic, noisy, the natives rush frenetically about, ever busy, even at night—the lights of the city drown out the stars overhead. I spend hours, too many of them, by the ocean—this is a seaport—when I should be in the libraries and museums, learning about these creatures. But I find the frantic pace they live at overwhelming. The sea brings me a measure of peace as I watch it ebb and flow and crash and murmur. It reminds me of home, even the natives swimming—*they* call it swimming, at least; to me it is clumsy thrashing, fighting the water rather than being one with it.

I take out the Link and stare at it. Among the decorative elements on its surface there is one stud that is meant for Recall, in case of such unforeseen and serious emergencies such as civil unrest, natural catastrophe, or war. Definitely not for use by homesick scholars.

We were originally a seafaring culture. Perhaps because the sea is so vast, and accidents are so random and sudden, my kind developed a formal and structured society: every situation noted, every situation with its appropriate actions, every situation accounted for.

I know in my heart I don't fit in very well. I liked to test myself against the sea too often. This was a sorrow to my family. When I should have been attending to my share of the clan duties, I was inattentive, my mind on the waters.

I am ashamed of this. I owe my family much, for they have supported me in the study of other cultures, a study I love. Many clans decide the paths their youthful members should tread, without taking personal preferences into account. But I am fortunate, for my clan is different. Our Mother Supreme is very old and very wise, and feels that children work harder and more willingly—and thus are more likely to do well—when they work at something they enjoy. So she indulges us. I owe it to her and to my parents to repay their trust and confidence in me.

I'm beginning to feel smothered under the weight of all these obligations and expectations.

I was daring today. The waves were high, crashing on the shore. I longed so much for the feel of the sea that I dared to venture into the water, yes, into the water in this temporary form I wear. I swam.

I attempted to swim, rather. Oh, but it is a feeble reed, this body. Clumsy, awkward in the water, unstreamlined, no harmony with the currents. Worst of all, no way to stay below the surface for more than seconds at a time—as I discovered, choking and spluttering. Of course, no water-breathing structures. Why didn't they warn me against this?

Because it never occurred to them. When the thrice-ignorant fools who surveyed this world did so, they reported no cities by the sea. I am certain they never bothered to look.

I staggered from the water and collapsed on the beach. I was fortunate it was early morning, and the beach was almost deserted. There was no one to see my humiliation.

But as I regained my breath, I noticed there were a few swimmers out there. No, wait, not swimming. They were balanced on long narrow boards, balanced on the very crests of the waves surging to shore, balanced like dancers.

My jaw dropped. My people have never even *dreamed* of such a thing. These people call it "surfing."

I inquire at the library. "I wonder if you can help me. I'd like to learn about the history of surfing, and I don't really know where to begin." When I explain

I was inspired watching the surfers at the nearby beach, the librarian laughs.

"Oh, we don't have serious surfing *here*—those are just baby waves. I think a tape of last year's Hawaiian championships has just come back in . . ." The helpful librarian brings me audiovisual records of surfing contests held in other parts of the world. I'm astounded when I view them. The local waves are indeed just "babies," and the surfers I saw are far from expert. The award-winning surfers do things I wouldn't have believed possible. Of course, I find the size of the waves they're riding almost impossible to believe as well, but the librarian assures me these are factual records, no trickery involved.

"Not like that new movie—I hear they used a lot of special effects in that one to make the waves look so huge."

Movies? Special effects? I decide to leave that for another day. I want to view the sequence called "shooting the curl" again.

There is clearly more to this species than I realized.

I wander the streets. Fortunately, the weather is mild this time of year and I can sleep outdoors, provided I stay out of the way of others. I am equipped with food concentrates and there are public water sources. But this is only a short-term solution; I need a place to store my equipment and belongings, to archive my research records, and—most importantly—to have a little solitude and be able to meditate. It is only by merest chance that I am lucky enough to stumble into a niche where I can support myself and study this culture more closely.

I see a street performer, who entertains the passing crowd; in return they drop money into a basket at his feet. He's a conjurer—misleading the audience by the skill of his hands and his clever patter. I realize my gadgets will be useful after all. It appears magic tricks can be entertaining, even if the culture no longer believes in magic . . . or at least claims it doesn't. And a street performer doesn't need an elaborate background history.

I become a magician. My tricks with lights and smokes and colors fascinate them, and they pay well, far better than I expected. They come again and again, bringing friends. I discover, to my relief, I don't have to talk. Indeed, my silence seems to add to my mystique. And I learn, also to my relief, that my evasive answers to questions after my performances are considered entirely appropriate. No one *really* wants to know how it's done.

My Supervisor is pleased with my inventiveness. "Well done, Student Candidate! I believe your achievement is unique—an illusionist in a technological society. Continue your research—this will make a fine presentation at the next colloquium. Communication ending."

Research. I should be spending much of my time studying this world's past and present knowledge. Its history, its science and art, everything about it. But there's so *much* knowledge. I could spend far more than a tenth-span just assimilating the knowledge of the one library near the apartment I now rent, let alone every library in the city. I could spend a lifetime.

I *like* performing; it's much more fun than doing research. It's rewarding to see the awe on the faces of the audience and hear the delight in their laughter at the climax of a trick. Children are the most fun of all. Their eyes grow huge and they squeal with joy and clap their hands. I find it impossible to resist them.

I watch my spectators carefully, and learn better pacing and timing. I begin to study magicians and the history of illusions in the library, and try to develop better tricks. I become a fixture among the street performers and begin to make friends. I have the usual cover story ready: a traveler from a distant country, learning about this one. Friendships form easily in this culture; apparently there is nothing like the cautious negotiation of mutual obligations that accompanies such a relationship on my world.

I have become such a fixture, in fact, that I'm beginning to recognize some of the regular attendees of my performances. The other artists tease me—they say I have a "fan following." (The concept is new to me, and I learn it has nothing to do with devices for moving air.) These "fans" strike up friendly conversations with me. One of them invites me "to the bar for a drink." I accept, somewhat nervously.

My nervousness was unnecessary. Bars are fascinating; there's no equivalent on my world. There, one can have relaxed social interaction with close family members of the same age cohort, but not with those of different ages—and certainly not with complete strangers in a public place. Let alone while ingesting intoxicants. I would never have believed that a social species could be so casual about such things.

But here . . . I can go into the Overtime Bar and Benny, the owner and bartender, will yell a greeting over the din of the chat and broadcasts, and have my favorite beer—I've become very fond of Coors, an extraordinary brew—waiting for me by the time I sit down. There are always people ready to discuss anything, from politics to sports to entertainment to local gossip to, well, anything. Invaluable for a cultural anthropologist. All I need to do is listen and pay for an occasional round of beers. Everyone loves a good listener; I'm one of the most popular regulars in the place.

I now know what movies are: a flat, nondimensional audiovisual projection; holographic projection is still in its infancy. This species is ingenious, I have to admit; it never occurred to me that one could use such projections to record fictional stories. Movies are a very popular form of entertainment in this society, and there are dozens available in a variety of genres at any time. I plan to sample each genre at least once. The one I saw today is classified as an "action picture"; apparently this involves much gunfire and racing about in automobiles. Why automobiles—and not bicycles, which would seem to me to be a more accurate measure of the stamina and determination, and thus the heroism, of the characters involved—is not clear to me. My new-found friends at the Overtime tell me that if I want to see special effects, I should sample the latest in the "science fiction" or "fantasy" genres; I'm not sure of the distinction between the two.

My Supervisor interrupts me as I am enthusiastically describing the latest *Trek* film. She is displeased with me. "You should be *studying* the culture, not *immersing* yourself in it, Student Candidate. By all means, attend one of these . . . movies. Attend several. Entertainments, particularly fiction entertainments, reveal much about a culture's values and way of life, far more than their creators recognize. The assumptions behind the fiction's underpinnings; the styles of dress, adornment, transport, housing . . ."

Despite the expense, the Supervisor is carried away into lecture mode, lectures I have heard many times through my student career. I find my attention drifting. There is a new James Bond film coming, and a popular young actor is taking over the legendary role. There's been a lot of discussion about it at the Overtime, with much speculation as to how he will handle the character. Will he have the sly, double-entendre charm of Roger Moore? The more serious and subtle sophistication of Pierce Brosnan? The bluntly honest and somewhat primitive style of the original, Sean Connery? I'm a Brosnan fan myself, but I'm looking forward to seeing how the new actor interprets the famous spy.

It opens next week—I can't wait to see it.

* * *

"Hey—I've got a spare ticket to today's game. Want to go see your very first baseball game? It's the season opener." Dave, one of my fellow buskers, makes the invitation. I haven't any idea what "baseball" is, but of course I accept; a study opportunity like this is invaluable.

It's as unlike the dignified sporting events on my own world as could be imagined. Attendees wear the colors of the team they support, of course, but in a wild variety of fashions. Some of them actually paint their face and body in team colors—unthinkable in my species, but I admit having fur is a barrier to such a form of self-expression; this species has generally hairless skin. (I wasn't able to determine whether paint is acceptable in lieu of clothing in this social situation. This society has taboos about dress and undress that are utterly confusing.)

The din is incredible. There is noisy music. There is shouting. There are announcements about players and their statistics. People react loudly to the play on the field—some even have portable amplification devices to make certain they are heard. There are vendors hawking food, beverages, and mementos. And to my shock, complete strangers will assist in such transactions by passing money or purchases back and forth the packed rows of spectators.

Despite such apparent chaos, I find the crowd around me is genial, and happily willing to explain the game to a newcomer. Though the finer points elude me, I do learn the city's team is called the Giants (though Giant what, I don't know), and that they're doing well in "the pennant race," whatever that might be. We cheer and applaud when a player performs well, and shout rudely at the officials when we disagree with their officiating. At first I'm reluctant to be so discourteous, but am assured by my companions that this is all part of the game, and indeed, the officials seem to take no notice. I get so involved that I find myself on my feet, shouting with everyone else, when a Giants' player hits the gaming-winning "home-ee."

I had a *wonderful* time. The next time I go, I'm buying myself a team jersey.

"Student Candidate, you have spent enough time studying this culture. It is time you moved on to another."

"But—"

The Supervisor ignores my protests. "You've become fond of these natives and their style of life. I warned you about this before you departed—it's a common reaction for a student's first time in the field, though I had not expected it of someone as gifted as you. Remember, these beings are not friends, they are study subjects. Do you understand?"

"Yes, Supervisor."

"Good. Make plans to move on. Let me know within three local days what your destination will be. Communication ending."

I'm upset. I find my way to the ocean and watch as the full moon rises over the waters, brilliant even in the light-washed sky.

I don't want to leave this city. It is heresy to disagree with one's Supervisor, but she's wrong: I *do* have friends here. Heck, I have *fans* here.

I take out the Link and stare at it. Then I put it back in my pocket and look out at the crashing waves for a long time.

Much is expected of me. I am a Prime. Always, I have been given the first choice at meals, the first choice of playthings, of worship position on holy days. I have been allowed to choose which course of study to follow. I have been given first choice of mates.

But "choice" for me is not the same as it is for these busy, chaotic, noisy human beings. For them, choice really *is* a choice. Even so simple a thing as food: any individual here may choose a meal, any meal, at any of a myriad of eateries catering to a wide range of tastes and income levels.

My choices were not like that. Clan and caste, honor and obligation, all form ever-narrowing circles limiting my range of choices.

Here, life partners select each other. My selection was limited to Primes of appropriate age from appropriate clans. And my parents and the Mother Supreme discussed my preferences—they care for me and want me to be happy. But far more than my personal happiness is at stake in this. Political alliances play a role; status of the particular clan of a candidate; financial means; and of prime importance, fertility, for children are the foundation of a clan. It turned out that my "choice" and I were not compatible.

The Mother Supreme was gentle with me. "Child"— she used the honorific that meant an especially beloved child, to show that she attached no blame to me—"such incompatibility happens. It is a bitter blow. We will make the necessary regret gifts to the other clan. And you will make another choice."

Regret gifts. My clan is known for its impeccable courtesy, but naturally rumors immediately circulated that the infertility was *my* lack and fewer clans were eager to offer candidates. Eventually a suitable mate was found for me. The preliminary ceremonies were performed before I left; our final union will take place when I return. And of course I will have to assume the burden of recompense for the regret gifts—it is the courteous thing to do.

Damn courtesy. Is there no room for *me* in my life?

"Your disobedience is unheard of, Student Candidate. I *insist* you move on to another culture at once." My Supervisor is angry with me. Her crest has even changed color.

"Forgive me, Supervisor." I use the most respectful tone I can summon. "You are right—I have allowed

myself to become fond of this culture. I see now that
my objectivity has been compromised, as you feared.
I apologize." I watch carefully and see her intense
coloring begin to fade. "I will gather my belongings
and records and move on at once."

"See that you do so, or I will Recall you immediately."

I realize that I must act quickly or yet another
"choice" will be forced upon me. For there is another
aspect to Recall—it can be activated at the other end
as well. Occasionally, in the long history of the study
of other cultures, scholars like myself have "gone
native"—a rarity, admittedly, but the institute is meticulous in planning for every contingency. Except sur-
veys, I think wryly.

"It will take me several days to pack my belongings,
sever my housing agreement, and arrange transportation. The island archipelago that looks the most intriguing is at some distance from this land mass. I will
contact you as soon as I arrive there. Communication ending."

I go down to the seashore. It's a stormy day, cold
and blustery, with few people on the sand or in the
water. I sit on a log and stare out over the steely
waves.

I take out the Link. The Recall field is effective at
some distance, I have been told, and is tuned to me
alone. (It would be unthinkable to accidentally bring
along unintended passengers.)

I reach back and hurl it as far as I can into the
roaring surf. The currents here are particularly fierce.
It will be carried away in the endless roll and beat
of tides.

Perhaps I will be thought of as one of those scholars
who paid the ultimate price for attempting to enlarge
my people's body of knowledge. My clan will mourn
my loss; I was a promising youth tragically snuffed out
before I had a chance to fulfill my potential. Other
clans will sorrow with my family.

Or perhaps my Supervisor won't be deceived by the dying of the Link's signal. She will remember my behavior and report it to the governing board. My parents will be informed that I "went native," and will be shamed. My disappearance will bring dishonor to my clan.

I realize I don't care.

A great weight lifts from my shoulders. For the first time in my life, I'm utterly free! No obligations or duties to the endless line of the generations. I feel light and giddy. School's out!

There's a Padres verses Giants game this afternoon— an important one in the pennant race. Benny's pulling two-for-one drafts and offering hot wings to all comers who show up in team colors. I must go home and get my Giants' cap and jersey.

I may even learn to surf one of these days.

XENOFORMING EARTH

by Tom Gerencer

I TOOK A MOMENT to construct myself from stray carbon in the atmosphere, since I'd been spending time, the last few days, as patterns in the static electricity across the surface of the television screen, the drapes, and every other ungrounded surface in the room, including the cat. Admittedly an incognito method of relaxing, but every time the maid came, I got nervous.

I was on a planet called the Earth, out past Centaurus. They had named it after some dirt. I'd arrived there some weeks ago, in the center of a masked implosion, and had quickly set up shop. I'd rented an apartment, bought a car, and had some business cards made up. I'd also altered my entire makeup for the trip.

I'd changed my physiology, my body type, my language, taste in clothes, political opinions, and I had developed a proficiency at gargling. I'd even grafted a mild seafood allergy into my anatomy, just to round the picture out. Still, "a rose by any other name," or so they say on Earth, and that goes double, I am sure, for aliens.

I'd been sent to catch a criminal. The Naag, to be exact. A purely mental form of life, his ancestors had

not been small and furry animals or even large and
slimy ones, but catchy songs caught in the heads of
other sentient beings. They had evolved from there
into entirely independent superegos, in complete control of whatever organisms they decided to possess.
Literally, the Naag were a parasitical and highly spe-
cialized variety of guilt.

The one I had been sent to catch had claimed to
be on Earth spending vacation time "in some of the
planet's magnificent Catholics." I did not believe a
word of that. I knew him all too well. He was a xenoformer. That meant he altered worlds illegally, changing their atmospheres, topographies, and biospheres
for large amounts of illicit cash. The Earth was his
next target.

It didn't take me long to find him. He found *me,* in
fact. Broke into my apartment with a borrowed human
body and a screwdriver. I stepped out of thin air right
behind him and I tapped him on the shoulder.

"Hello, Naag," I said.

You should have seen him spin around. The centrif-
ugal force of it restyled his hair. I decided that it
suited him.

"How are the Catholics?" I said.

He went white. "They're wonderful," he said. "I
like the Jewish mothers, too. And most of the rest of
humanity in fact. Although some of the marketing
people make me nervous and I try to steer clear altogether of Los Angeles."

I shook my head. "It's crap," I said. "You're xenoforming Earth."

"I'm not."

"You are. What is it this time? An ocean planet for
the Hyrrions? Or what about something hotter, for
the Nuwa Chythicans?"

He shook his head. "I don't know what you're talking about."

"Oh, really? Then why did you break in?"

He looked down at the screwdriver he still clutched. I saw his eyes go hard.

"Don't even think it," I said. At the same time, I pressed a short gray cylinder up against his head. "You know what this is?"

He rolled his borrowed Earthling eyes to get a look at it. "A psychological injector?"

"Good. You know what's in it?"

"How many guesses do I get?"

"Forty millicogs of pure, uncut forgiveness from the Monks of Xalia."

"You didn't even let me guess."

"The most guilty beings in existence," I went on. "They think everything's their fault."

"Even shaving?"

"Especially shaving."

"They sound fantastic. I'll have to visit sometime. Bring the kids. Now if you'll excuse me—"

I shoved him up against the wall. "They train themselves for centuries in self-forgiveness. It's painstakingly harvested and concentrated in mental collectors. Do you have any idea what this stuff does to Naags?"

He did, evidently, because he dropped the screwdriver, and he didn't fight me when I used the cord from one of the venetian blinds to tie him to the credenza.

"No, no," he said. "Never mind me. I'll be fine. You go have your fun. I *like* being tied to the credenza."

I didn't listen, as on the one hand this was typical behavior for a Naag and on the other I had locked myself in the bathroom, where I'd dropped a tab of standard issue, psychoactive, prepaid calling acid. It was time, in other words, to call the cavalry and I planned to do it through a telecommunicative hallucination.

The walls melted. My head became a spray of huckleberries. The huckleberries grew and morphed into an office with a few inspirational wall hangings, a potted plant from the Dehutan sector, a desk, and, sitting at it, Remsee, my superior.

I use that last term lightly. You see, Remsee was a Wiee—a form of life evolved entirely from hand puppets. It was called inanimate evolution and it was all the rage some centuries ago. Manufacturers had started it to get their products to improve themselves by natural selection. They'd introduced accelerated recombinant evolution into household objects, then let nature take its course. The craze had ended in a flurry of lawsuits when a politically active band of intelligent suppositories attacked a ladies' historical society luncheon, but certain vestiges remained.

"Xzchsthyl!" Remsee said. "It's great to see you!"

I stayed wary despite this pleasantry. It was said the Wiee had no innate intelligence and so derived mental nutrition from the minds of everybody they conversed with. The process was not fully understood, but every time I talked to Remsee I had the distinct impression I was getting dumber.

"Where are you?" Remsee said.

"On Earth. Remember? I was sent to catch the Naag?"

He tipped his head to one side, making his eyeballs jiggle. "Oh, right. I hear they've got some wonderful hands on the planet."

"I'm a poor judge," I admitted.

"Fantastic knuckles," he went on. "Very good bone structure. Some of the fingernails can snag, I hear, but wonderful overall."

"Right. Listen, Remsee, I caught the Naag."

"An aunt of mine got a job there working with a ventriloquist. Totally freaked everybody out. What did you say?"

"I said I caught the Naag. I've got him in custody."

He looked thoughtful. He managed that by scratching the red fur of his forehead. "Right, right," he said. "Xenoformer, isn't he?"

"One-hundred plus worlds," I said.

He nodded. "I remember. Thing is, Xzchsthyl, you've got to let him go."

I couldn't get sense out of that comment any way I looked at it. It was like drilling for orange juice inside a goat. "Did you say, 'let him go?' "

"I did."

"But he's a known xenoformer. And he plans to xenoform the Earth. Under article six million three hundred thousand eight hundred and fifty-two, any planet hosting indigenous intelligent life—"

He was nodding like people do when they can afford to concede your point because theirs is bigger. "And the human race does not meet the criteria for intelligence."

I was mouth breathing by then. "Come again?"

"The council held a special meeting," Remsee said. "They cited strip malls. Overdevelopment. Pollution. And Minnesota."

"Did you say Minnesota?"

"Mmm. The council thought Minnesota was a particularly dumb idea."

All the strength went out of me. It was obvious enough what had happened. The Naag had bribed someone. It wouldn't be the first time. Only a year ago, for example, I'd nailed him for xenoforming a small reddish-brown world out by the Crab Nebula, and the judge had thrown the case out, saying the witnesses for the prosecution were a bunch of no good clowns. He had a point—they were second-rate performers from the victim planet. Kept snapping the bailiff's suspenders and throwing cream pies at the jury. But the Naag had also bribed the judge, and the larger issue was, the Naag had money. In the face of that, a mere bureaucracy is helpless.

"You're to return to base immediately, Xzchsthyl," Remsee said. "And bring a couple of hands back with you if you get the chance."

I tried to talk some sense into him, but he was ada-

mant, and by the time we disconnected I could not
remember how to tie my shoes.

After my talk with Remsee, I stood looking through
the bathroom window. In the playground near my
building, a little crowd of children played. They were
singing, laughing, jumping rope. One of them pushed
another's face into a mud puddle. They reminded me
of another child, on another planet, many years ago.
That other child was me. Granted I'd had several
limbs, an exoskeleton, and had propelled myself around
by means of air expelled through one giant nostril, but
I'd been just as oblivious and innocent.

The Naag had xenoformed my homeworld all those
years ago. His *modus operandi* then had been to move
in, drive up the property values, slaughter 98 percent
of the indigenous population, and then experience
vague guilty feelings afterward and let the survivors
open up casinos by way of partial restitution. My family had only made it out by becoming excellent croupi-
ers, although I never mastered that particular skill
myself—a fact that almost killed my father. Literally.
The dice we used weighed several tons and I fumbled
one and dropped it on his thorax.

I'd been chasing the Naag ever since, with gills one
month and tentacles the next and feathers the next
until I could not remember what I had originally looked
or felt like. And finally, I had begun to see that I
would never catch him. Because xenoforming paid
well. Because he could afford the bribes. Because (as
they also say on Earth) money talks, and there's another corollary concerning ambulatory bovine fecal
matter.

But I decided, then and there, looking out my
rented bathroom window at those laughing Earthling
children—playing, jumping, sticking chewing gum in
one another's hair—well, I decided Earth was off limits to the Naag. And if I couldn't stop him legally. . . .

I went back to the living room and aimed the psychological injector at his head.

"Call it off," I said.

"Call what—"

"The bribe."

"What bribe?"

"I mean it, Naag. I'm not afraid to use this."

He took a second, apparently to gauge how serious I was. "Okay," he said. "I'll help you. But I can't call off the bribe. It's too late for that now."

I paused, my finger trembling on the trigger. "I'm listening."

"The human race. You can get them legally protected." His voice dropped to a whisper. "They produce the cure for chronic ullnik."

Chronic ullnik. A terrible and fully hypothetical disease. It attacked organs that its victims had never bothered to evolve. The phantom pain was said to be excruciating.

"The human race produces the cure," the Naag went on. "By accident. It is a mix of waxy yellow buildup, unsightly nail fungus, and household soap scum. I came across it by accident in a public lavatory."

"And you expect me to believe that?"

"I've got proof. It's with my partner."

"What partner?"

He answered rapidly, possibly because I'd put the injector's business end in his left ear. "The Sublukhar," he said. "I'm working with the Sublukhar."

I shuddered when I heard that. I knew the Sublukhar as well. Another xenoformer, huge and sluglike, brutally efficient.

"She's outside of town," the Naag went on. "At a place called Breakneck Mountain. The Earthlings call it that because a cow fell off it once and broke its neck. If you ask me it is a lucky thing for the local civic organization that it didn't break its reproductive organs. That would not have sounded half so rustic."

"What's she doing there?" I said.

He shrugged his shoulders. "You know how Sublukhar are. Temperamental, but excellent with machinery. She's setting up the xenoforming equipment. And doing other things."

I grabbed my jacket and a blaster. "What kind of things?"

"Unnatural things. With monkeys. But I don't ask questions where the Sublukhar is concerned." He frowned. "You're not going to leave me here, are you?"

I didn't answer. I just headed for the door. If the human race really did hold the key to curing chronic ullnik, my troubles were as good as solved. If I could get the proof . . . get it to Remsee . . . no bribe in the universe would stop me from saving Earth.

"Well, that's fine," the Naag called after me. "The rope is starting to rub my wrists raw, but I don't mind so much. And anyway, I'm sure you've got more important things to think about."

Breakneck Mountain rose out of suburbia, an undeveloped pile of rock and tree, a lonely shred of evidence that Earthlings were intelligent. By the time I reached it, night had fallen from it like a cow, and it hung caught and broken in the thousand orange streetlights bordering the highway.

I parked in the breakdown lane and climbed the slope, ascending through the musky darkness in between the trees. Near the top, a blue haze filtered through the branches. I crept forward, catching glimpses of machinery. I approached a clearing. In the center of it loomed the Sublukhar. She squelched, cursing, glistening, tinkering with something. For some reason I could not yet fathom, monkeys hung from branches overhead.

I stepped into the light.

"Nice night," I said.

She spun around fast for a Sublukhar, her knobbed antennae shrinking. "Well, well. The great Xzchsthyl." She pronounced it wrong. "I thought you'd be slimier."

"I haven't been feeling well," I said. I'd never met her before, but I knew all about her. She was of a race of incredibly possessive sluglike creatures. They had no word for "yours" in their language, but over seven thousand words for "mine." When the concept of property possessed by others was first explained to some of their linguists, they laughed hysterically for weeks and finally had to be hospitalized.

"I hear you're xenoforming Earth," I said.

"That's the plan," she admitted, gurgling at me. "We're going to turn it into a filing planet."

"Filing?"

She nodded her slick and eyeless head. "In three days' time, the machinery you see around you will create the cataclysmic, simultaneous appearance of over three trillion billion trillion manila folders, burying every major landmass on the Earth. It's for the Griggons. You've heard of them?"

I hadn't. "I've been busy lately."

"An interesting civilization. They reduced forty centuries of history and learning down to a simple, beautiful mathematical equation, then misplaced it. They keep hard copies of everything since then."

"And Earth is going to store those copies."

"Only G through K. We'll need other planets to take up the rest. That is," she added, "if I can get the job done."

"Something wrong?"

"I'm having problems," she admitted. "And I don't mean you." She swung her head in the direction of the device she'd been repairing. "I was supposed to be in human form three weeks ago, but my ZrrfCo Somatorific here is on the fritz. Keeps turning everything to monkeys."

That explained a lot. But she was still slithering

slowly toward me, so I held my blaster up where she could see it. "That's far enough," I said. "I'm here about the cure for chronic ullnik."

"Oh, that," she said. "Why didn't you say so? It's over there, in that compartment."

I looked where she had gestured, and saw a hatch in one side of a domed machine. I kept one eye on her and walked to it. I had to scare a crested gibbon away, but I popped the hatch, pulled out a manila folder, and looked inside.

I am no scientist, but the papers in the folder seemed to be the real McCoy. There was even a budget analysis of the cost of harvesting the cure for chronic ullnik. Evidently the Naag had thought about selling the cure himself, but had decided he'd make more money from the xenoforming.

This was it. If I could get this evidence to the government, they'd have to protect the human race. I'd stop the Naag. I was so excited by the prospect that I completely failed to notice that the Sublukhar had pressed the button on her defective ZrrfCo Somatorific, and that I was standing in the active area.

Metamorphosing into a monkey stands low on my list of enjoyable sensations. Growing the hair was the worst part—like someone pulling a million needles out of all the pores on my entire body, all at once. I had to bite the Sublukhar in order to escape, and all the other monkeys chased me through the canopy. I did manage to get away with the evidence, but I was in no condition to drive, and don't even talk to me about the use of public transportation as a monkey. I particularly and personally hated it because, although I had never met an Earthling monkey myself, I had spent three weeks as a binkled ape one time on Ratcheon in punishment for excess parking violations, and my love of primates was, therefore, a sickly thing at best.

"You're looking well," the Naag said when I came in through the window.

I screeched at him.

"I see your point," he said. "We've all got problems. Look at me. I've been tied to this credenza for hours. Not that you care about *my* suffering, of course."

Trying to guilt me again. Typical. I pivoted on my knuckles and loped into the bathroom, leaving him behind. Once there, I dropped another tab of prepaid calling acid, and after staring at the pretty colors that resulted, I found myself face-to-face again with Remsee.

"Good God," he said, doing an exaggerated double take. "Xzchsthyl! Is that you?"

I screeched. The hallucination compensated, translating. "That's right," I said.

"My God. What happened?"

"I've been turned into a monkey."

He nodded. "Parking violations," he said knowingly.

"Not this time. But never mind that now." I held up the manila folder.

"What the hell is that?" he said.

"Evidence. The human race produce a cure for chronic ullnik. We'll have to protect them now, Remsee, intelligent or not."

He grabbed our mutual hallucination of the manila folder and leafed through its contents. Then he looked relieved. "Thank God," he said. "I was beginning to think I'd never get a crack at those hands. I was looking through your research this morning. I found—I think it's called a television show. They called it *Howdy Doody . . .*"

I was feeling dumber already. I cut him off before he could get into it. "I've got to go, Remsee. Just send backup, will you? I'll have to bring in the Naag and his partner and I'm in no condition to do it alone."

We disconnected. And it wasn't that I didn't trust Remsee . . . Okay, it was. Either way, I made a few more calls, and showed the evidence about the cure to other higher-ups within the government. Things were looking up, in other words. I sat down on my rented Earthling couch and waited for the cavalry.

I picked at fleas to pass the time.

I had run out of fleas some hours later and I was starting to get nervous. Especially nerve-racking was the look on the Naag's face. If he grinned any wider, he'd be in danger of an embolism.

"Anything seem strange to you?" he said.

I thought about it. Apart from my having been turned into a monkey, there was the lack of a patrol troop materializing in the living room.

"They're not coming," the Naag positively gushed. "And do you know why?"

I was starting to have my suspicions, to tell the truth.

"It's because your friends know by now I'm on your side. By now, they've got a message from the Sublukhar. They know that I have every reason to protect the human race."

I hopped up on the armrest, glaring at him.

"Oh, yes," he said. He cocked his head. "The human race. Don't they strike you as odd?" He tried to stand up, but the ropes jerked him back down. He went on talking anyway. "Think about it. After a billion years of competitive evolution, with organism after organism fighting for a niche here, a niche there, one species out of countless others wins the game in an evolutionary eyeblink."

It did seem strange to me. But I'd been busy tracking down the Naag and hadn't thought about it much.

"It was the Sublukhar's idea. Her species, anyway. They paid a visit to this place a hundred thousand years ago, and saw that it was bad. Too cold. Too much ozone. Too little latent radioactivity. The oceans were too small, too salty, and didn't have the right levels of PCBs or mercury. There were too many of the wrong kinds of plants and animals around. Too many mountains. Forests."

I felt my heart leak out through the bottoms of my padded feet.

"So," the Naag went on, "the Sublukhar said, hey! Why not tinker with the DNA of one of the existing species? Hardwire it to xenoform the planet? They did that thing, then told their creation: be fruitful. Multiply. Spread out and seek dominion over all the Earth. This was before the age of quick and easy xenoforming machinery, of course."

I slumped back against the couch cushions. I'd been duped. Why hadn't I seen this? The human race themselves, the perfect intra-biospheric xenoforming organism. No matter what they thought, no matter what they wanted to do or talked about doing, they'd been designed to do one thing: to turn their homeworld into a paradise which they could not inhabit.

"Simple. Elegant," the Naag went on. "It takes a long time, I'll admit, but the results speak for themselves. Another few hundred years and their work will be done. They'll self-destruct in cataclysmic biological attacks, and the Sublukhar will have their paradise." He chuckled. "Only one small problem. With all the scrutiny over xenoforming lately, the Sublukhar were worried someone would find them out and stop them. So they hired me to get the human race protected. Of course, it takes someone with pull inside the government to protect a species." He did a little half-bow. "I thank you for your help."

In that moment, centuries of guilt caught up with me. My own world, gone. My father, crushed (literally) by a roll of the dice. Hundreds of planets, xenoformed right under my nose. And now I'd failed to save the Earth.

And in that moment, the Naag moved in.

"Hello, Xzchsthyl," he said from inside my head. His Catholic slumped forward on the credenza. "You know, I'm sick of having you on my back all the time.

Sick of having to bribe judges because of you. Sick of you in general. I'm going to enjoy this. I'm going to devour you, Xzchsthyl, and when I'm through, I'll use your empty husk to get offworld."

He walked around, using my body like a puppet made of bone and meat. I didn't try to fight him. I deserved it, after all. That was clear enough. It was my fault that the Earth was going to be xenoformed, and there was nothing I could do about that now.

But there were other, future worlds the Naag would xenoform, and anyway he had really pissed me off. So, even though I'd earned my guilt, I knew I had to ditch it.

"You're off the hook," I told myself.

Now, I'm no Xalian monk, and my forgiveness wasn't much. But it was just enough for me to take back a small amount of motor control.

"What are you doing?" said the Naag.

For an answer, I reached out and grabbed the psychological injector, and I aimed it at my head.

After he recovered, the Naag was brought up on charges under article five million three hundred thousand eight hundred and thirty-one: conspiracy to use an officer of the law as interstellar transportation. He bribed the judge, of course, but I had had about enough of him by then. In other words, I bribed the jury. It took my life savings, but it was worth it to see him brought to justice. He was incarcerated on Earth, in California, Pismo, in the mind of a marijuana-smoking, ex-competition surfer whose favorite phrase was "Hey, man, ain't nothin' but a thing."

Remsee came out to supervise the procedure and, after he was told the surfer also ran a puppet show at county carnivals, they fell in love and Remsee left the force.

The Sublukhar, meanwhile, was badly injured when, pursued from Breakneck Mountain by a pack of enraged monkeys, she was struck by a public works truck hauling fifty tons of road salt.

As for the Earth, well, by their very nature, the human race will turn it into a paradise they can't inhabit, but even if they hadn't been protected, what was I supposed to do? Have them destroyed? It's just one of those things. And anyway, there's always hope. Not much, I admit, but it does exist. I visited the planet a few years later, and by that time, Remsee's consumption of ambient intelligence had mellowed out the population as far away as Idaho, and the environmental movement in that area had subsequently grown by leaps and bounds. He'd taken a particular toll on the Naag, who had become so idiotic that the last time I saw him, he actually apologized to me for being such a jerk.

I felt just the tiniest bit guilty.

THE SKEPTIC

by Jennifer Roberson

ODD CREATURES—*(Sidebar: yes, even I admit it, honored colleagues [note the irony, won't you?]; I'm not blind to reality)*—but that doesn't change anything. They're fascinating all the same.

They come in a wide assortment of sizes, colors, scents, and textures, even though they all approximate the same basic shape. They're a massive jumble of contradictory data. I mean, the vast majority of otherwise intelligent beings—*(Sidebar: yes, I said "intelligent"; they found us didn't they?)*—waste huge chunks of time sleeping, grooming themselves, playing games, copulating, and eating.

Since my rep is that I love to conduct empirical studies on new spacefaring species rather than playing around with theories—*(Sidebar: going native, my peerless colleagues—[yes you; you're still reading this, aren't you, with some kind of perverse fascination?] may call it)*—it wasn't too difficult to get myself assigned here to check out the latest arrivals into our part of space. So as usual I learned the language and the slang, reshaped my body, donned appropriate female guise and clothing—*(Sidebar: the males are easier to manipulate; dare I say it's the same with us?)*—adopted incomprehensible habits, and headed out to

125

experience reality such as they know it. *(Sidebar: How else do you really learn a species without getting inside its mind?—and no, don't tell me it's easier to use the scanner. This species has no idea why they do what they do, they're just a bundle of biological wiring. How could a scanner uncover anything of actual value? Besides, laboratory experiments are* boring *when compared to going into the field.)*

So, here I am. In the field. On the inside. Learning by doing. I scouted ships, found a likely one bound for a rimworld called *Paradise,* bought myself a license, and set up an office.

Pheromones are pheromones, regardless of the species; and yes, even in this guise I receive as well as exude. So I confess—*(Sidebar: and won't that amuse all of you, now?)*—to being a sucker for the studly young types who enter my place of business with a lazy grace and try to charm me. Some of them mean it. A few of them don't.

I've gotten very good at sniffing out the *skeptics,* as they're called. Some are innocent enough, trying to figure me out so they can say they have; others truly don't believe a word I say.

And then there are the self-satisfied ones who find immense amusement in poking holes in my job, which also means in my cover. *(Sidebar: and yes, they* are *intelligent enough to figure out I'm dissembling. They may think differently from us, but it doesn't make them stupid.)*

Anyway, it had been a slow day on the job—and in the study—until he sauntered in, all sleek and smug and elegant. Not a hair out of place, not a foot put wrong, with the faintly superior air of one among the blessed, sanctified by whatever power had endowed his kind with enough intelligence to find their way to deep space.

Silver hair flecked with black and brown. Clear hazel eyes. A tilt to his head and a negligent stride as he eased inside my office.

He halted, letting the door slide closed behind him. He struck a pose, eyed me a moment, then yawned.

Ah. *That* kind of skeptic.

I arched a brow at him, waiting. When he didn't offer anything beyond a stare replete with self-indulgence, I smiled and began the game. And the game within the game.

Incense, lighted. A candle brought to flame. Silks and velvets and carpets; an endless supply of cushions. They expect certain trappings in this line of work, and if I want to really get into their heads I have to live up to those expectations.

Lastly, the cards. I took them from the casket, from the scarf, and set them down on the table with its green cloth. I looked at him again, studied him, the attitude, the arrogance—and turned up the Knight of Cups.

"So," I said, "it begins."

Now he moved. With an elegant stride of no wasted effort, he arranged himself in the chair across from me. The stare was fixed and unwavering.

His nails were long. With a skilled flexing of tendons he flicked the pile of cards set on the table before him. They toppled, slid, spilled in a river of painted pasteboard across the green surface.

Commentary. Or challenge. Oh, yes, they love their games.

"You must think of a question," I said.

He blinked, unimpressed—and clearly disinclined to answer.

Inwardly I sighed. Handsome, young, elegant, ineluctably self-confident. So typical of his kind.

My turn to move quickly, with no wasted effort. The next card, turned up to cover the King of Cups. I opened my mouth to speak—and the card blanked.

I managed not to gasp. Wondered if he'd think it was some stunt *I* was pulling. Or had someone snuck into my office last night and replaced my cards with another set? That would suggest someone—maybe even he—had learned my true purpose. *(Sidebar: No-body likes to discover they're the subject of a study, after all.)*

I shot him a quick searching glance from lowered lids, raising my pheromone levels to distract him. *(Sidebar: trust me, it's worked before, even with a few of you.)* He merely stared back at me, undistracted. Patience personified.

With economical haste, I worked my way through the balance of the deck: covering, crossing, crowning.

And all of them went blank.

My mouth dried. I summoned the slang. "Okay," I said, "give. What's the scoop?"

One slow, casual blink. Then he leaned forward, hooked a nail beneath the edge of the card that had once been the King of Cups, and flicked it from under the other.

He yawned. Displayed teeth in a feral grin. Fixed me again with a stare. "You should know better," he said. "I and my kind make our own fortunes."

And with a disdainfully high hook in his tail, the cat jumped down from the chair and sauntered out of my office.

NATURAL SELECTION

by Laura Frankos

I MADE MY WAY into what the Terrans had dubbed the Drones Club, the refectory of the Selection Center to which I had been assigned. Some of you are no doubt aware that "Drones" is one of the numerous—and often rude—appellations the Terrans have given us Hripirt. Unlike many of my colleagues, I see no point in taking offense at these jibes. They aren't a bad race, not compared to some. My assignment, screening potential Terrans to find those best suited to journey to Hripirt, is largely a pleasant one. The Terrans tried submitting lists of candidates chosen by their governments, but our leaders quickly rejected those. As if we'd let just anybody visit our home, without meeting proper criteria and being able to contribute to our society!

That was one reason I enjoyed relaxing in the refectory after a long day evaluating humans. It was exclusive even by our standards, and offered a fine array of both Hripirt and Terran food. I hadn't gotten much past the entryway when someone noticed what I was wearing. "By the spoon of my great-aunt, Mullnor, what is that you've got on your foretabs?"

Such a screeching voice could only belong to one Hripirt: Bingokk. He was at his customary table, feasting on the usual greasy lavender mound of *frobrill* eggs. I don't know why he goes to the added expense of ordering them. Terran chicken eggs aren't that different in texture, and the fried salty pig-meat that often accompanies them is quite tasty.

His noisy remark caused everyone in the refectory to stare at me. Afttabs buzzed far above the level of ordinary conversation; one could understand why the rare human visitors had deemed this a Drones Club.

I addressed the room at large. "They are an example of a Terran handicraft called knitting, purchased from a human in my survey region. I find them quite fetching." I removed one with a finger-tentacle, waved it about, then slid it back on. The articles are small, and shaped rather like right angles, so they fit nicely on my foretabs. As foretabs are relatively useless appendages, the covers do not interfere with communication, as they would if placed on afttabs. My demonstration concluded, I joined Bingokk and his shipmate, Delip, at their table.

"That is most intriguing," Delip said. "When I first saw you, I was reminded of those long-gone days when rebellious youths tattooed their foretabs or had glimmer-nodes surgically attached to them, all for the sake of gaining attention."

Bingokk began coughing loudly and turned his face away from the table, but not before I noticed the thin line of scar tissue on his foretabs. He is vain, as well as extravagant. Why should anyone care what youthful follies he once perpetrated? To save him further embarrassment, I asked Delip how his meal was. He is partial to Terran black beans, cooked in the style of some tropical island, as am I.

"Do not order them today, Mullnor," he said. "They taste scorched."

Heeding his advice, I logged an order of Terran pastries called crumpets with several pots of jam. I am especially fond of orange marmalade, and have shipped a container back home for my many relatives.

"How goes your screening?" Bingokk asked me, his ears swiveling forward with interest. It was common knowledge he has started gambling pools based on when the selections would be finalized. He truly is incorrigible in his various appetites. Our leaders were wise to forbid him to visit the city of Las Vegas, for fear of what chaos might ensue.

"Very well. I think I am ready to register my choice."

"So soon?" he howled. "But you were still reviewing *three* different groups only last week! How can you be ready to recommend a human? From which group did you make your selection?"

An angry low hum sounded from a nearby table. "Stop that racket immediately, Bingokk, or I shall fine you for violating the decorum of this establishment." The rather slight Hripirt, an individual unknown to me, glared venomously, then knocked back a large glass of fermented *azot* juice. The murmur of his afttabs continued to broadcast his annoyance, despite Bingokk's feeble attempt at looking apologetic.

"What's the matter with that fellow? I asked.

"Depression," Delip said. "He despairs of ever finding a suitable candidate. There are many, he says, who score well on duplicity and slyness, but they uniformly lack common sense."

"What is his region?" I asked.

"Washington, District of Columbia, United States," Bingokk said through a mouthful of eggs. He also muttered something indistinct about my family background which I carefully pretended I did not hear.

"Strange," I said. "Washington is a major population center, as is your region, Delip. New York, is it not?"

Delip's snout wrinkled in the affirmative. "Perhaps his candidates demonstrate the herd-animal mentality of the ones I encountered on the thoroughfare called

Broadway. Many of them dress the same, act the same, and stand in the same endless lines for performances of live actors."

Bingokk smirked. "It's not so entertaining watching dead ones."

His comment reminded me of the worst planet I ever surveyed: the sentient race, who resembled Terran peapods, had made decomposition into a religious cult. We found no suitable candidate there, and it smelled terrible. We left after one of the natives killed a Hripirt solely to see her rot. This, however, is not a pleasant subject to discuss at a meal, so I remained silent. Unlike Bingokk, I know the meaning of restraint.

"Most of our jokes about Terran entertainment are well-deserved," Delip said, spooning up some beans. "But one of these shows amused me, though not for the same reasons the humans liked it."

I gave a short *blat* with my afttabs, but not loud enough to disturb the noise-sensitive fellow. "Call the medical forces; Delip is clearly ill."

Bingokk shoved aside his empty plate. "I don't know which bothers me more: Delip enjoying human entertainment, or Mullnor attempting humor."

"Let me explain," Delip said. "This particular entertainment involved the humans dressing as small domesticated beasts and cavorting in a heap of garbage."

"Are you certain the Advance Teams screened this race for suitability?" Bingokk asked. "They sound delusional."

Although I hated the notion of agreeing with the disreputable Bingokk on anything, I had to concur. "How is animal-mimicry a form of entertainment? I mean, aside from foolish characters who can pucker up and snort like wild *gronkree,* hoping to induce laughter at dull parties." From the corner of my eye, I saw Bingokk's afttabs relax in mid-pucker. He is as predictable as the Terran satellite's cycle.

"The show is more complex than that," Delip admitted. "The actors playing beasts represent human characteristics, such as vanity, gluttony, and so on."

"Ah, it is a morality piece, such as Tipli the Humble wrote!" I said. My cousin is a noted scholar of ancient literature, so I am reasonably familiar with it.

Bingokk, obviously sulking, took out his all-purpose unit and flicked his finger-tentacles over it. I suspect he was revising the odds on his Candidate Selection Pool. "Humans portraying animals who act like humans. Madness! I truly hope I find my candidate soon, and can leave this planet."

Delip, well-accustomed to her shipmate's tantrums, ignored him. I do not know how she endured them on the long voyage to Terra. My patience will survive occasional encounters with him, but not daily ones.

She continued: "The beasts parade before their Elder, hoping to be chosen to ascend to animal paradise, or so a devotee of the actors informed me, for it had made little sense to me. She explained their characteristics determined which one is selected, and this amused me, for it seemed so similar to our job of screening the candidates for the voyage back home."

Delip is a pleasant being, but every so often, she falls prey to flights of fancy, and this, I fear, was one of them. For while certain personality traits are common to sentient beings—without them, civilized life would not exist—others differ from race to race. We Hripirt had already learned that while we share much with Terrans, we value some characteristics that they view with distaste. Some of their religions even regard them as moral crimes. For Delip to equate our search with a silly Terran entertainment showed poor judgment.

A young Hripirt, her foretabs still velvety, brought my order of crumpets and jam. "I hope this is satisfactory, Screener Mullnor," she said. Her afttabs were faintly humming, so I knew she wasn't finished. Highly unusual, for here at the refectory, the staff interferes with members as little as possible. Serve and scoot, that's the policy.

Still, I thought I knew what was coming, and I was right. The little thing hummed louder and asked, "If you don't mind, Screener, could you tell me where you got the Terran handicrafts you are wearing? I'd love to purchase a pair for myself."

"Perhaps we could come to a financial arrangement," I said.

The server practically trilled. "Oh, thank you, Screener!" She looked around, probably to check if her supervisor was watching, then presented her all-purpose unit. I produced mine, and, as she was eager, we completed the transaction in moments. She slid the human articles onto her foretabs and scurried back into the kitchen.

Delip's afttabs murmured humorously. "I fear you may have started a trend, Mullnor."

"I've no objection to making a small profit from the foolishness of youth," I said, sampling the crumpets. They were nicely done, and I quite enjoyed the boysenberry jam, a new flavor for me. I logged a note to order some.

Bingokk continued messing about with his unit. Finally, he put it down and *blatted* sharply. "I still can't figure it out. You must tell me how you came to a decision so quickly. As I had it, you were screening three groups, each with twelve to twenty individuals. How did you narrow it down?"

"Last Sunday, I immediately eliminated the entire group known as the San Fernando Valley Rowdy Riotous Raider Nation on the basis of irrational behavior."

"An entire nation consisting of a few entities?" asked Delip.

"They do not comprise a recognized state. They are supporters of an athletic team."

Both Delip and Bingokk *zzurbed* in understanding.

Our leaders prepared special lessons on Terran sporting rituals, mandatory viewing for all Screeners. I found them appalling. Had I had my way, the Rowdy Raider adherents would never have made it onto a shortlist for screening, but then, I confess to being something of an elitist.

"I did not mind their outlandish face-painting and peculiar garb," I said, "but while at the sporting event, they all became 'drunk and disorderly,' violating numerous local laws. Nor, I discovered, were these their first infractions. Obviously, I could not select a lawbreaker as a candidate."

"No, for if they break their own laws, they might not respect ours," said Delip.

Bingokk waved his tentacles. "And the next group you eliminated?"

I hummed pleasantly, remembering. "A gathering of fans and authors of speculative fiction. I enjoyed being with them; of all humans, they are most at ease facing the reality of visitors from another world."

"So *why* did you not make your selection from there?" Bingokk asked. The low desperate tone of his afttabs made me wonder just how detailed his pools were. Perhaps he was not merely wagering on which of us would make our selections quickly, but from which of our focus groups we would choose.

"They scored extremely well on intelligence and creativity; some of the authors had also high marks for cunning, avarice, and duplicity—you should hear some of the wrangling they engage in regarding their internal political offices and awards. But they showed too much individualism and initiative. Our leaders want visitors who are not herd-beasts, like those Delip encountered, but neither do they want Terrans too inclined to stray from the path and explore on their own. Finally, they are definitely unusual sorts, even among humans, and not truly representative of the species."

Bingokk *blatted*, "I should have known you'd be this stuffy! When will I ever learn?" He pounded his unit on the table until the Washington-screener began buzzing again and the server, her pretty pink-garbed foretabs twitching, motioned for him to stop.

I scooped the last globs from the bottom of the jar of strawberry preserves and started on the plum jam. Bingokk's financial troubles were no concern of mine. "One odd thing happened when I surveyed this group," I commented. "There is apparently a famous fictional piece in which the aliens arrived on Terra and took away humans, intending to cook them on their home world. At the gathering, people kept asking me if I was there 'to serve man,' and laughing rather nervously."

"That is not odd, Mullnor, it's disgusting," said Delip. "What a concept! I am relieved you did not choose from this group of candidates."

"So you picked one of the ornithologists," Bingokk said gloomily. "I never would have expected it."

"They are not accredited experts on avian species," I said. "Merely well-educated enthusiasts. They journey into undeveloped areas, looking for birds."

"Then what do they do with them?" Delip asked.

I didn't answer immediately. I was watching the little server chatting with yet another diner and giving a demonstration of the foretab-covers. Most amusing.

"They don't do anything. They count the different species," I finally said. "It is a pleasant pastime."

Delip mused, "Well, perhaps this is a good test of the Terrans, to see how they fare in the wilderness in which they evolved."

Poor Delip. She obviously did not pay attention to the human history lessons. Terrans evolved on another land mass altogether different from this one. I chose not to reveal her ignorance, but merely said, "No, they only stay for brief periods in the wildlife regions, so it is not indicative of their survival skills."

"Which one did you pick?" Bingokk asked. "I must know."

I trilled lightly. "I shall describe my final four candidates, all of them high scorers for intelligence and common sense. You tell me which one I chose on the basis of the other factors. Come, we shall have a wager." I slid my unit toward his.

"Very well! Maybe a chance to get some of my losses back!"

"The first was the group's leader, Joe. He is a strong man of middle years, well respected by the others. He organized the trip, as he has done many times before. This included scheduling transport—the site was some distance from the organization's headquarters. When one individual damaged her optical equipment, he developed an ingenious solution to her problem.

"The second candidate was the youngest, a teen-aged boy named Spencer. He proved the best at identifying bird species, made numerous realistic sketches of the creatures, but generally was silent. He spent the entire bus journey playing with a small gaming unit and wore a shirt emblazoned 'New York Knicks.'

"The third was another middle-aged man, this one called Mort. Mort showed an inconsistent ability to identify birds, often loudly proclaiming a sighting was of a particular species, only to be corrected by Spencer or Joe. I mention him only because of an incident at the end of the trek.

"I explained to the humans that while the fresh mountain air and unspoiled surroundings were delightful, I found their hobby rather pointless. I then demonstrated the Sense-Surround feature of my unit, and provided them with an exact total of the avian species in the area: twenty-one Stellar's Jays, thirty-eight California quail, nineteen white-breasted nuthatches, and so on."

"What did Mort do that was of interest?" asked Delip.

"He approached me, wanting to buy my unit. Claimed he would win the Birding World Series with it, an event of competitive bird-counting."

Bingokk *zzurbed:* "Ah, avarice! Good score!"

"The final candidate, a woman named Agnes, was elderly, but in good health. She regaled me with tales of her many grandchildren, and spent the long journey creating clothes for the smallest ones. As the organization's secretary, she kept track of the birds they identified, and planned to publish the list for the members who could not attend the trek.

"So, which human did I select?"

"Spencer, Joe, and Agnes displayed creativity," said Delip. "Mort, obviously, was the only candidate to show avarice. I would pick Joe, for overall qualities."

"I would choose Spencer," said Bingokk. "Talented youths often make good candidates, and those who play with gaming units often exhibit other useful characteristics."

Now it was Delip's turn to *blat* derisively. "Ah, but Mullnor said the boy wore a New York Knicks shirt. He is undoubtedly a sports fanatic, and this negates all his other good attributes."

"You are both wrong," I said, shoving my unit at him. "Pay up, Bingokk. I chose Agnes."

He yowled and buzzed, and the Washington fellow got up and left. "Why, Mullnor! It makes no sense, and you are esteemed among screeners."

I slid a tentacle into my travel-sack and pulled out another pair of Agnes's hand-knitted *booties* and placed them on my foretabs. "Don't forget, we evaluate Terrans on what they can contribute to Hripirt society. Agnes claims she can knit many pairs of these foretab-covers each day. She and I have already registered our trading firm, Earth Socks, and have some seventy orders pending." Perhaps more, given that I transmitted the relevant information to the server's unit and she had shown hers to at least four diners.

Bingokk abruptly cut off his buzzing. "You astound me, Mullnor. I must go."

"Where do you suppose he's going in such a rush?" Delip asked.

"If I had to guess, I'd say he was going to survey his candidates for knitting ability. Pass the last jar of apple butter, if you will."

AORTIC INSUBORDINATION

by Batya Swift Yasgur and Barry N. Malzberg

I DON'T WANT TO go, I said. Let someone else do this. Not me. I never wanted it. Please don't make me—

Ah, they said, you will change the world. The needle twinkled. And the world certainly needs changing; we have had enough of this.

But, I said. Speaking as I did "(speech" of course is a converted term for what I did). But no, not what? They said. No change so great ever started with one so small. The syringe poised, hovering lovingly.

Until we understand what we are doing, I said.

We understand, they said. The syringe struck. I was propelled into the River of Memory. Swimming along its currents.

Was that how it happened? It is my best approximation. It must have been something like that as the Priests methodically unlocked and sent me on. Surely it would not have been in silence; surely I would not have gone without protest. And yet who is to know? Out of circumstances we create consequence, link a chain of events to a source, even if that source is a dream. A dream from which I will awaken safe and warm, no enclosure, no lessons, no orientation, no Priests, no mission, only circumstance itself.

Circumstance, I can handle. Haven't I always? That is why they chose me, but perhaps I was not chosen, maybe it was just a dream that I was taken to change the world.

A dream that I begged for this cup to pass (my capacity for protest was inexhaustible then), a dream that my plea was ignored, a dream that I found myself—

—Falling, falling and rolling and tumbling and bouncing, bounce and jounce, tumble and jump, roll and folderol, surrounded by the thick, viscous, oily fluid. So they did it after all, they really did make me go and it had worked, the protocols correct.

—And disbelieving to that last scoop, swoop, loop, and whoop, I thought they would desist, that someone else would be taken to prowl the darkness. But no, no passing cup, so there I was falling and rising in that tunnel, propelled by rhythmic pulsation.

Thump. Thump: it's dark, I said, and I miss my—
—Best not to think of them. Of origins, of the way it had been before and of what had been taken from me. I must live in this new world. This world, my mission.

Orientation Chamber earlier. Lecture topic: Meet Your Neighbors. You will be coursing through tunnel-like vessels in a stream of *blood*. You will be surrounded by discs, oddly concave at the center. *Red blood corpuscles*. These new neighbors are important, yes, but not as important as the white blood cells: *Leukocytes*.

Remember those. That's what you'll be.

And even before: I don't want that, I said. I don't want that. Silence, I was told, and shattered and complicit I acceded.

Follow your fellow leukocytes: watch and copy

them. Then at a crucial moment you'll make that one
critical change and then—

And then what?

And then you'll see what is needed and why.

And then they obliterated me.

Into that blood of memory. *Leukocytes, corpuscles,*
my new family. Two cells in front, fellow members of
the White, fellow soldiers of the Immune System. Behind, a mass of them: some round, some ovoid, and
some horseshoe shaped—as, fetchingly, am I. Eccen-
trically located nuclei too like mine, surrounded by
cytoplasm that glistens in the slick and random darkness of the blood. Cytoplasm just like mine, except
for that one crucial difference, the infinitesimal message of change given this humble Voyager to carry.

I, Voyager, greet them as they greeted me. We communicate in the bloodstream's ancient code. Their language comes easily as we signal and call to others of
the Family: *Monocytes. Macrophages. Eosinophils.* All
that instruction I have endured facilitates communication. I mask my origins and darker, higher purpose
with the words of cells, commonplaces hiding the
deeper codes of exile and ruin. The Leukocytes and
I, burbling small confidences as we await the call: the
true summons.

The call.

A nasty virus this, they say. Herpes zoster. Kill it
now is the command. So it's off to the hand where
Herpes Zoster has pitched camp. We are armed and
ready for battle. We jog and swim to the Herpes Fort.
My own substance is grim with the knowledge that
my battle is not with Herpes. Not at all. Herpes is not
the enemy. I know this.

I plan my address, then.

Herp, I will say: Herp, old pal. We're allies. Friends.
Herp, I will say, you are the smallest life-form known,
nothing more than a package of DNA with a dirty

assignment. I have an assignment, too, and these missions are not dissimilar. Your mission is to replicate yourself and so is mine. You will use the body's own reproductive process by taking over a cell's internal machinery. And I—

—And I

—I stop. That would be too blunt. I might have said that I would take over Herpes' own machinery, but that would alert him and then I would have to take him by force then instead of having his cooperation. Try this, Herp, I will say instead: I will assist your takeover by sending false signals to the Leukocytes. They will disperse, the dumb things. By the time my deception has been discovered, Herp and I will be sharing a cell and the process will begin.

This seems more reasonable.

Accordingly, I volunteer to lead the attack. The Leukocytes agree. Why not? They are so dumb, so gullible, so easily led after all. Furthermore, they are relieved. Let someone else lead the charge to the enemy camp. Find someone as willing as I.

Wait ten heartbeats I say to them. Then move to the fifth capillary along the digital crease of the third right interphalangeal joint. I will be waiting for you there.

They are dumb but imprinted. They waver. It should not be, they suggest. This seems peculiar, they bleat. We are not at all certain, they whine. We have doubt, they mumble.

I am persuasive, intense as I have been trained. This is the best way, I say. This is the source of the signal. They grumble and mumble a kind of agreement. They bounce and jounce, hobble and bobble.

I will be waiting for you there, I say. Go ye heroes, etc.

Mutual salutes, wishes of luck, and then I forage my way to the fifth capillary where Herp perches, indistinguishably.

I speak to him just as I planned. It goes as I knew it would.

Herp is persuaded.

"Mommy, it itches!"

"Itching is normal when you have chicken pox. Let me prepare an oatmeal bath for you."

"Oh, that feels better. Can I sit in the tub all day?"

"If you want."

"I want. But, Mommy—"

"Yes, dear?"

"There's one spot that is still itching. Like it's on fire. And the oatmeal isn't helping."

"Show me."

"Here. The middle finger of my right hand."

"Oh, my, that is some blister. I've never seen one quite like this. Let's try some lotion and see if it helps."

"But, Mommy—"

"What is it?"

"I feel weird. And all the other blisters are starting to itch more. Something is happening. Something's happening! The blisters—look, they are getting bigger and bigger. Help, they're growing and growing! Look at that one on my pinkie, it's as big as my whole finger. And that one over there—"

"Oh!"

"Mommy what's wrong with me?"

"I don't know. Hello? We need an ambulance immediately. Something terrible. Terrible!"

"Mommy!"

Of course I don't kill him.

That was never the assignment, of course. Never. What would be the purpose of that? The mission can be accomplished only through a live carrier, an active host. And a good thing, too, because killing him— well, that would have been malevolence, nothing else.

Seven years old: innocent and adorable. Cute as a button. That's what the nurses have been saying, now that the swelling has receded.

But before that: doctors in and out of the room, the kid's little face now a bowling ball, his fingers and toes fat little sausages. And the arms and legs unrecognizable in their edemic monstrosity. Massive does of benadryl to control the itching, sedatives to help him sleep in the fever's furnace, antibiotics to kill the alien invaders . . . if only they knew, if only they knew.

No one told me that it would be this way. The Priests, they kept me in the dark. That was certainly wise of them. I was already protesting and if I had known it would be this way, would I have still gone on with it/ The burning, the excruciating itching which has made the merge possible.

The merge possible. The next step.

The transitional step as the host and the Voyager become fused.

Now I am him: now he is me. I am Mikey in the fire, here we are in the flame, close to death, but we won't die. We sill survive. We have survived and are so cute once again.

They say we are cute again. Cute as a button.

Merged to Mikey in the fire. Mikey the fiery, Mikey the funny, Mikey the redeemer. Listen to our song:

> *I am Mikey*
> *And Mikey am I*
> *I come from the sky*
> *And I can fly.*
> *Why, sky, fly, oh my, so high.*
> *Never shy and never will die*
> *I am Mikey*
> *Mikey is me*
> *And we can change the world*
> *Just wait and see.*
> *Me, we, he, hee whee!*

I am Mikey
Mikey is laughter
I was serious before
But this is after
Ha ha, Mama, Papa, ha, ha, ha, ha

So that's it. Laughter. My mission. From the solemn emerges the irreverent, and it is the Road of Redemption. Make 'em laugh. Shake 'em up. Sacred sounds, as their bellies jiggle, the hips wiggle when they giggle.

Like the vase. It's funny. That's what it is. To watch that vase sail across the room, banging into the wall and then the little pieces of glass showering the floor. How they twinkle in the sun, those colors streaming in rainbow splash as they fall. The rainbow shower is ever so much prettier than a dumb old vase sitting on the shelf.

A flying vase is funny. As funny as telling my teacher that I was born in China, adopted by Mommy, had plastic surgery to make me look American, but couldn't do the homework because my English skills were still poor. And talking fake Chinese the rest of the day. Ong. Pong. Ching chong. The other kids laughed. They liked it. The rest of the day, we were all going around saying Ing, Ping, Ong Pong, Ching Chong. Only the teacher didn't think it was funny. Why?

It was as funny as the sound of tinkle in the kitchen sink. Sinkle. And watching the mailman slide along the path on the yellow thing I left there just for him. Squeal on a banana peel!

Why won't Mommy see that?

Because she just won't. Not when I'm the one doing it. Oh, she laughs at the guys on television—or at least she used to. The big fat man and the short man. She laughs when they get pie in their faces and when they slip on banana peels and when they throw things at one another. She laughs at circus clowns, doesn't she? So why won't she laugh at my red nose and my cheeks? My flying vase and banana peel. And if I can't make her laugh, how will I make the rest of the world laugh, too?

Because that is my mission, to make them all laugh. Clever of the Priests to make it so serious—classes and lectures and that scary injection—when it's really all about being funny. Your mission will emerge, they said. You will learn by going where you have to go. And so it has. To turn everything topsy-turvy. To get them to shred their assumptions. What makes a vase pretty on the shelf and ugly in pieces on the floor? What makes a banana peel funny on television but not in real life? Only those stupid beliefs passed from parents to children. Change those and you can change it all.

How will they learn to change their assumptions?

By laughing at everything.

Everything!

Down the railing and up the stars, bet you can't catch me, Mommy! Funny, how you run! You weren't made for this, were you? Whoops! And when you put the salad on the plate, I suddenly whisk it away so the salad goes right on the table. And when you try to catch me, I say you can't catch me. No one can catch me! Catch us, I should say. Catch me and Mikey.

And the look you give. Oh, Mikey, you've changed, you say. Your forehead wrinkles and that new annoying line comes between your eyes. Tears on your cheeks. I was supposed to make you laugh, not cry. What's going on? Why do you take me to that lady, Mrs. Burton, the one who tries to look so important with her silly dolls dressed like doctors and nurses. Why do you get so angry when I make the dolls fly across the room? I've got great aim, haven't I? And Mrs. Burton herself when she reaches clumsily for them. A flying Mrs. Burton!

Oh, ladies, stop whispering. All those long, serious

words about "trauma and adjustment," "aggressive tendencies," "repressed rage," and "inappropriate affect."

Laugh and dance. Dance and laugh. Light and fun. Come on, Mommy, watch me run. Mommy, you can help me change the world. Get everyone to see everything different. Hey, is your world so great? War and terror and cheating and pain. Wouldn't it be better to just laugh and laugh? Mommy, you're not laughing—

Mommy is crying.

"I understand, ma'am," he says. "There's nothing more painful than having to institutionalize a child. But you've tried everything for this boy. Thirteen years since that bizarre early childhood illness. Thirteen years of treatment. Individual therapy. Family counseling. Psychotropic drugs, acupuncture, herbs. There's nothing more you can do. But your son is in good hands here and he'll do very well. Won't you, Michael?"

I thought it would be simple once Mikey and I became one. To get them to laugh. To turn sadness into happiness, to change the world, shatter their assumptions, break their idols and make them happy. Simply happy. They were so aggressive, so destructive, but laughter would solve it all.

But they wouldn't laugh. Why didn't the Priests understand, in Orientation Chamber, that they could not laugh? They are not like us. Their complexity, their convoluted, crazy world, it cannot respond to laughter.

The Priests didn't know. They did not understand the situation. They had misappraised. But I know now. I have learned.

The question is—what do I do now? To get it back. Retrieve the mission. A serious mission, to bring frivolity? Infect with laughter, infect the world? What can I do, stuck away in this loony bin, with all these—

Then all at once I know what to do. And fall down

in awe, for the Priests understood after all. How to bring the mission, where to execute it, my very failure the necessary stepping stone to my success.

Begin right at home, of course. What better place than a nuthouse for laughter?

So I hold a meeting after lights-out and before the meds kick in. Tommy is sleepy and mumbling as usual about the Government. James is preparing for his Second Coming. Arnold is moaning and rocking. Dorian— Well, you don't want to know what Dorian is doing. The orderlies are somewhere down the corridor, of course. They don't care. A typical night.

"Well, folks," I say, "Do you want to change the world?

They become quiet. No more Government or Return of the Son. They have never heard me say anything serious before. They have barely heard me speak. I sure have their attention. The orderlies yap on, I hear their voices from down the hall.

"If we change the world, will you change the Government so they won't be after me anymore?" Tommy asks.

"We'll have a different Government, sure," I say.

"But will they show any compassion? Will they leave good citizens alone?"

"Great compassion. All the compassion you could possibly want and more of it."

Tommy considers this. James says, "Government can't change. The world can't change until the second coming."

"I am the second coming," I say. "I begged pass this cup and they did not listen and now I am here."

They say nothing to this.

"Blessed are the light of heart because they shall uplift the world."

"Amen," James says and crosses himself.

"The Lord God is a God of Laughter," I tell them. "Just read the second Psalm." Psalms had occupied a lot of my time years ago. When Mommy went off to cry.

"You get a lot of good information from the Psalms," I say. "You'd be surprised what is in there. Harps and lyres and whatnot."

"I don't know what lyres are. What we gotta do?"

"We laugh," I say. "That is how it begins. And then we do things to make everyone laugh. If each of us make two others laugh, and each of those take on another two, we can take over the world."

"Just laugh?" James says doubtfully.

"That's it.'

'Seems pretty silly to me," Arnold says. "But it beats the crappy therapy and basket weaving. Sounds like more fun than Basic Living Skills, too."

Carlo, Ben, Jamal, Kenneth, Dorian, and the others come to join us. The whole men's ward. "Try it," I say. "Ha."

"Ha."

It begins so feebly.

Ha.

But it builds. Piece by piece, sound by sound, we give to the world the sounds which the world deserves, which it has always needed. Ha and ha and ha again. And the orderlies come with their syringes and restraints, but there are too many of us, so they call the nurses, but there are still too many of us, as we hear the sacred syllable of redemption from Wards 3 and 4, so they call the doctors, but there are still too many of us, as the women's wards begin, ha and ha and more ha.

And the plates go flying, the people go flying, until the top of the nuthouse itself is levitated by our laughter, lifted by that sound, twinkles and twirls at that sudden elevation and as Arnold and James and Jamal and Carlo and Ben and Dorian and Kenneth and I continue that levitating laughter it seems to overtake the world itself; manifest silken strands of light and laughter penetrating the closed and open spaces.

There is much more to this, but it is not for me to tell that story. My story is of origins, masques, and the sudden flight of running blood. Of contagion, cell to cell, voice to voice, echo to echo. From here, it is for the Kings and the Popes, the Presidents and the Preachers, the Priests and the Headquarters to take over that fierce obligation of laughter, laughter as hot as the sun, burning into all the spaces and places of human habituation.

Hi, Mikey.

Good-bye, Mikey.

Finita la commedia.

HARVESTING

by Nina Kiriki Hoffman

I STEPPED OUT of the dimension gate at the forest's edge. The sun was high overhead. It always disconcerted me when I wound up in a different time zone, which was ridiculous, because I always did. At home, it was the hour before the evening rush at the restaurant; here it was before noon, a good time to harvest.

It was hot and humid in the half-dark below the trees. Unfamiliar, sparkling bugs whined. The air smelled swampy. Sweat started all over me. I shifted the packstraps on my shoulders.

A small dirt-brown boy with only two arms and legs stooped among low, light-green plants in a clearing nearby. He had a string bag in his hand. He was picking wild lettuce. On his back was another string bag, with three glass balls the sizes of fists in it, separated from each other with moss, each visible in subtle, glowing colors, gleaming in the green-filtered forest sunlight through the meshes of the string. I had never seen anything like those globes before, but I could tell just from their sight and scent that they were valuable, full of promises.

Anger rose in my throat. I wanted to kill someone. I drew my big knife.

151

"Hey," I said to the boy. He looked up, startled, then thumped back on his heels. "Let me help you." I sliced through the stems of many baby lettuces at once, angling my blade so that the severed plants flew toward the boy.

"What?" His eyes were wide, his eyebrows up.

"Pick fast. You shouldn't be here. It's too dangerous." Who would send a boy alone into a demon wood with such globes strapped to his back? Home in my hive, we wouldn't let such little ones out at all. His skin wasn't thick enough to survive brushes with reality.

What if I were hunting meat instead of fungus? Such a young, soft creature, tender and tasty. I wasn't the only one who came to gather in these woods. Node pull was strong here.

He put the sheared lettuce into his bag, glanced at me and away, his face flushed. I squatted nearby, the blade dangling between my foreknees. "Who sent you here?" I asked.

I could hardly concentrate on my own words. The globes on his back glistened and called to me. "Own us," they whispered. "Caress us. If you have us, everything snarled in your life will straighten out. All you need is us."

"Who sent you here with those things on your back? Don't they know you're in danger?" I scythed more lettuce for him.

He licked his lips. He placed the lettuce in his bag one small plant at a time. Why wasn't he picking them in armfuls? He had to be quick.

"We want to be with you," the globes whispered. "We don't like it where we are now. We'll make all your heart's dreams come true. Take us."

I grabbed the bag out of the boy's hand and stuffed it full of lettuce. I handed it back. "Go home," I told him. Why was I bothering with this boy? I was only on this world to get swamp truffles for tonight's special dish at the most expensive restaurant on my world.

All ingredients guaranteed fresh and organic, but don't ask where they come from. My leash was pretty tight. If I didn't return in the next hour with the truffles, someone would tug it, and I would suffer.

"Take us," sang the globes. "We will free you of everything that binds you. That Over who plagues you in unfair tasks and orders? Become an Over yourself. That Other you've had your eye on? Show her only one of us and she will come to you."

Swamp truffles! I'd forgotten my mission. I'd visited this world often to gather produce. There wasn't much heavy industry here; everything from this world tasted wonderful and fresh. I knew where I was. There was a truffle patch only a little way from here under some ancient oaks.

I took the boy's arm and pulled him to his feet. "Go home," I said again. I shoved him toward the edge of the forest.

A flood of people came out of the trees. One tossed a leather rope-thing with weights on its three ends. It wrapped around my upper arms and torso. One of the spinning weights hit a globe on the boy's back, shattering it. It screamed as it broke. Its despair at its own wasting filled me with echoing despair. I had resisted the call of the globes, and for what?

The stones at the ends of the rope slapped into my sides with bruising force. Pain burst through me. Once my upper arms were immobilized, the weights dangled, swaying.

"You don't want to do this," I said to the people who gathered around me. One darted forward and tugged the big knife from my upper right hand. Another made a loop in some rope he held, and reached for my lower right hand. I tucked my lower hands inside my shirt, gripped the handles of the little harvesting knives in their sheaths.

A woman broke from the line of people and ran to the boy, hugged him to her.

"It didn't hurt me," he said. "It only helped me."

"You caught it for us, Kutu," said one of the men. "Good work."

There were provisions for gatherers who encountered disaster on harvesting forays. In the best-case scenarios, gatherers were abandoned. There were too many of my people on my world, and we were too easily trained for us to be very valuable as individuals.

Worse-case scenarios involved self-destruction. I wasn't important enough to rate a bite-down poison, though. Worst-of-all-case scenarios meant that the gatherers were gathered for something unpleasant.

I had worked my way up from fuel gatherer to fungus hunter. My masters valued my special sense of smell; I could find funguses others missed. But I wasn't the only one like me.

If only I'd gone for the truffles and left the boy alone.

I slid a knife free and slipped my hand up under my upper arms. I sawed on the rope thing that had caught me. Even though I kept my knives super sharp, they couldn't saw through the ropes that bound me.

Who were these people? Where did they get their ropes? Usually on this world I avoided contact with the natives. Wrong-shaped people in other dimensions got upset when they saw me, so I had made stealth my practice.

I had no interest in being a meat-hunter. Fungus was what I liked to harvest. It didn't fight back, and I could snack on it while I gathered. I had finally gotten the job I had always wanted.

A line of fire striped the backs of my legs, then another. My homeworld handlers were jerking my leash a little early.

Some of the people around me stirred. They brought out more ropes, made loops, dropped them over my upper parts. Many of these few-limbed people spread out around me, gripping ropes that ended in loops that restrained me, tugging from different directions.

When there were enough ropes, they dragged me out of the forest into the hot wet daylight.

"But it didn't bite me," Kutu said.

"You were lucky," someone told him.

"You told me it would eat me or kill me for the wishballs. It just cut leaves for me and told me to go home. It didn't even try to get the balls."

"You were lucky."

He pushed away from his mother and came back to where I walked along, responding to the tugs of eight different people with ropes on me, all going in more or less the same direction.

"I'm sorry, Monster," he said.

"Me too."

"Kutu, get away from that thing!" said someone.

He pulled one of the globes out of the bag on his back. I saw where the first one had cut him when it broke. Black blood.

"Would you like this?"

I sheathed my useless knives and grabbed the ball from him with one of my lower hands.

"Yes," the globe told me. "I want to belong to you. I want to serve you." It felt warm in my hands.

"Kutu!"

What to wish for?

Six more lashes hit my legs. I stumbled. I felt the hot green blood flowing down my calves toward my ankles.

I didn't know what the people who had captured me wanted with me. I couldn't do anything to satisfy my handlers. Even if they pulled me home, I wouldn't have the truffles, and that meant punishment, maybe becoming an entree.

I held the globe tight in my lower hands and wished for freedom.

Nothing changed, and everything changed. Part of me still walked along in the grip of ropes between these villagers, suffering from cuts to my back and legs from the handlers on my home world. Part of me lifted out of my body and rode up into the sky, free of everything. The sky part almost let go of the body part, but not quite. The sky part watched everything below.

The globe didn't work. Or only a little. Not enough.

I threw it on a rock, where it broke wide open. It screamed. My sky part flew back down to become trapped inside my body part. I shuffled on toward the village with my captors.

Entree at home, if they jerked me back? Or entree here, where the natives had ropes that could withstand my best knives, and wishballs nobody in the gathering community had ever mentioned?

Either way, entree, I guessed. I hoped I would meet a chef with skill and go to the shadow hive in glory.

WHAT MUST BE

by Josepha Sherman

YOU ARE MY FRIEND, Human though you be, and so I shall tell you the tale I have told no other Offworlder.

I am Krahelk, a warrior as are all Gratarikai. Our world is a sterner one than yours, with more power to its gravity than yours as well. And so your people are smaller and less powerfully built than is our way of being. Your eyes, too, are strange to me, Human eyes with their strange variety of colors. Gratarikai eyes are always one shade, the proper yellow that is the color of fierceness. Our hair is always the proper black, and worn by most in traditional warrior knots.

And we are beings of honor. Honor, yes, it was honor that ensnared me—

Wait. I am aware that Humans are quick with questions. I will tell you of my world, my family, but you must promise not to interrupt.

So now. I will begin by warning that Humans do not truly understand our Gratarikai government. We are not a monarchy, yet my father, Kratarel, is the people's ruler. So I would, in turn, have become his heir, if the council so approved and the rites were all propitious. And . . . if what must be had not been.

Yes, I know that is not yet clear. You must listen.

Here is our world: Rugged as we are, our beautiful, fierce mountains and red earth. Here is my father's mansion or, if you prefer, palace: A long sprawl of compounds, each separate as a bead on a necklace. We do not live close together as you Humans, for our warrior spirits will not permit that, and one clan will not overlap the territory of another.

All is elegance in that palace, clean white or sleek and gleaming metal walls, green things growing for food or ornament. We have no need for beast-pens. We do not eat tame creatures, since there is no honor in killing something that has no freedom.

And here, now that you can understand a little more of us, the tale can truly begin.

Youngling was I then, still bearing nothing more than my child-knife, my jaws barely strong enough to tear the throat from a tiny *kragi*—a creature, maybe, like your sheep—assuming that I had the skill and speed back then to *catch* a *kragi*. But I was learning quickly, as a Gratarik child must. The weapons teacher did not knock me down half so often, nor was I quite so covered with slashes and bruises. I need not mention that I was learning other things, since we do not deny ourselves the worth of art and music. Politics and cunning I was being taught as well, being the son of Kratarel, as well as the way things must be.

There was more to learn. I knew, of course, that I was not my father's only child. There was another son, my half-brother, though I had never seen him, nor he, me. We lived in separate wings of the compound. His name, I was told as soon as I was old enough to understand such things, was Erekal. And as soon as I was old enough to have the concept, I was taught to know him as my enemy. How else? There can be but one heir.

Akkkh, you give the Human dip of head that says you understand. You do not. Not yet.

There could, of honor, not be a reckoning till he

and I were both of age. For now, I was a child, curious
as a youngling must be, and stealing silently through
the compound, stalking I knew not what, practicing
skills I was only just learning. There was the smallest
tangle of undergrowth, a long hedge of dark green-
and-silver *watik*—not large enough to hide prey or
predator, understand, but large enough for a child to
creep into. It was beyond the territory permitted to
me. But I would not have been true Gratarik-kin if I
did not test boundaries.

I quickly found as I crept along the ground under
the tangled green cover of prickly leaves that another
had the same idea. Yes, it was another young one,
and yes, it was another male.

We did not instantly state challenge at each other,
too startled, I think, at coming face-to-face with each
other to do more than stare. His face was just a touch
stronger than mine, a little closer to the fierce lines of
adulthood. He still bore a child's knife, though, just
like me.

"You do not belong here," he said, not quite in
a snarl.

"Neither do you," I retorted, and saw from his in-
voluntary blink that I was right.

Now what should we do? A challenge seemed foolish, since we were both trespassing. No, do not interrupt! That concept you just stated, "retreat"— surely
you see that is not our way. No, we knew even then
that we must resolve this encounter in a way of mutual honor.

The problem was suddenly altered by the sound of
grown Gratarikai. Finding us here where we knew we
should not be would mean punishment. Neither of us
wished that.

We fled together along the line of green, under the
bushes, pricked by leaves but soundless as two determined young of our kind could be. At last we came
out in a little pocket of greenery where the bushes
hadn't quite grown together. It was just wide enough

for us both to sit back on our haunches and study each other. Now I saw a faint likeness to myself in him. And his *gyag*-hide tunic was just as supple—and thereby costly—as my own.

We knew, I think, even at that moment. We should have instantly attacked each other. But we both hesitated, and the hesitation grew just a moment too long for action. Now neither of us really wished to attack. Curiosity was too strong, yes, and with it a certain child-rebelliousness against the way things must be.

"I am Erekel." He said it almost defiantly.

"I am Krahelk."

The names sent their trained thrill of *enemy* through us both. We accepted that: We were brothers and therefore enemies. Yet at the same moment—

This is why heirs are not meant to meet so young, before the lessons of *enemy* and *kill* are firmly implanted. Before a youngling's rebellious nature can be tamed by adult needs and honor.

Akkkh, but there we were, not quite enemies. It seemed too strange, I think, after we had both escaped together. We parted without fighting.

After that, the name "Erekel" had a face to it. That bothered me. I could not hate, not when I remembered a face that looked something like my own—a face that had borne the same confusion as my own.

We met again. Of course we did. How could such a situation be left unfinished? But again we could not fight. There seemed no honor to it. And sweet, sweet, too, the taste of rebellion. Sweet to say, *I am not bound by every rule adults have commanded.*

We talked together, Erekal and I, comparing our lives and experiences. We even, when no one else could see, play-hunted together, stalking and catching an *aldu*—a small thing like what you name a lizard, inedible but swift as a flash of light. We let it go, of course, since there is no honor in killing for no reason. But the hunt gave us laughter, quickly cut off so no adult would hear.

Yes, my formal training continued, warning over and over again, *Erekal is the enemy, Erekal wants your life.*

But I found it increasingly easy to disbelieve. So it was with Erekal as well.

We should have outgrown this. After all, the years were passing and we were no longer truly younglings. It was nigh impossible for two nearly-grown Gratarikai to meet in secret. Those meetings grew more and more rare, more and more brief. But despite that brevity, I realized that the unthinkable had already happened: Two brother Gratarikai, two heirs, had become friends.

"Why do we need to fight?" I asked my brother.

"Ekh, yes. Why should I kill you?"

"Or me, you!"

He waved that possibility away. "But it is so: We are the only two brothers in history who do not hate each other."

"Then we do not need to kill."

Erekal hesitated. "There can be only one heir."

"Why?" I asked bluntly.

"Why . . . because . . . you know why!"

"I know the schooling, yes: We are Gratarikai, we are fierce, we cannot share a throne. But we are both heirs and yet we both live."

"What are you saying?"

"If we are friends, if we do not fight . . . why not build *two* thrones?"

He stared. And then Erekal grinned. "Why not, indeed?"

But what might have happened then never was completed. We were interrupted by the outside world. The war against the K'ritqa had begun. Our people are, of course, sworn members of what you call the Alliance, our loose-spun gathering of trading worlds. The K'ritqa threatened us all.

I went to war. Erekal did not. He had no choice: It was forbidden, with guards and locked doors to see it stayed that way. Unspoken on many lips was that if I died in battle, there would be mourning—but there would also be relief that the two-heir problem had been so easily resolved.

I had no intention of obliging them. And Erekal smuggled me a message, one word only:

LIVE!

Of the war itself I need not speak. You know as well as I how fierce it was, in space and on world after world, how short but brutal, how many died, and how the K'ritqa, never really understanding the concept of different species in alliance, were beaten back. They are, so we all believe—and hope—no more a threat.

As for me . . . I had gone into war a youngling yet. I had fought before, of course, but never slain sentient beings. Now . . . one does what one must. I came back from the war a seasoned warrior with the taste of enemy deaths sharp in my mouth and the memory of Gratarikai deaths dark in my mind.

I had scarcely thought of home in all that while. But now, as the homeworld filled the warship's screens, I felt the same surge of joy as every other returning Gratarik. But in my mind, the joy was mixed with thoughts of what must come.

Had Erekal changed? Was he still friend to me? Was he still sworn as I was to change the way of things? We were both adults now. It could not be long until the day when we must fight or dare defy our people's ways.

First, though, came the requisite ceremony of return. I went before my father—he whom I so seldom saw. Picture one my height but more burly. Gray streaks his warrior knot of hair, but there is nothing of weakness or age in the cold yellow fire of his eyes.

That fire did not warm for me. Even as he honored me for deeds done in war, I could all but read on that grim face a calculating, *Which of my sons should be the one to live?*

No, you misunderstand. I agree, it was not what one of your species would call a "charming welcome home." But it was no more, no less than could be expected from a Gratarik ruler with two living heirs.

Upon the spot, my father set the date for the Day of Destiny, when he would learn the answer to his question.

That simply made me all the more determined that Erekal would not slay me, nor I him. I will not deny feeling a thrill of relief when I finally heard from Erekal. He managed to send me a wary message: *I have not forgotten.*

My message to him contained only one word in return: *Friend.*

We would do this, then. We would refuse to fight. We would rule our people together, and show how strong two wills united could be.

The Day of Destiny came. We do not fuss or add undue fanfares to such serious events. I was left to make my own way to the Courtyard of Ritual. I bore no weapons, of course. You have seen that we do not enter death-duels with other than our own strong arms and jaws. There is no honor, after all, in injuring bystanders. And of course there were bystanders, a ring of them, watching as they must watch to see all was done properly. They stood with fierce eyes and impassive faces: They would not interfere.

Yes, my blood was surging by now, but not from fear. Today, I repeated to myself, we would bring Custom down, yes, and tear out its throat.

Akkkh, there on the far side of the Courtyard was Erekal.

In that one cruel moment, hope died within me, and cold despair took its place. Erekal approached in a hunter's stalk. Erekal's eyes were hot, blank fire, insane—

No. Drugged.

By whom, scarcely mattered. Some courtier, perhaps, some slighted rival, even our father himself. Obviously, someone had known. Someone had betrayed our friendship and us.

Oh, my brother!

Erekal clearly was not able to know me as other than *enemy*. He roared out a Death Challenge on me. The words would mean nothing to you. The intent . . . yes, that you do understand.

I could do nothing else but fight. You have seen Gratarikai in combat; you know how swiftly we move. We fought, Erekel and I. We fought. He bruised me, clawed me, once even nearly closed his jaws on my throat. I . . . did what I could to stay alive. I battled instinct, battled custom, battled myself more than poor, drugged Erekal. And I—my mind wasn't clouded by drugs. I won.

Standing over my brother's dazed body, I roared out my defiance: *"I will not kill!"*

For that . . . dishonorable crime, for that refusal of my rightful duty, my father did as he must. He declared blood feud against me and gave me only time enough to find a ship off-planet.

Akkkh, now you are truly shocked. What else was there for him to do? He now had lost both heirs.

Yes. Both heirs. I had not saved Erekel's life. He had lost the fight, remember. My brother was slain as being "unfit to rule." I learned of that much later.

So I wander the star roads in exile. Honorless? To my people, perhaps. To my father. Not to me. I have lost my brother, I have lost my world. But *I did not kill Erekal.* It cost me much—but I kept my vow. *I did not kill my brother.*

In a strange and lonely way, I have won.

AND I WILL SING A LULLABY

by Paul Crilley

MUMMY TOOK ME to see her friends once. She's not my real mummy, but I call her that in my head because I don't have a mouth, which daddy says is good because if I talked the way I looked it would be a horrible noise.

Mummy put the chain around my neck, which is For My Own Good so I don't get lost. Lucky for me! Sarah also came with. She is my sister (but not really) and she is six years old. I've known her since she was one when all the people came here in their flying ships and built farms and little towns.

I don't like mummy's friends. They sit around a table with a very white sheet on it and drink drinks that make them act strange. Daddy calls them horrible hags, which I think is funny.

I even got a dress to wear! It is strange and heavy, but mummy made it specially because it is not right that decent people should have to look at my elephant skin and giraffe neck. I'm not sure what that means, but I don't want to be mean to decent people so I try not to scratch too much when it hurts my skin.

You're probably wondering how come I can speak so well? It is because when Sarah sits down in front of the see-through man for Lessons I watch also. I learned words and numbers and other things.

Two plus three equals five. That is math.

When we were at the ladies, they all laughed at me and said how adorable you dress yours up! Mummy gave me a drink which I couldn't drink (because as I have previously shown I have no mouth) and one said it was like watching a monkey playing human.

A monkey is an animal from Earth and it is quite clever, so that was quite nice of her. (I learned this.) Another said mummy should be careful or I'll get a big head, which I think isn't bad as my head is only a quarter the size of theirs and could do with some growing!

Sarah didn't enjoy herself. She said she was bored and would use the knife that is supposed to be for lunch to make holes in the white cloth. This is naughty. I watched her but not a lot as mummy says I'm not allowed to and especially I'm not allowed to look at her eyes. I'm not sure the reason for this. Another thing I'm not allowed to do On Absolutely No Account! is touch anyone at all, especially not Sarah. Mummy says I have dirty skin, so I don't as I wouldn't want anyone to get dirty.

I got tired standing in the sun, so I closed my eyes and visited my brood. They live far away and I try and teach them things I have learned, but they are still young and confined to their sacks. Maybe when they come out, they will show an interest and call me mummy, but in the meantime I carry on feeding and shaping them with my thoughts. This is how they grow. I decide to make their heads bigger than mine so they will look more proper. I look forward to teaching them all the wonderful things I have learned from the see-through man and my family.

For daddy's birthday Sarah made him a card which said "Happy Birthday Daddy" on it in orange pen. I made one as well and drew a picture on it so I wasn't copying Sarah. When daddy got it, he stared at it a long time then went and showed mummy. I heard mummy saying it was wrong and they should tell someone and daddy said he thought it was sweet and anyway look at the picture it was a perfect likeness. After that daddy asked me to draw lots of things which he took away. He said I was Very Good, which made me happy.

One day I was sitting in the garden. I was speaking to my brood sire who lives with his own family many many places away. He is learning how to grow things that his family eat and also clean the house they live in. He says it takes him a long time and he sometimes gets hurt when he breaks his family's things. (Not on purpose of course. His hands are not small like mine and he cannot grip things properly.) His lady (that is what he calls his family: lady and man) also teaches him other things which I do not understand, but he says his lady is happy so it makes him happy. He didn't say anything about his man teaching him, so I suggested he try the same thing for him. Maybe the lady and man will both be happy!

On Sarah's birthday (which is my birthday as well but not really, only in my own head) we went into town so Sarah could pick a present. She wanted a doll which I knew already and I have been trying to make her one from the broken wood in the back garden, but it never looks right. It is not like drawing or as easy as forming my brood where all I have to do is think a thought. But I couldn't make a doll and daddy put it in the fire anyway, but I don't think he knew what it was and I didn't tell him or he would feel bad.

We went to lunch first, but I had to stand outside in the dusty road holding their bags with a dog which kept barking at me. I wished I had a mouth so I could say *shush dog,* but I don't so I couldn't. The owner came and untied the dog and he said good boy, you tell the ugly alien, which I didn't think was very nice of him.

After lunch we all went to another shop where I

had to wait outside again. I wish I could go in and look at all the things. But I had to look at the window instead and stood making faces at my reflection which was fun.

Daddy came out and went across the road to a shop filled with bottles. Mummy and Sarah were still looking for dolls.

Then at the same time, which is funny if you think about it, daddy and Sarah and mummy came out of the shops at the same time. Sarah saw daddy and ran toward him waving her new doll which was very pretty. Both daddy and mummy shouted no, then stop her! stop Sarah! catch her! which I don't think they were saying to me because I am Not Allowed to touch Sara.

Sarah ran to her daddy and one of the floating cars hit her in the side while she was waving her doll in the air.

Sarah's arm came off and landed on the car. She flied through the air and landed on her neck in front of the shop where she got her doll. People screamed and dropped things. People shouted at me why didn't you stop her? You stupid alien! You killed her! And I started to cry because I thought I wasn't allowed to touch her and now they wanted me to and I didn't know.

Daddy came up to me and his face looked horrible and angry. He hit me in the head so hard I fell down and he said to me get out of here you fucking beast I never want to see you again, and he kicked me. Then he turned away and fell onto the ground crying and I went away from my family.

I ran away over the dust for four days. (I took my dress off first and folded it into a bag so it wouldn't get dirty.) I ran away to my brood because this is where my clan have sired For Ever and it is a peaceful place.

I lay down in the hole where I was born and cried.

I didn't mean to kill Sarah. I wondered if they would ever forgive me.

I closed my eyes and let my mind join my brood. I listened to their minds and their hearts beating in time with each other. It was like a tune for a lullaby and I sang myself to sleep, a song I heard mummy sing to Sarah.

> Golden slumbers kiss your eyes
> Smiles await you when you rise:
> Sleep pretty wantons, do not cry,
> And I will sing a lullaby

I dreamed that Sara was alive and we were a happy family again. We ate lunch in the garden and little bugs sat at the table and shared our food. They talked about bug things which are secret and much more important than anything we talk about, but we were all allowed to hear the secrets because everyone was happy. Then the bugs gave everyone kisses on the cheeks and flew away making *bzz bzz* noises.

Then it was my birthday and mummy and daddy gave me a room of my very own inside the house and not in the garden where I used to live. Their was a sign on the door saying *Mary's room* because this is the name they decided to give me as it was daddy's own mummy's name.

Then we all laughed and laughed, but then I cried because I was the happiest I'd ever been in my whole entire life.

I woke up with A Plan about how to make mummy and daddy happy again. It would take a long time, but sometimes those are the best surprises because you have to wait and wait and then you get it and it's really nice.

I dug the dust and earth away from my brood. Their sacks throbbed and moved which is good because it means they are still alive. But not all the time. Sometimes a creature burrows into the sack and eats the babies and the creature wriggling around in the sack munching only looks like the babies are alive.

Munch munch.

But that is not the case here as I touched them all with my mind and they are happy.

It took me ten whole days for me to make my own sack. It is very horrible because it grows in my tummy and then when it is too big I sick it out and it hurts. But then I climbed inside and the wet edges joined together and Just Like That! I don't have to move or feed from the air because my sack does it all.

I closed my eyes and my brood joined me and I started to work.

I wake up after many days. A hundred and a hundred and another hundred! My sack has split open and the wind rubs dust onto my skin which hurts a bit. But then I look and see that my brood has also wakened. They have all gone away except for one that I made stay because it is part of my plan. It is sitting in its sack looking at me and I laugh and clap my hands because balancing on the long neck is the face of Sara smiling at me. Her head is still too small and it wobbles a lot, which is funny, but I don't think mummy and daddy will mind because they will have Sarah back and they will be happy.

I gather her up and run back along the dust because I want to give them their present as quick as I can run.

But I still wait. Because I want it to be a surprise. So I sneak in the house at night and take New Sarah to her bedroom. A Wonderful Surprise awaits me. Mummy and daddy have had another baby! Now we will be a big happy family. I put New Sarah into the bed with her sister and tiptoe back downstairs. (Although this is just a Figure Of Speech that means very quiet as I don't have tiptoes.)

I wait in the garden and I shake because I am so happy. I put on my dress that I have kept clean all this time. I sit at the table where we will all have picnics and laugh and tell stories. When the sun starts to come up, I listen to the bugs, but they are keeping their secrets.

Then I hear a scream. It is mummy and she is screaming for daddy. It must be about something else though because it does not sound like a happy scream. Then daddy shouts and then mummy runs into the garden with her new baby. She sees me and starts screaming Samuel! Samuel! (For that is daddy's real name.) I see daddy at the window then he goes away again and I get up and walk to mummy, but before I can get there, New Sarah vanishes from my head. It is hard to explain, but she is just not there anymore.

I wonder what is wrong because I feel all horrible and twisty and I want mummy to comfort me like she did Sarah when she was upset, but she is still screaming and so is the baby, and then daddy comes out and he has something against his shoulder. He screams for mummy to get out the way and she runs away and leaves me. I still feel horrible and I think New Sarah has gone. I wonder if the creatures that eat the sacks are in the house as well. I should tell mummy so nothing happens to the new baby.

Then there is a loud bang and I jump backward and sit on the wet grass although I didn't even mean to! There is lots of smoke in the air and I try to catch it with my fingers, but it slips through them.

I think the run has left me tired because I can't keep my eyes open. I decide I will sleep, and then when I wake up, maybe then we will all have lunch at the table.

Then we will all be happy.

AQUARIUS

by Susan R. Matthews

I BECAME AWARE in the warm part of the year, resting and growing in the litter of the leaves, drinking the cool dew from the night breezes, growing and gaining in understanding of the world that was around me. I had siblings; all of the aware one was my mother, and there were others destined, like me, to be fruiting bodies—children of the aware one, and part of the aware one.

I lay in the warm moist comfort of the tree-floor as I formed, as I grew stronger and throve in the nourishing forest. I had nothing to do but to eat and drink and listen to the voice of the aware one, the thousands of voices of the aware one, speaking quietly in the night of the moment of Creation and the nature of the world. We are old, very old, millions of dayblinks, thousands of warmcolds, but until only one hundred and thirty warmcolds ago we were not aware.

How did it happen? Just as it happened with me, I supposed. In the natural progression as the caretaker of the tree-floor we grew in size, we grew in complexity, and in the course of time we became aware—not only aware, but able to communicate with the rest of our being, and know that we were with the aware one. I am of the aware one. I am the aware one.

And at the same time I was only one of a generation of fruiting bodies, and there was something wrong, something that puzzled the aware one, something that had not happened in our memory which reaches back to long before the time at which we became aware. Something was happening.

In my infancy I cultivated the tree-floor where I lay for nourishment, breaking down the litter and the debris, taking the material the insects made for me and processing it further for the smallest of insects to complete the cycle and free the food that the deadfall contained for the use of the trees and the insects and the aware one, and me. The aware one was hungry, I was hungry, I was not growing as quickly and as well as I could have; I felt it as something that was wrong, and wondered if I was working hard enough.

The moisture was not there. The moisture was needed for the insects, but the moisture was even more important to me for my use. I could not make use of the nourishment without moisture. I cultivated my area, I sought out the moisture in every warm breathing spot where it could yet be found, and there was not enough.

Without adequate moisture I would die. I would not be able to complete my development, I would never fruit, I would wither into the tree-floor to nourish the fruiting body that would come next; I would fail.

I sought the warmcolds-old wisdom of the aware one for assistance, and there was no comfort in the answer. *There is no moisture,* the aware one said. *Not throughout the forest as we travel in your direction. The others are being called back to the Body. Find moisture, or surrender your substance back to the aware one.*

During the brights I could do nothing but hide in the moistest places to be found, stretched thin, almost out of touch with myself from place to place. During the darks I could sometimes find enough moisture in the cool air to seek out my siblings to one side and the other side of me and ask for their report. *No moisture,* they said, *something has robbed the forest of its water here, and dryness increases. We must return to the Body, or be lost.*

But when the wind blew through the forest from the one direction, the one that was in front of me, it was fat and rich and pregnant with moisture, delicious moisture full of nourishment. I rose up to the surface to capture the treasure in the wind, spreading myself as thinly as I could to drink the most deeply, watching always for the bright to come—knowing I had to protect my moisture from the bright—but filled with so much joy and delight in the dark, when the wind blew toward me, that it was as though something was different in my awareness, something very light and filled with happiness. I had no word then for intoxication, but I learned to be drunk on the night breeze's moisture, and grew strong on its treasure while my siblings faded back to either side of me.

Thus I grew and prospered, thinking only of myself, because that was my purpose at that time—the aware one had made me to be a fruiting body, it was my function to gain and grow fat, but before I could achieve my mission in life, the aware one took thought for the treasure I had found and changed my instructions.

You are strong, my child, the aware one said. *You thrive while others fail. What is the explanation?*

I sent back my information, the flavor of the moisture on the night wind, the riches that came into the forest when the wind blew from the direction in which the aware one had not yet gone.

The wind that travels over us is dry, the aware one said. *You must go out and seek this moisture. Separate, my child, and when you have found the answer, send back to me so that we may live.*

Separate? But I wasn't ready to fruit yet. If I separated now, would I ever get to fruit, would I become just one of the forgotten processes, and only share in the awareness as an afterthought—

Separate, my child, the aware one said. I didn't want to. I wasn't ready. But the aware one said that it was more than just my siblings on the fore-line of our growth who were at stake; it was more than just my need for moisture that impelled the aware one. If I could never fruit, if I had to sacrifice my place in the history of the aware one, if I was going to be a sterile scout—well. I am of the aware one; I am the aware one, if only a very small part.

And past the grief and the anxiety I felt in separating, in the loss of my identity as a fruiting body, I felt some interest and anticipation. *Go out,* the aware one said. *Find out where the wind that bears the moisture is coming from. Bring back the news to us, so that we may live.*

It took me several dayblinks to collect sufficient moisture; it was the warm part of the year still, but the wind was very rich at that time, and I fattened on the treasure that it brought, spreading myself as thinly as I dared over the blanket of debris on the tree-floor to absorb as much as possible.

On one night I fattened and grew full, and knew that the time had come. I called my substance back into myself, I made myself solid with my flesh and the water that sustained it, I rose up out of my bed in a form that I had borrowed from a small eater of vegetation, and I walked forward into the woods—past the boundary of my life, past the far edge of what was familiar to me, into the woods in the direction from which the treasure-wind came.

It was frightening and exciting at once in a sense I'd never experienced but one time before—when a small animal had died and been buried in my leafmold by the insects for processing. The richness of the feast had sustained me in fullness for almost an entire warmcold. That had been in the warmcold of my coming to awareness; I could still remember it, but the husk of the memory was fragile.

There was so much new to eat here, so much untouched food to process and to harvest. There were others here, too, others like me, in their unconsolidated state; but when I touched them, I could sense nothing that was aware, and wondered. They were not like me, then. They seemed to be the same, they seemed to do the same work, but they were not aware.

When the bright came on, I sank deeply into the embrace of a bed I prepared in the tree-floor and rested myself, taking nourishment from the substance that was like me and yet not aware. Perhaps the aware one had been here before, and just forgotten, and left this food for me. I was very tired after traveling on footlike-things above the ground, carrying my substance with me; I shuttered up my sense-of-light and rested for some time.

But I had a purpose, and could not rest for long. When the next bright dimmed, I spread myself out along this new piece of the tree-floor, to absorb the moisture in the wind; there was more of it, here, but as I was about to collect myself to rise again something new and unique came through the forest, treading upon the tree-floor, breaking through my substance with its weight.

They were creatures such as I had never seen before, with two footlike things to travel on, and the only animals that I had ever known with only two footlike things were feathered. These animals were not feathered in the same way, though perhaps they were feathered, because they seemed to be wearing dead leaves of some sort upon their flesh. There were some of them, I couldn't tell, more than two, then another two, but it was difficult for me to sort them out.

They stopped in the middle of the blanket I had spread of myself to catch the moisture and made sounds to one another. One reached down into the tree-floor and lifted in its branch or paw or claw a piece of me—they had four footlike things, then, even if they only used two of them to travel—and, in contact with warm flesh uncovered by the dead leaves or

the tangled hairs the nesters use or whatever it was
that they were covered with, I tasted moisture.

It was moisture with mineral salts, and I was greedy
for it, and sucked it all up as quickly as I could. It
wasn't all there was. There was more moisture. There
was so much moisture, juicy, warm, bursting with nu-
trients, and I couldn't get to it through the rind of the
creature; what was I going to do?

The one who had lifted the portion of me dropped
me from the height to the tree-floor once more, but
another came down to the tree-floor as the first one
dropped me, putting its other footlike things into the
tree-floor where I could harvest the moisture and the
minerals on its skin. I wanted through its rind. I was
near frantic with desire, so much moisture there, the
aware one would feed from this for an entire warmcold as I had with the smaller beast. What could I do?

I fruited. It was my only chance to get closer, to get
in. I could smell the moisture when they made their
noises to each other, and they had breathing-places
that were similar to the other warm animals I knew.
If I could only reach . . . I fruited, then and there, in
front of the creature, and thrust my spoor as hard as
I could up toward its body, aiming for its mouth and
nostrils. It wasn't a full fruiting, no, of course, only a
small process, I hadn't had the time to do a better job
of it; the creature fell into the tree-floor heavily, making sharp movements with its body, but I was in.

Oh, it was heaven. Moisture, minerals, salts,
nourishment—preprocessed nourishment, the rarest of
treats, flesh bursting with the moisture that the aware
one needed for survival—but it had been only a small
fruiting, simple, and when the creature expelled me
from its body too little of me remained behind to
make an effective use of the resources.

The creatures withdrew across the tree-floor in the
direction from which they had come, but now I knew
that some of the wonderful juiciness in the wind came
from the creatures. And I knew what to do next. For

several dayblinks I traveled after the creatures, resting during the brights, feeding in the darks, sure of my purpose.

In the dark of the fourth dayblink since I had seen the creatures for the first time they came back. I smelled them coming in the wind; I sank into the tree-floor where I stood and spread myself, carefully, seeing myself shining in the night with the blue-white glow of the aware one, and concentrated my energies to fruit. There was only one creature who came, though. That was a disappointment; I wanted at least two, one to have and one to send ahead, but I could make use of this one, I could experiment.

Hesitantly, the creature came, pausing at the edge of my glow-field. I increased my bioluminescence in the place where I was nearest to being ready to extrude a fruiting body; it came closer, it put itself down into the tree-floor, its mouth and nose and eyes were so near that I could have reached out and had them then and there but I wanted in through the rind. Carefully, I formed a fruiting body, a much bigger fruiting body this time, and made it like something that a warm-blooded chewing animal likes to hunt and hide and eat, so that it might look familiar and appetizing.

The creature reached out for the fruiting body, plucked it from my substance, put it in its mouth where it dissolved into the pith and filament I needed to propagate my substance throughout its body. I waited. There was nothing. The fruit failed. The moisture in the creature's mouth, was it too unfriendly to my fruit?

The creature lay down in the tree-floor, then, and was quiet.

I scouted it carefully, wondering what was going on, trying to understand what was happening. The creature had not stopped breathing; I made a net over its face to capture its moisture, so that it would not go to waste. I tried to comprehend the dead leaf covering, the hair covering, sending my processes into every ap-

erture I could find; just as I was about to give up
hope . . . I found it.

The creature's rind was broken in several places,
not large places, and most of the breaks had a shield
over them so that I could sense the aperture but not
get to it; but some of them were still building their
shields, new breaks perhaps, and I could get in.

Oh. I cannot describe the wonder of the experience.
I had only been inside a dead thing ever before; this
one was still alive. Its body did things when it recognized that I was other than itself, so I took its chemistry, I borrowed its moisture, I adjusted my processes
until its body could no longer tell that I was not the
same as it was; and then I learned and fed and fed
and learned, and when the dayblink came I covered
it up with leaf-litter and mold and continued to learn
and feed as it lay on the tree-floor. It breathed quietly
and slowly for the entire bright before it died.

It would have been too much for me to process, but
with the strength I gained from the nourishment and
moisture it provided I sent substance back across the
tree-floor floor where I had walked and traveled; that
absorbed substantial excess nourishment, and when I
touched the skirts of the aware one in the place of
my origin—the aware one fed through me with the
hunger of the almost desiccated.

I hadn't understood how close the aware one had
been to discontinuity. It troubled me; but I was more
pleased than troubled, because I was there, I was entirely the consumer of this wonderfully succulent creature, and I was the one who had saved the aware one
from discontinuity. I was the one. I am of the aware
one, but there were parts of the aware one that were
not me, and I hadn't truly understood that before
then.

The aware one wanted more. Needed more. From
the first taste of the moisture I sent back I knew the
thirst of my siblings, the seeking along my path. When
the bright dimmed, I could feel the drawing from me

quicken; I was first, but many were coming. It was frightening, because I wasn't ready to fruit and didn't want to be absorbed in the aware one. This was my accomplishment, the acquisition of nourishment; I didn't want to stop there and be content, because this one had come from the direction of the wet wind, and there had been more of them.

I gathered up the leaves that the animal had used to cover itself. I gathered up the nourishment that I had not fully absorbed, I arranged it in its original pattern, I stood up in the manner of the creature and walked into the wet wind. There was something so rich and promising in that breeze that I could hardly grasp it, more nourishment than seemed to be possible.

When the bright came, I sank back into the tree-floor to rest and feed. Creatures came through the forest, many twos and twos and twos of them, but I kept quiet and fed from the hard long and bony parts of the one I already had. I made an error in judgment; I used too much, drunk with moisture and replete with food. The hard bony parts would no longer support the weight of the water in my substance when I stood up to walk, but crumbled.

I needed another. I knew how to get one. I left the pieces of the animal where one of my siblings could find it in a dayblink or two, and went on. When I felt some of the creatures coming in the dark, I spread myself, as I had done before, and set my lures glowing in the dim light.

These were new creatures, it seemed, because they seemed wary or unsure, and kept to the outside of the field that I made for them. I waited. One came, finally, to take up the fruit I offered; this time I tasted the air all around it, quickly, and found where its rind was recently broken, and went there.

The creature didn't try to eat the fruit I made for it, but it didn't matter. I was there. I was in. I sealed the place where the rind was broken and went out into the creature's body, remembering what I had learned from the last one about hiding from its internal defenses, reveling in nourishment.

I didn't want to make the same mistake that I had made before. I didn't harvest the creature; I merely fed, quietly, and only enough to keep my awareness. For my reward the creature stooped down and picked up the fruit I had made for it, and took it in a container of clear leaves; turned around and signaled to the other—and started walking back.

Terror paralyzed me as the creature stepped past the field that I had made, and carried me past the forward edge of my knowing. The aware one had never been here. There was no connection anymore between me and the aware one; and yet I was still aware. What was going to happen to me? Had I become lost? Could I ever get back?

I was alone. There was no aware one. There was only me, and the creature, and the creature's companion. It walked vigorously with confidence, it moved so much more efficiently than I had moved the remnants of the last one, and with every step it took we traveled farther into the wet wind.

Through the forest. Out onto a hard place in the forest, something wide and stony with very strong substances in its composition, chemistries I had never sensed before; there was no way for me to send back the news to the aware one, we were severed from each other, so I didn't know if the aware one had ever encountered anything like this in our life.

The creature had a fir-cone on the hard place, something that was in a way similar to a fir-cone, something that would carry its weight and could be moved over the surface; a very large fir-cone, and with little that was forestlike in it, but much more of the very strong chemistries all around. It sat in the fir-cone, its companion sat inside the fir-cone with it, and the fir-cone started to travel very quickly across the hard place, still into the wet wind.

I couldn't tell where we were going. It was going too fast, and the messages in the wind were gone before I had a chance to truly taste them. I recovered from the paralysis of fear; I had to know, and my desire was stronger than my fear, but I didn't know how I could slow the progress of the fir-cone.

The creature's body protected one part of it more than any other; that is where I went. I didn't care any longer about concealing my presence from its body. I went into the protected place; it was where all of the sharp brightness of warm life was concentrated, all of the quickness of the creature. I had to stop the fir-cone. I exerted myself, I infiltrated its brightpaths, I slowed the quick bright sharpness of its messages.

The creature fell forward in the fir-cone, and its companion became agitated, but the fir-cone stopped. It stopped very suddenly. The creatures were both damaged, but I was not damaged within the creature. It was a shame that the creatures had been damaged. They were interesting creatures. Was there something I could do to restore them? I had caused the damage, after all, in some sense.

I went carefully across the surface of the strong and very bitter chemistries to the other creature and crept in, since there was no lack of places where the rind had been broken. This creature had not been as badly damaged as the one I occupied. I used the nourishment of the one to try to repair the other, encouraging its body, transferring fuel; after a while the other moved its body, shifted itself out of the fir-cone, and stepped onto the hard surface.

I let it carry me. It walked back in the direction from which the fir-cone had come, but not very far. The wind was still blowing in the same direction, but the wet was different. I harvested some nourishment from the creature to strengthen me and went out of its body to go look. There was a steep bank there, with a smell of sharpness as though the steepness had been made not very many warmcolds ago. The hard

surface bridged the gap between one steep bank and
another, and beneath—in the low place—there was
wet. So much wet. Unimaginable wet.

As though the rain that falls in the forest, all of the
rain that had ever fallen in the forest, had collected
in one place, so much rain that it did not soak into
the tree-floor, so much rain that it stayed whole and
wet even though it lay upon the ground. That was
where the wind picked up the water, blowing over this
huge wet; and behind the wind, instead of a forest,
there was a flat land with soil that was so fat with
nourishment that the taste of it was dizzying.

There were things growing in the flat land, things
in regular array, juicy things with fruit in them ripen-
ing in the warm. I left the creature; I needed all of
my substance with me to explore, and lay the creature
down softly on the hard surface before I fled into the
flat land.

The bright came. But I was safe below the surface
of the flat land, feeding from the juicy things with a
hunger I had never known before. There was so much.
It was so good. The juicy things grew sere and with-
ered as I fed, but I didn't care, there were so many
of them—nothing that I could sense as far away as I
could sense but food.

I could no longer sense the aware one. I was in a
new place, on my own. I no longer even thought of
the aware one. I knew my purpose. I fruited and fed,
and fed and fruited, and when the creatures brought
poison into the flat land I crept into one of them and
traveled to more food. There was no end to it. There
were fewer and fewer creatures, and poison in the flat
lands behind me; but they could not keep me from
the food.

Now the warm is over and the cold is coming, but
I will not sleep. I have found a place in a nest of the
creatures, full of moisture, full of food, and I will keep
myself aware there for the cold. When the warm comes
again, I will try to get back across the hard stony thing

to the place where I was born to find the other, to share the nourishment I've found.

I am of the aware one; I am the aware one. There was only one: now there are two, and with the nourishment I have found we will feed and multiply, and be the caretakers of this wonderful new world—and all the creatures in it.

FIRST CONTRACT

by Linda J. Dunn

MY NAME IS TWEEN dy Kula Niiam and I can justify my existence. I am a Tween. I facilitate communication. I have years of experience and adapt quickly to new situations.

I repeat these words every morning while facing the judgment wall and wait to learn if I continue my duties or expire. I stand still and calm, keeping my skin color a reverent shade of pale blue, and oozing the sweet scent of dedication. When the wall flashes life colors, I bow three times and back out of the room.

I have performed this sacred ritual every morning of my life. The difference now is that I know I will not die as long as I am assigned to the negotiating team on Earth. Our work is important. We cannot pause to wait for our home world to send a replacement.

Once the contract is signed, a new team will arrive to oversee the construction of the three factories and sublight delivery systems. They will hire humans at a fraction of what we pay our lowest caste laborers on any of our colony worlds.

Then I shall return home and once again face the possibility that the judgment wall will find me no longer useful.

This will not happen, though. Not to me. I am efficient, meticulous, and highly useful. I shall merit at least one life extension for my work on Earth, and I would not be surprised to be granted immortality. Such a reward is rare, but I have done very well.

I was thinking about this when the shuttle arrived to take us to our meeting with the humans. I sat down in the first seat behind our human escorts and turned a happy shade of blue. Vaaishya dy Muwa Feerow sat down beside me and emitted the pleasant odor of success.

"Today, we will sign the contracts and our work here will be done." He punctuated his statement with the rich aroma of satisfaction.

"I pity the vaaishya who must stay behind to assist the new team overseeing construction and management." I turned a sickly shade of yellow to convey my thoughts about that particular task.

"Pray it will not fall upon my shoulders." Feerow turned a matching shade of yellow and the richness faded into the tangy scent of concern.

"They are all idiot savants," Feerow added, "except for those who are not. Some are merely idiots."

We flashed laughing shades of purple and filled the shuttle with the thick aroma of humor. Our Earth escorts at the front and back of the shuttle stood watching, deaf to most of our conversation.

Poor idiots. They lacked two of the basic components of language. Their bodies could turn only one color and that was a reddish tone that indicated embarrassment. As for scents, they could only emit one and that was a most unpleasant odor that none of us wished to encounter again.

How tragic that the first oxygen-breathing, intelligent life-form we encountered was two-thirds mute!

The first Tween to encounter humans was terminated by the judgment wall. So were the next three Tween representatives to Earth. I was warned that all had gone mad from their efforts to learn so many different languages, each of which were splintered into numerous dialects.

I am the fourth Tween, but I do not fear insanity. After the deaths of the other Tweens, the Earth representatives selected their best communicators. They speak one common language clearly, consistently, and without any of the neurological problems that afflicted the first group of human negotiators.

Those humans, according to the notes left behind by my predecessors, were subject to fits that caused their faces to twist in odds ways and their limbs to flail about while they were speaking.

Feerow must have been thinking along the same lines. He said, "Have you ever paused to think about the problems our brethren will face after we sign this contract? The humans have so many strange customs and they only expect to work five days out of every seven. I cannot comprehend a species that can set aside their work like it is something other than part of themselves."

He turned yellow-almost-green and added, "I would rather expire than live among these people. I pray I will not be selected."

"Blessed is our judgment wall," I said, "and perfect in its choices."

Feerow turned blue again and emitted the scent of contentness. "Yes. Thank you for reassuring me. Perfect is our system, unlike the chaos of Earth."

I nodded and then the impossible happened. I heard the screeching of the shuttle's brakes, the crunch of metal hitting metal, and a loud whooshing sound that I could not identify. Airbags exploded and we struggled to free ourselves and see what had happened.

I smelled smoke. When I escaped the airbag and stood up, I saw fire at the front of the bus. Our human escorts rushed forward into the flames and I, being wiser than they, ran toward the emergency exit at the back of the shuttle.

My fellow team members all did the same and I feared I would be the last to escape, if I escaped at all.

"The window!" Feerow shouted. I was closer to the window than he was and thus I stood on the seat and pushed my body through the shattered window while he faced the approaching flames.

I fell and hit my head. I could hear people screaming, and over all the noise someone shouted, "Get them away from here!"

Rough, human hands grabbed me and I saw blurry images that I knew were not our guards. They dragged me toward soft grass. A moment later, I saw someone carrying Feerow and, as they reached the grass, the shuttle exploded.

People screamed and I heard a man's voice clearly, "A bomb! Get the hell out of here. There may be another one."

Hands touched me again and I was too groggy and confused to respond.

"I don't think we should—" Whatever the woman was going to say was interrupted by a different man's voice.

"It's a gift. Fate. We've got to take them."

"We'll never get away with this," a woman said. "The police will think we did it."

"Shut up, Amy, and follow me," the first one said.

They pulled me upright and I heard someone ask, "Where are you taking them?"

"To a hospital," the man said. "She's a nurse. Clear a path for us, please."

So I was safe. I thought I would wake up in a hospital and all would be well.

Except they didn't take us to a hospital. I barely remembered the jostling ride down unfamiliar streets into a part of the city that must have been undergoing major construction. I could think of no other reason why the building's doors and windows would be covered with wood.

I lost consciousness sometime during the ride, and I woke up in a small, dimly lit room.

"About time you came around." A male human of

dark complexion loomed over me. "It's been an hour. You are our prisoner and you will remain here until your government agrees to go away and leave Earth alone."

I struggled to sit upright and realized that I was injured. My head ached and my extremities burned like I was still inside the fiery shuttle. I looked around and saw three other Earthlings and one other of my race.

Feerow. He was stretched out on the floor beside me. His body was a sickening shade of green that was far too dark.

"He is dying," I said.

"Then you had better hope your world meets our demands quickly," the man replied.

"You said you were taking us to a hospital." I could not comprehend saying one thing and doing another.

"I lied." The man's mouth opened wide to expose his teeth. They were not clean, white, and beautiful like those of each human I'd met thus far. These were grayish-yellow and there was a gap between two lower teeth. I could smell his breath and it was not pleasant.

Then I realized that I stank as well. My hands were charred from the fire and blood encrusted. My tunic was ruined and heavy with sweat.

"We both need medical treatment and the room's temperature needs to be decreased for our comfort."

The pale-skinned woman beside me made an odd noise in her lower throat and spit on me. Me! A Tween! The spittle ran down the left side of my face and when I tried to wipe it away, I realized that my upper limbs were tied fast to my sides and I could not reach that high. I had to sit there, wearing this female human's body waste.

She smiled and said, "It's different when the shoe is on the other foot, isn't it?"

I glanced down at my feet. Both shoes were there and they were correct.

"He doesn't understand, Glory," the dark-skinned

male said. His arms moved up, like he was attempting
to toss something into the air.

"Of course he does, Bill," Glory's voice was loud
and she squished her face tight so her eyelids nar-
rowed into tiny slits. The effect would have been comi-
cal had I not felt my life imperiled. These people had
bombed our shuttle!

Glory stood up and moved closer to Bill.

"He's the Tween! Just look at his cloak."

Her arm moved to point at me in a straight line.
For a moment, I considered the possibility that it was
not a neurological problem, but an intentional action,
that caused her to point in my direction.

Not possible! I could not have overlooked anything
that might facilitate communication.

"We hit the jackpot," Glory pulled her arm back
and now both arms were waving in Bill's direction.
"Not only did these two fall into our hands like gold
falling off a Brinks truck, but we got the one member
of their group who can speak our language."

She glanced in Feerow's direction and grinned in a
way that made be feel cold despite the heat of the
room. "The contract's not signed yet, and if he dies,
that'll scare them off."

"Feerow is a vaaishya," I said, scarcely believing
that even humans could set themselves up as judgment
walls. "He is important and needed."

The light-skinned male made a snorting sound.
"Hey, Bill, maybe this Feerow guy can get you a record contract."

"Shut up, Trey."

A record contract. So this was another musician.
What was rare on our world was common and cheaply
available on theirs.

"There will be many opportunities when our factories are completed," I said.

"I don't want a frigging factory job!" Bill hit the
wall with his fist and I could no longer deny that these
seemingly random limb-wavings, which I'd attributed

to some neurological problem, were actually controlled and deliberate. In fact, they were a method of communication.

The earlier Tweens had not gone mad. They had learned that humans were not the mutes we had thought. The idea was so bizarre that the judgment wall must had thought them insane.

And would think me insane as well, should I live to report it.

"I am an artist!" Bill's voice nearly broke on the last word. I could clearly see the pattern now.

"I am not a hack." His face was redder than any I'd seen before and I could not reconcile his words with embarrassment. Years of training and experience led me to believe he was angry, although I hadn't a clue why I thought that.

Hack meant a cab driver. A writer. A computer coder. All of these were jobs that no longer existed in Earth's society. Ah! There was another definition that might apply. Art without imagination and originality.

Feerow was growing darker by the moment. I was not a vaaishya and I could think of only one thing to say that might persuade them to take us to a hospital.

"I am certain that I can arrange job interviews for each of you in return for Feerow's life."

Bill kicked me. In my face. I fell backward and when I finally managed to open my eyes again, the dark-skinned woman was leaning over me and wiping my face with a rough cloth. My face hurt. I tried to speak, but my mouth felt so huge and numb that I couldn't form words.

I panicked. Never in my life had I been unable to speak in any one of the three forms until now.

The room filled with my smells and I could see my limbs cycling through one color after another. I would die. If the judgment wall was here, I would be judged useless and die immediately.

Feerow lay mostly dead a few feet away from me

and he reeked of pity. He was dying and he pitied me. I fell back and turned the darkest shade of green that I could imagine. This was worse than death.

"Nice going, Bill," the dark-skinned woman said. "He can't speak."

"Shut up, Amy," Bill muttered. "It's an improvement. Damn lying alien. Trying to rape our culture. Turn us into slaves. Ought to slit them open and drop them at the UN's doorstep. That'd convince them to go away and leave our world alone."

"What we need to do," Trey said, "is get out of here. The police have to be looking for us. That woman who asked where we were taking them probably gave the police a description of our car. The hell with saving Earth from little green men. Let's save ourselves."

"He's too sick to move." Amy pointed toward Feerow.

"Leave him behind." Trey shrugged his shoulders. "They'll find him."

"He'll be dead when they find him!" Amy put her hands on her hips and thrust her face forward. How odd. In a strange kind of way, this reminded me of the ballet that had been presented for us during one of our initial meetings.

"Let him die." Bill muttered. "Look what they're doing to us."

"I won't be an accomplice to murder," Amy screamed. "Besides, it'll kill the cause, not help it. Those idiots who bombed them probably undid everything we've managed to accomplish."

So someone else did this. It was logical. These four humans were too disorganized to have planned anything successfully.

While they argued, I glanced around the room and began easing toward the door. I didn't know what these people wanted, but I knew I couldn't give it to them and Feerow was dying. If I escaped, I might be able to find help in time to save him.

They weren't looking in my direction. They were too occupied with their internal dispute.

I reached the door and struggled to turn the doorknob with my upper limb's digits. The door creaked when I opened it. I glanced quickly toward the humans, but they were too busy shouting at one another and waving their arms about to notice the small noise.

I ran, screaming fear in the strongest scent that I could possibly release. I felt like I'd run 100 kilometers, but they told me later that I had only gone a single kilometer before a hovercraft descended and six huge Earthlings dropped to the ground around me.

"We're from the government," the first one said, "and we're here to help you. Just let me fasten my harness around you."

The next thing I knew, I was being pulled off the ground into the hovercraft.

"You'll be fine in a few days," the doctor told me.

I opened my mouth and strange gurgling noises were all I could manage.

"Don't worry," he said. "There's no indication of any permanent damage. The swelling will gradually subside and you'll be talking normally again in no time."

I struggled to find some way to communicate and remembered the way my captors had gestured with their hands. If my theory was right, I might be able to convey a question with the right motions.

I rolled all but two digits into my upper limb. There had been two of us. He stared and I could see his eyebrows furrow together. I wish I understood what that meant.

His eyes widened and he asked, "You want to know about your friend?"

He looked away and said, "His injuries are much more severe than yours. I'm afraid I don't have much hope for recovery." He looked back at me and added, "I'm sorry."

I stood there, unmoving, hoping for more. One of the human escorts moved forward and said, "They arrested the people who held you. The people who bombed your shuttle died, but they belonged to a fringe organization. Authorities don't believe they acted alone. They're investigating."

If I lived forever, I would never understand humans. Their actions were insane. I bowed slightly to the doctor and followed my escorts out of the hospital.

I said little to the others when the humans returned me to our lodgings. They apparently assumed I felt ashamed because I had lost one third of my speaking ability.

They were half right. I felt shame, but I felt that emotion because I had made some horrible misinterpretations which no Tween should ever have made.

I stood before the judgment wall the next morning and struggled to form the words to the best of my ability. The wall blinked puzzlement. I knew death would come, as it had to my predecessors, and I waited, half-longing for the end so I would no longer feel shame for my earlier failure.

The wall told me to step forward and place my digits against it. I did, and waited to feel the softness of death.

Instead, I felt a sharp tingling sensation that traveled through my digits to my upper limbs, and then up my body until it reached my jaw.

The pain was almost as intense as the original injury. I leaned forward and pressed my forehead against the wall. I would not scream. I would die with dignity.

The vibrations stopped and the wall exploded with the colors of life.

"I don't understand," I said in a perfect tirade of spoken words, smells, and color. With that speech came full understanding.

The wall had cured me. It had performed a cost

analysis and had determined it would prove more cost effective to cure me.

I was blessed. If few had been injured, even fewer had ever been cured.

I bowed low and thanked the wall profusely. The wall, as always, remained cold and nonfunctional after dispensing its verdict. I would never know why it had gifted me with healing and life, but I accepted this blessing as an opportunity to correct my errors of omission.

We had not yet signed a contract. My fellow teammates had decided to withhold even the three site names while they contemplated this latest development. By the time I arrived for our private meeting, they were considering abandoning Earth and forfeiting our option payment.

"It's bad enough that they are idiots," Vaaishya dy Keem Briice said. "But they attempted to kill us. If they had planned better, we would all be dead."

"What if they wait until all our factories are built and then destroy them?" Vaiishya dy Baase Roitz asked. "The potential losses could be devastating."

"They are not idiots," Vaaishya dy Ziam Toolan oozed the scent of repulsion. "They are madmen. We could never trust them."

Toolan turned to me. "Why didn't you recognize this? It is your duty to facilitate communication. Should you not have led them to reveal their insanity?"

I waited for the sound and scent to die down before speaking. "I have had a learning experience," I said. "I spent some short time as their captive and I learned that some of our original beliefs about their communication were incorrect."

The room filled with silence louder than any I had ever experienced in my life. "I confessed my failing to the wall just a short time ago and waited for termination. Instead, the wall healed me so I could stand before you now, able to communicate normally. The wall would not have spared me if I didn't still have something to contribute."

"The wall spared you because it would take too long to send another Tween!" Roitz said. He turned yellow and emitted the scent of contempt.

No one else said a word. They all sat there with their smooth faces and perfectly still limbs, secreting scents of dissatisfaction and turning yellow with displeasure. They all agreed with Briice.

"We should meet with the humans tomorrow and discuss our concerns," I said. "I will facilitate the conversation."

With that statement, I left the room and did not return. I spent the rest of the day and most of the night using the Earth viewing machines to study everything I could find about humans . . . with the sound off.

I saw patterns.

The humans sat stone-faced and motionless at our table the next morning. They said all the right words. They disclosed all the right details. They performed all the proper rituals.

But I was not fooled. Not anymore.

I saw patterns. Layers and layers of patterns.

The woman beside me wore a silk suit that fit her perfectly and shoes made of fine leather. The man across from me wore an equally well-fitting suit and shoes made of crocodile skin. Behind us, the escorts wore ill-fitting uniforms made of inferior cloth and their shoes were identical, black, and of inferior quality when compared to those shoes around me.

Even their clothing was a form of communication! It shouted their caste standing.

The human representatives sat stone-faced, without any of the gestures I'd seen during captivity, and I realized then that this was more for their benefit than our own. Without gestures and expressions, it was easier to lie.

They were sorry to announce Feerow's death, which they all felt deeply. They had arrested my captors and they would be punished. They were still looking for those who had bombed our shuttle and would not stop until they, too, were punished. Nothing like this could ever happen again. The factories would be secure. There was no reason to deviate from our original plans.

My brethren looked to me for guidance and I led them, brilliantly, to a conclusion in which Earth government agreed to compensate us for any damage that might occur at any of the factories due to similar events in the future. They also agreed to provide their own security forces to guard our plants for the next fifty of their cycles.

Briice named the three sites. Siberia. China. Pakistan. All three offered isolated areas and a population eager and willing to work seven days out of seven.

I noticed the tightness of shoulders among the losing representatives and the relaxed limbs of those humans who represented the three sites selected. I also recognized, for the first time, the difference between polite smiles and genuine smiles of joy.

At the end of the day, I gathered with my brethren in blueness and pleasant scents while we congratulated one another upon overcoming the impossible.

"You facilitated well," Briice said. "I had not expected to change my mind."

"The humans were willing to sacrifice much for this," I replied.

"How could you tell?" Tooland asked.

By the jaw muscles that twitched on one representative, and the way two of them flinched when various counterproposals were offered.

"Body language." I turned a deeper shade of blue and emitted the scent of satisfaction. "I learned that their language is far richer than we'd ever imagined."

Roitz flashed purple. "The muties? Well, you are the Tween. If you say they are rich, then they must be so. I do not see it."

Because they did not wish you to see it.

In the morning, I stood in front of the wall of judgment and I could not stop myself from turning a rich shade of blue. I had done well. I had learned much. Surely the wall would recognize my value and reward me with a new position whose duties would occupy me for many years to come.

My name is Tween dy Kula Niiam and I can justify my existence. I am a Tween. I facilitate communication. I have years of experience and adapt quickly to new situations.

The wall flashed life colors, as I had expected, and rewarded me with the immortality that I had always wanted so very much. I thought my life was perfect. But then it gave me my new assignment, which was to last until completed. It would take longer than eternity to complete this task.

I turned dark green and almost brown. I could not restrain myself. This time, the always-silent wall broke its usual silence about assignments and offered me insight.

The reward for a job well done is more challenging work.

An old proverb. One I should have remembered.

I watched most of my brethren leave. Soon, a new crew would arrive to construct the factories and hire employees. Another crew would arrive not long thereafter to provide continual oversight.

I would not be at those factories. I was to walk among the humans and convert them to the way of truth, light, and profit margins.

I will live forever and I must spend that eternity among the heathen humans, attempting to save them from themselves.

How I envy Feerow!

ANAKOINOSIS

by Tobias S. Buckell

DAYS AGO MY AEROKRAT left me at the edge of the forest. Now I ran back toward the break in the thick, tall woods, hoping to find him again. I wanted to return to his safety and bondage.

The sun fell behind the knobby trees, and heavy clouds killed the light. Rain exploded through the leaves, drenching the world in so much darkness and moisture I could hardly breathe.

Before long I fell down, and crawled on my hands and feet, slimy with mud, leaves, and sticks plastered to my thin clumps of fur.

I felt very alone, trying to find my way home. The trees loomed over me, threatening in the darkness. Creaks, snaps, and the sounds of animals skittering around in the darkness scared me.

Stumbling around in the night, I found a burrow in the space between a large root and the moist ground. Dirt caked my hands as I dug in for the night.

Overhead, streams of water cascaded down through large leaves and drooping limbs to soak me.

It would be a shivery night. My fur was only just starting to regrow after the anakoinosis.

I wasn't sure what to do next. There was no advice,

or past memories, to guide me on my path. It would be a shameful, lonely night, devoid of new learning.

When I was born, I broke free of my shell with my own hands. I picked the insides clean until I had a full stomach, and the brittle remains fell apart easily with a few punches and kicks.

I remembered this, as I remembered all things from long ago, and far away.

Many aerokratois stood around me when I broke free. They were pale and twice my height, with disgustingly smooth skin. The only visible fur grew on their heads.

Yet what fascinations they brought!

Until this point all the memories of my parents had swirled around through my body, mixing and intermingling, growing with me as I knit myself from egg.

So I understood what they said when they looked at me. Many of my parents understood their languages, though it had taken fifteen generations of anakoinosis to spread those memories all throughout.

None of my kind could absorb aerokratois memories, not the way our own foreparents' memories were etched in each of us. The aerokratois defied true understanding because of their alienness. So we observed, watched, and learned to imitate the aerokratois ways.

Maybe, we thought, if we imitated them long enough, we could come to understand them without anakoinosis.

"Bob," one of the aerokratois pointed at me. "This is your whiffet."

"My what?"

"It will be your . . . assistant."

Bob, I knew from the memories, looked upset.

"Assistant? I don't want one of your little slaves, I want nothing to do with this."

Another aerokratois stepped forward. "It is merely indentured servitude. Look, the leaders of the whiffets gave us their young willingly in exchange for the technology we gave them. It's a fair trade."

The memory of the aerokratois descending from the sky on a loud wind popped into my mind. They came with gifts: glittering objects, rare metals, strong spear-tips for better hunting, and diagrams for even more interesting machines.

"That doesn't make it okay," Bob shouted. "It's wrong. You know it. Just because they were given to us doesn't make using them right."

The conversation, and my new master's concern made me nervous. I walked forward and grabbed his hand. I formed words.

"I will serve you well, aerokrat. You will teach me all I can absorb."

Bob's mouth hung upon.

"How can it learn to speak so soon?"

The other aerokratois made *laughter* noises and shook themselves.

"They learn in the egg, we think."

"You think?" Bob shouted. "Why haven't we thawed out anthropologists yet? This needs to be studied. To be learned."

I was excited. I would understand new things, things my foreparents had not known. Very few of the aero-kratois seemed to care about learning. They had a desperate air about them, and only cared about one thing: the Great Repair.

But this aerokrat seemed different.

"We don't have time," the others told Bob. "The repairs must continue if we want to make the launch window. We have to fix the ship first, then we can study the whiffets with whatever time we have left. We can leave the scientists behind." They made *laughs* again.

"That would be all right by me," one of them said.

I stood and watched them all.

That was the day I was bonded to my aerokrat. The cycle of learning new things continued.

Huddled under the root of the tree in the steady rain by myself, I sorted through long buried, and a few recent, happy memories. They comforted me.

More of my fur had grown in by morning. I took a few moments to carefully groom myself with twigs, trying to comb over the few bare patches still left in my fur.

It was the fourth time I'd lost and regrown my fur. I was proud of the memories I imparted to each of my children with every new generation I sired.

The mud hadn't dried, but it was walkable. Outside the treeline, bare ground stretched for miles and miles. Big yellow machines roved over the roads, driven by aerokratois inside.

The yellow machines shoveled and ate dirt. They burrowed into the ground sniffing for Metal. Then the Metal got taken back to the Hopper, which digested Metal in huge, fiery belches, and created Spare Parts for the Great Repair.

The bare ground of the aerokratois had spread outward quickly. When the first of us were taken over the ocean to work here, there were only trees and the Hopper.

Whiffets clung to the backs of the yellow machines, waiting for their orders. Others walked along the roadsides with picks, keeping the roads in good order.

More worked deep in the earth, their fur thick with dirt, pulling Metal from the ground.

I knew every inch of the land. From generations back, the memories swirled inside me. Sometimes I remembered the land across the sea my kind came from. It was very similar, but without wild animals, aerokratois, or big yellow machines.

Time to walk the many miles of road back toward my aerokrat's home.

My aerokrat looked down at me. I stood on the steps to his small hut. His eyes looked puffy, and the fur on top of his head was unkept.

I extended my forearm to show him the numbers on it. NN-721. The fur didn't grow around those markings.

Bob flinched. He recognized me now.

"Oh, god," he said. "I helped you run away. I freed you. What are you doing here?" His voice sounded like an angry hiss. I flinched. "No, no," Bob stepped back. "I won't hurt you."

"I am back." I was happy to be back, and in the presence of aerokratois again.

"But why?" Bob shook his head. "Do you know what it took for me to get you out there?"

I give him the aerokratois gesture of understanding: I nodded.

"You," and I recalled it exactly, *"faked a pass to use a flier to drop me off far, so I could get far away from this hellhole of bondage."*

It had been an exciting adventure.

And now I was back.

Bob leaned toward the side of the doorway and repeatedly hit his head against it. I watched, trying to understand his actions.

I walked over next to him and did the same.

Some ritual of returning?

Bob stopped and looked around.

"Get inside," he ordered.

He closed the door behind me quickly.

"Didn't I drop you far enough away, so you could get away from all this?" Bob moved to the back of his hut and mixed different colored liquids together from elaborate jars into a glass. His face twisted when he lifted the glass and swallowed.

The liquids must not have tasted very good.

Bob drank things that didn't taste very good often.

"Yes, you did drop me far enough away," I said.

"Then why have you come back?"

"How can I leave my master? You guide me, teach me, and command me." I would learn more new things, things not in my memory. The moment I came out of the egg I had become bound to him. This was our way.

Bob drank more liquids.

"We are missing each other, I think," he said. "We don't understand each other."

I was excited.

"Yes, we must understand."

He grabbed my hand.

"Come on, we're going out."

Bob took me to the graves. Tiny white crosses spilled out over the hill like strange saplings.

"In just two years since we first came to this planet, look at all the whiffets worked to death." He swept his arm at them.

I looked at the hill, thinking of all the foreparents there. Many of their memories swirled through me like a storm. They were not lost, their memories were all over the place, in other whiffets working for the aerokratios.

"They are remembered." I looked up at Bob. "What is your complaint?"

"You are being exploited." Bob walked around in circles. "It is bad."

"Why?" I sat on the bare ground. "What else would you have us do now that we are here, an ocean away from our homeland?"

Bob's lips moved, but nothing came out for several seconds.

"It's not just you," Bob said. "That is bad enough. But we are also destroying ourselves." Bob crouched next to me and put his head in his hands. "Losing our self-sufficiency and innovation. You know, the other day one of the trucks broke, and instead of fixing it they chose to build a wagon pulled by whiffets . . . it's easier and quicker than spending time trying to figure out how to fix the truck." Bob looked at me. "It'll keep going like that. First we used you to serve tired workers drinks and get into small areas we can't. They said it was better to relocate the robots into dangerous areas, we needed more help than just the people we'd unfrozen. But soon they will use your labor to replace other things. We'll be taking away the greenhouses and using whiffets out in the fields to grow crops. And then, when the robots break down, you'll be doing that work, too."

A thrill shot up my back. All these new things we would be doing!

"This is wonderful." I stood up. "You came from the sky and blessed us with all these new things. And now you tell me you will give us more."

Bob pushed his fingers through his hair.

"You make things worse thinking like that." He pointed down at the direction of the Hopper. The great legs poked out. Smoke rose from its pipes. The maw gleamed with fire. "We were just passing by this system when our ship's shield failed. We were moving so fast the interstellar dust just ripped through the hull. Half of the passengers died, and hardly anything of use survived. This was the best place they could find on short notice. The engineers dropped down planetside near the best resource-rich area they could find. They think the hopper can manufacture enough of the parts they need." He pointed up at the sky where aerokratois came from. "They say we can, but I don't think they're going to be able to fix the damage. It's been two years and we're hardly any closer, and the hopper is beginning to show signs of failure." Bob poked at the dirt. "They're many more passengers in storage up there that they're going to have bring down before more life support systems fail on the ship. That's why they're making the roads and buildings: temporary housing."

More? More aerokratois?

I jumped up.

"This is marvelous!" I wanted to share this new

information, to ask if I could leave again, but Bob heard sounds from the tiny machine on his hand and sighed.

"Time to work."

Bob directed teams of whiffets. We built huts for the aerokratois. It was long, hard work. Others around me, their fur thick, clumping, and ready for ana-koinosis, talked with me as we sawed wood and hammered the buildings into shape.

Even though I could talk to other whiffets while I worked, we all knew this did not bring true understanding. For us speech was just a shadow of the truth. Only through constant anakoinosis could we truly be a community, and know what lay in each others' hearts through the shared memories of our foreparents.

Because we could not understand the aerokratois, we were happily there to work, observe, and struggle to understand them.

And Bob had told me interesting new things.

Bob kept me out of sight. He let me work with other whiffets, but then hid me in his hut at night. He was worried about other areokratois realizing I had returned.

"They might decide to do something to you," Bob said. "Some of the men are worried that one day the whiffets will start running away."

"Do not worry," I said. "We will not leave your side."

That did not make Bob relax, it made him drink more of his different colored liquids.

It took several days of work before Bob talked to me about leaving again. My fur had thickened considerably, and was full of healthy clumps. Bob and I sat at his table. He turned away my attempts to cook dinner for him, or mix his funny liquids.

I asked Bob if he would let me leave again.

"Won't you just come back?"

"Yes," I said.

"Where are you going?" Bob stood up and looked out the window. "How long?"

I was excited.

"Anakoinosis! I will share what I have learned about your ships in the sky and your prediction of more of your kind coming to live among us."

Bob's voice sounded like it was cracking. "You will not try to escape, then?"

"I could not do that," I told him.

He shook his head.

"What is this anakoinosis? The men told me you mean sex," Bob said. I stared at him blankly. "Reproduction?" Bob continued.

I grabbed his hand.

"I will show you what it is."

In all my memories, in the last two years, and so many generations of whiffets since the sky broke and aerokratois came among us, I don't think any of the aerokratois had taken the time to understand what anakoinosis really was.

They were too busy worrying about the Great Repair and how to feed the Hopper with Metal.

Two years was not long to them.

Bob followed me out of his hut.

A small group met on the far side of a hill an hours' walk away from the lights and buildings. They didn't know what to think about Bob, but I talked to them gently until they agreed to let him stay.

Bob sat in the grass and watched.

One of the four whiffets still had patchy fur, but he was excited. He had learned how to operate one of the yellow machines by looking in through the windows at the aerokratois while they operated it.

It would have been better to wait until his fur was thick, but he was in a dangerous job. I chose him.

The other three faced each other, a triple act of anakoinosis. I turned away from them and grabbed the arms of the other.

His tattoo was NL-501.

I leaned forward and brushed my cheek against his, hugged him, and felt my skin stir. He smelled of machinery, aerokratois, and dirt.

I slowly began to molt as we held each other tight. The fur on my arms and chest intermingled with his. We rotated, pushing our backs against each other, then rubbed our legs together.

Fur sloughed off, responding to touch, and drifted into a compact ball on the ground. Naked, we both sat next to the new egg and watched it bind itself tight.

The loss of fur made me very hungry, and tired.

I let go of 501 and walked over to Bob, who sat very still.

"Explain this to me." I could barely hear his voice as I sat next to him. We watched the trio standing over by their own egg.

"This child, when it matures will have both the memories and understandings of my insights with you, and the insights of learning how to operate the yellow machines," I tell Bob. "That is anakoinosis; true understanding. The egg will be brought to our masters, and they will choose who to bind the children to, as that will let them learn more than I could ever teach them. They know everything that I have known."

"But these are your children!" Bob was loud now. He got up and walked in slow circles again.

"They are us." I followed him around in circles. "They will be bound. They will be paired with those who know different things. If you had been one of us, before you died, we would share anakoinosis, so your knowledge would not be lost, and the memories of those after us increase. Only after our masters die are we free, and alone."

Bob's mouth hung open. He was trying hard to understand. It was the closest an aerokrat could get to anakoinosis.

"It must be a survival mechanism. You commingle to pass on all your knowledge. Your fur . . ." He stopped and ran his hand over my bare skin. "It's protein, right? The DNA must combine, they . . . I don't know . . ." He looked up into the sky. "I cannot believe they decided against unfreezing anyone to study you all. We need the scientists down here!" A new thought caught him, and he whirled on me. "What happens to you when there are no new masters with new memories, when you share all?"

I spread my arms.

"Those are happy times," I said. I remembered generations of pleasant times in the woods. Times when you knew, from all your prior foreparents' memories, which trees could produce fruit every year. How many could gather in a copse and not go hungry. The feel of the sun on bare skin by the coast. Communal anakoinosis of hundreds together. Stasis for thousands and thousands of generations, with no new ideas to be found.

"These are not happy times," Bob said.

"These are learning times." I pointed at the Hopper. "We must learn everything you can teach us. And then, when there is nothing more to learn, we can have happy times. We will be just like you."

Bob shook his head.

"It won't work like that. It won't."

"But it will. It always has. In memory, there were other threats. Great predatory animals, others of my kind who knew very different things who came from different parts of the land we lived on before you took us away. We incorporate them, become them, reflect them, remember them, their thoughts, and their essence. We will do the same to you."

Bob walked away from me. I ran to catch up with his long strides.

"There is never stasis with humans." His feet hit the ground hard. "We always change."

"Then we will learn this, and . . ."

"Not as long as you consider us different, or masters of any knowledge. You will always be bound. And

since we have longer lifespans than you, you will be
bound forever."

I could barely keep up with him.

"Well, yes. Eventually your young will need to become bound to us if they are to learn new things."

Bob stopped.

"What?"

I smiled happily and said nothing.

"We can't share memories with you," Bob's hands
waved in the air. "Humans barely understand and
agree with each other."

"We will come to be just like each other. That is
how things must work. We will become just like you,
and once we are just like you, you will be just like us.
We will do all the same things to each other."

Bob looked down at the ground.

"Oh, god!" He rubbed his forehead. "You might
just do that."

He walked in silence back to his home, me right by
his side. Inside he made liquids and drank them late
into the night, while I watched.

He shook. It was not *laughter,* but something else.
His eyes watered over.

When he thought I had fallen asleep he picked up
a blanket and spread it over me.

"I think we fucked up real bad here, whiffet," he said,
his voice slurred and funny sounding. "And I don't
know how to stop this mess. I just don't know how."

My aerokrat became strange. He avoided me, refused to let me work, and he stayed out late. That
went on for many nights.

It seemed like he was trying to induce anakoinosis
in the other aerokratois in his own way, but not doing
well.

He finally came home one night with bruised eyes
and a bleeding lip. People gathered outside Bob's hut,
screaming and shouting at him.

Bob said some of his companions listened to him

and were sympathetic. But there was the Great Repair to be thought of, and most ridiculed him for questioning the need to get everything fixed on his ship as soon as possible.

"They say we have to return to civilization, or our machines will eventually fail us and we'll all die as savages here on this planet," Bob says.

We sat at his small table.

"I'm really sorry." Bob took a long drink of his liquid. "I think they've had enough of me challenging them. I tried to organize, but there are too many of them."

I nodded like I understood, but in truth, I was not sure why Bob would try to break the entire process. It served learning well. It served anakoinosis.

But I didn't say anything. I did not want to agitate him. I only wanted to learn from him, and pass that learning on to all my children.

Bob leaned close to me.

"The people outside, they've come to take me back."

"Where?" I wanted to know.

Bob pointed up at the ceiling, indicating the sky above.

"The ship in the sky. There are places aboard it where I will be frozen again, so I can't speak up anymore. They're putting me back in storage with all the other passengers."

New things to learn. I was excited.

"When do we leave?"

Bob looked at me strangely.

"You must do me a favor," he told me. "I need you to run out of the door, and go toward the forest. I will follow you in a bit."

"Okay." I said.

"I think," Bob stared at the door, "I think I may have found a way to do something good, something that might help you, something that might help all of us."

When I opened the door, twenty loud aerokratois shouted at me. I walked toward them, scared of the yelling. The nearest aerokratois kicked me. I was lifted up and beaten, tossed from hand to hand. In seconds, blood ran down my face. My newly regrown fur was torn out of my skin by the angry aerokratois.

I barely crawled away from the mob into the grass, and as I collapsed I heard a loud explosion. Nothing was visibly damaged, but the aerokratois fell silent.

"He killed himself," one of them shouted.

I learned something very new about the aerokratois.

Bob was the only aerokrat buried in the hill. His white cross was much larger than the other small crosses that covered the grounds.

I imitated the shaking and wet eyes ritual he had done before his death.

And I was alone, my own master.

On the second night of being alone, I tried to join in anakoinosis behind the same hill where Bob had watched us, but was refused.

"You have nothing new to give," a trio of whiffets told me. "And maybe what you bring is bad."

They even refused to let me work with them, and learn new things. Among the thousands there, none would look at me.

I fled away from the areas near the Hopper to go toward the forest.

At night I walked the roads, and during the day I found places to hide and sleep. The forest, when it came up, was welcome. For a whole month I disappeared into it.

There was food in berries and roots. Other animals sometimes came toward me, but I ran from them. They were dangerous and rough. They were not like the docile animals in the land we were taken from to bond with the aerokratois.

My fur soon became shaggy, matted, and long. My skin ached for anakoinosis.

A gang was working on the edge of a new road. They jumped when I came out from behind a tree. I had visions in my mind of being a master to other whiffets. I thought about being alone, and that maybe I could spread the memory to other whiffets. If they were like me, alone and their own masters, but with me, maybe I wouldn't be so lonely.

Was this what it was like to be an aerokrat? I wondered.

A cool wind blew over us and rustled the falling leaves on the ground.

I held my hands out.

"Do not be alarmed."

"Who are you?" they wished to know. I showed them my tattoo and told them I had lived near the Hopper.

"Such thick fur!" they said. They gathered around me. "We have not had time for anakoinosis for a while. We have worked so long and hard."

I stroked their arms.

"Then let us," I said. "All of our fur is thick."

They found me strange, but relaxed enough to let me into the group. Our egg was thick when it formed on the ground by our feet.

"We'll give it to our aerokratois," they insisted afterward.

The road was getting hotter as the sun rose higher into the sky.

"No," I told them. "I will take this one."

They were shocked.

"You are too similar."

"I know."

They watched, quiet, as I took our egg with me deep into the forest.

*   *   *

When my child hatched several weeks later, he stood up, full with pieces of my own knowledge and the knowledge of the road crews and the knowledge of all their foreparents.

He didn't bond with me. Just like I had been free since Bob killed himself, my own child was somewhat free. I could see that he was a bit confused, and that he had much on his mind. Just as I did.

We stood with each other for a long while.

"We should go find other road crews," my child finally said. "If we both have anakoinosis with others, then others can be their own masters with us."

I was happy he felt the same way I did, and did not feel so alone.

My child told me where the nearest work camps where, and we split company to spread our new revelation.

It was a rainy day when I found the work camp.

The sun remained almost invisible behind the clouds, but it occasionally broke out to illuminate the rows of tents behind the barbed wire. Several aerokratois walked around the edges of the camp, giving orders to the multitudes of whiffets bonded to them.

I stopped. I was about to return to being ruled by the aerokratois in there. Maybe it was better to stay in the wilderness, taking eggs from work gangs. It would be better to remain free, and spread my memories, than return to a work camp.

The memories of my foreparents bonded to aerokratois overwhelmed me, telling me to return to the camp. The memories of foreparents who where their own masters remained distant.

It was comforting to think about returning to a workgang, and being told what to do, and when to do it.

Would I ever be my own master again?

The desire for anakoinosis tugged at me, and with a strange feeling in my stomach I walked to the edge of the camp. At the gates I stood in the mud and the aerokratois let me in.

My fur was thick with dirt.

The aerokratois were such exciting creatures. They brought these new concepts, new behaviors, and many other things we never could have come up with. I had so many things to learn from them yet. It was good that I was returning, I reassured myself.

There were many whiffets in the camp behind the sharp wires.

I hugged the first one to reach his arms out to me behind one of the tents. I touched his cheeks to mine and shared my memories of my foreparents, my life, and Bob's strange gift to me.

I wondered if there would ever be stasis again, now that I was trapped inside the camp, working for the aerokratois again. I hoped my child spread some of the very new thoughts Bob gave me.

Those memories would never die, but live on. My fur fell to the muddy ground as I gave new memories to another.

The next morning I was awakened by an aerokrat with red hair. He handed me a pick.

"We'll be breaking rock, today, whiffet," he grinned. I was slow to stand up, so he yanked me to my feet with a shout, hurting my arms.

As I walked out into the sun, blinking, I knew, deep within me, that the longer we worked for the aerokratois, the sooner we would become just like them.

Then both would have true anakoinosis.

THRESHOLD

by Terry McGarry

THE SOUTHEASTERN VERANATHOR Center for Neurosuppression has been grown in the shape of a tree. It is not a tree—it is ordinary plant tissue designed to mimic the form of a broadly spreading warmwood. In older, more affluent parts of Veranathor Island, homes are grown over generations from genuine hardwood stock, the earliest chambers burrowing farther from daylight year by year, the outerwood hardening and darkening into an impenetrable encrustation of bark. Here along the sunny coast of the island state, professional accommodations are grown cheap and quick from production-grade cellulose, and the walkway I stand on winds among anonymous clusters of the simplest, most common designs: bulbous mushrooms, cylindrical stalks.

Why couldn't one of those have been the place? Why must my destination stand out so sorely? This faux tree is a profound aesthetic deception: the intricacy of leafless branchings suggests the fractal density of the neurons they destroy here, while the gracious spread of boughs supersedes the technical with the hortitectural, making you forget that what goes on inside is illegal in every other nation on the planet.

This is the only place in the world where it is legal

to evict ghosts from your own mind. This is the only
place in the world where it is legal to reject immortality.

My name is Nethón. The community knows me as
Tollisdelá Nethón Arimthorá, vocational ceramicist.
Nethón is my selfname, Arím was my bearer, and
Tollís was my quickener. It's best to be clear on that,
since naming conventions differ so widely and change
over time. I don't know where this record will ulti-
mately end up, or who will read it. I'm not even sure
why I'm making it. Procrastinating, I suppose. Enjoying the feel of my claws scoring the tablet putty.
Enjoying being me, just me, alone with myself. Trying
to decide if that feeling is worth committing murder
for. Trying to decide whether or not it is murder.

I thought I'd know, by the time I got here. All that
long way, loping past windfarms and moss refineries
on four sore feet, I thought that when I stood in front
of this entryway the decision would bubble up from
inside me—truth and right chiming like a clear bell,
calm and certain. But I'm more terrified now than I
was when I set out from home.

And more lonely, in this shell of mortal flesh. It is
a pleasant shell. Arím, who did not know Tollís personally and wants no part of this decision, has a mus-
cular build and a beautiful glossy chestnut coat, pale
shadow striping in the underparts, fur so thick as to
afford barely a glimpse of dermal ossicle. Here in Veranathor, boasting is socially unacceptable—but you
can praise the physical attributes of your bearer or the
cleverness of your quickener, and it's considered to
amount to the same thing. That's fine where my bearer
and I are concerned, since we're genetically identical.
But until I reach puberty, I am me, not my quickener,
or all the quickeners that came before mine.

I think I might do anything to stay that way.

I can't let them strip my self from me. I can't let
them take over. They might outnumber me hundreds,
even thousands to one. There's no telling how many

generations Tollís carried. They can impose their interests, their pursuits on me, shoulder my learning and my passions to the side. I am a talented ceramicist—not the best or brightest who ever lived, at least according to those who were around at the acknowledged height of the ceramic arts, but consistently original and pleasing. And I love my work. It is unique to me, imbued with my personality and no one else's.

And yet . . . can I be sure of that? Can I be sure that I'm not somehow being directed by the ghosts I carry, that my work is not somehow improved by their presence? Can I take sole credit for anything I've ever done?

"Oh, their personalities are in there," my friend Melén says. "It's just all subconscious. You're not aware of it. You're not aware of them. But they're in there, those souls. In you. They may be dormant but they're not comatose. Glaciers look dead and frozen, but they expand, contract, make forays and retreats— they breathe and move and behave. They influence you whether you know it or not."

If Melén is right, it means that I have a microcommunity of ancient minds nesting under the floorboards in my head. A haunting of ancient minds, whispering to me in my sleep, influencing me, prompting me.

The thought of that blanks my sight white with rage.

Melén cannot be right. Melén is only a bearer, a fleshgiver, and knows nothing of quickening. The engrammatic neuroencoding perpetrated on me by my quickener is inert, nonfunctioning, until my maturing body secretes the neurohormones that can stimulate the designated receptors. Children do not produce those hormones. I do not yet produce those hormones in sufficient quantity to wake Tollís' ghosts. Until I step off the cliff of puberty, the pathways of the past are closed to me—and I am safe from them.

But I'm nearing the cliff. I can hear the winds whistling up out of the abyss. I have begun to have bad dreams. Dreams of places I have never seen, feelings

I have never felt. Alien emotions, alien sensations, alien attitudes. There are monsters in me and they are shifting, stirring. I perceive them in brief bursts of firing synapses in the small hours, like looming shadows silhouetted by sudden glare, the eye-searing shock of lightning in the coal deeps of night.

They will wake. They will engulf me. They will submerge me. I will drown in them. Drown in ancestors.

Unless I get them first.

I want to blame it all on Tollís, but that would be unfair. Tollís was a victim, and can't be faulted for the cruelty of others—or for possessing the memory of that cruelty. Tollís had no choice in what happened, and no choice about whether to remember it or not.

But I do.

The trouble with freedom of choice is that at some point you have to exercise it. Once I make this choice, there will be no going back. And I don't have enough information to be sure I'm choosing correctly.

I have only external knowledge of Tollís: a lightleaf imprint of Tollís' bearer, found in Tollís' carryall and passed on to me by Arím (why carry an imprint of your bearer when you can just look in the mirror? yet people do); news stories I researched myself; and Arím's verbal description of the stranger on the trolley platform. I know of Tollís' trauma only through hearsay. The one who was Tollís, a dark, coarse-coated native of some mountainous northern land, with ice-shard eyes, a ready grin, and a burred accent, died when I was quickened. There is no one I can ask, "How many lives did you carry? How many did you pass on to me? Will you live quietly inside me once you're freed, or will you enslave me to your foreign desires?" I have asked prepubescent and postpubescent quickener friends to describe their experience, and nothing they have said convinces me that they remain entirely themselves and have not become puppets of their forebears.

The news stories of Tollís tell little of the quickener

and focus predominantly on the horror. Quickener, bearer, one offspring, two parents, and two visiting siblings attacked in their Veranathor home, beaten and tortured, all but one killed. The details are gory and I don't like to think about them. If I receive Tollís' memories, I will have to live with that experience for the rest of my life, and it didn't even happen to me.

For all I know, Tollís might have wanted to end it all that day. Who can say for sure that Tollís, standing on that transit platform, didn't plan to jump under the trolley's wheels, or ride it to an observation tower for a fifty-length dive? But there was Arím, full of me, standing beside Tollís on that station platform, and there was I, overeager then as now, tearing free of the pouch prematurely. Arím had no idea I was coming. Tollís simply happened to be the only quickener there. Stimulated past resistance by the pheromones and bloodscent, by Arím's cries and mine, Tollís, willing or unwilling, slid my small body from the fleshgiver's blood-slick claws and did what millennia of biological evolution compelled:

Quickened me. Electrochemically stimulated my brain to think, forging pathways that in other species' young would take weeks to years of experience to form, forcing myelinization to flash-pave those pathways against erosion. My cardiopulmonary, sensory, and nervous systems, allowed to develop in safety within my fleshgiver's pouch, were fully prepared for use; with the exception of the armor plating that would later form in my skin, physically I was already a fully functional miniature replica of Arím; but until Tollís quickened me, I lacked motor skills, coordination, spatial perception, tactical and strategic comprehension. Tollís bequeathed to me a full set of survival skills—enough, in the primitive, predator-rich environment that bred us eons ago, to keep me alive long enough to reproduce.

And then Tollís passed on life and spirit, memory

and identity as well. Quickening me past bearing. Quickening me into a quickener.

That degree of quickening—soulgiving, the elder cultures call it—is death for the quickener. No one knows why, any more than they know why we sleep or why we dream; there are as many theories as there are sophists. No one even knows precisely how, any more than they know precisely how it is that we think at all. Consciousness and memory are hotly debated topics within the sophistries. But it seems to me that there's more to this than neurotransmitters and electrochemical copying, or quickening wouldn't kill you. There's some sort of transfer of spirit, of soul, something profoundly more than mere brain chemistry. . . .

Why did Tollís quicken me? It meant that that experience of torture and bereavement and rage would live on for at least one more generation. Was it ego, or sacrifice, or cowardice? Did Tollís feel it was preferable to continue suffering than go into oblivion? Did Tollís shy away from selfdeath when the void roared, and grab panicked, desperate hold of neural immortality? Or did Tollís courageously agree to live on with trauma rather than end a line of predecessors?

Allowing puberty to thaw the memories in me, and passing them on in turn, could be consigning Tollís to eternal damnation.

Denying the hormone surge of puberty could be wiping out millennia of ancestors.

I don't know how many predecessors there were. How many were quickened by those who'd been quickened by those who'd been quickened before them. Everyone who knew Tollís, who could have answered my questions, is gone. By choosing suppression, it could be that I'd destroy only two of us—myself and Tollís—and one of those deaths a mercy to a tortured soul.

There is only one way to find out, and there is no way back from it. The only way to find out if something will break is to break it. The only way to know the future is to go there.

And so I sit here on a bench in sight of the entrance of a clinic that can excise these ghosts from me permanently, and make no move to cross that threshold.

Memory-murder. Killing the mind or minds I host. There's no way to pass them along unsampled. There's no way to give them to someone else to hold. If I die without passing them on, they die, too. And I will die without passing them on if I walk through that entryway, because it will burn out the parts of my brain where the ghosts lie dormant. Someday, perhaps, there will be better therapy, temporary suppression, denial of integration; perhaps someday you'll be able to let the ghosts wake, get acquainted, and then decide if you like living with them or not; perhaps someday you'll even have the choice of storing predecessors and passing them on to the next child undamaged while you yourself forgo the next life for restful oblivion.

But not now. For now, it's all or nothing. I must jeopardize my identity by allowing an unknown number of strangers—one of whom I know for a fact has experienced unspeakable horror—free reign in my head, or I must silence them all permanently, whoever they are, however many of them there are.

Bearers live one life and then they die. If they can bear that, why can't I? What gives me the right to impose myself on the next generation?

I know now why I'm writing this. Because I had decided not to go in to the center. Because I couldn't take the risk of committing murder. Because I had decided to go home, and let nature take its course, and let the neurohumors wash over me and float me away into whatever half-life I am destined for. I wanted to keep some record of my own voice before it merged into the voices of the ages. I'm still me, right now. Just me. Nethón, alone, on the cusp of adulthood, unpolluted by adult hormones or adult memories. I just wanted to be me for a little longer before I gave up and turned for home.

But I'm not willing to give up. I'm not willing to give up my self. Maybe it is murder. But if it is, it's in self-defense.

I am under siege, and I have a right to protect myself.

I'm going in.

Yes. In the end, I went in. And I saved these tablets—I'm not sure why, but most likely for the same reason that I saved my predecessors: because every echo and reflection of thought and identity is precious, however fragmentary, and in whatever form; and because change comes when and where we least expect it. In a clinic chair. On a trolley platform.

I stepped over the threshold of the suppression center and saw a neurosophist and told my story, much as I told it to these tablets. And, just as at the end of these tablets there was a little room left to write, which I use now, at the end of my interview there was a little room left for the sophist to comment. A little space of time and consciousness as I laid my arm out to be shaved and used my claws to lever the dermal plates apart to admit the injection. Just enough space for the sophist, leaning in to administer the neurophage, to say, "Wasn't Elindelá Tollís Noranthorá killed by anti-neurosuppression extremists?"

No. But Tollís' family was. And that memory is worse than my worst fears. But having Tollís' conviction and courage to draw on is more wondrous than my sweetest dreams. And Tollís is only one of the precious many who share this lifetime with me.

I let the armor plating close on my flesh before the injection could go in. I snatched the arm back and ran. My memory may be degrading after all these years, but as I recall, I ran all the way home.

If I was relieved at the choice I made, I will never know whether it was because there were so very many spirits collected in Tollís and I had avoided by the thinnest wisp of chance becoming a mass murderer, or because my dearest Melén was right, and our forespirits have their own survival imperative, just as our forebears did. The survival instinct of consciousness is no less potent than the genetic imperatives of flesh.

Unlike my adolescent self, however, I do know who I am writing this for, and why.

You bear Melén's genes, not mine. Your body, your reactions, your speed, your physical proclivities will be Melén's. That is a glorious thing. It would be a poorer world without Melén's verve, Melén's keen eyes, Melén's kind heart. I love Melén deeply. And just as I suspect that the minds stored within a quickener have fundamental urges and requirements and defenses, I suspect that flesh has its own personality. Soul is as much a thing of flesh as of mind. In that, as in so many things, you are the child of us both equally. I cherish that. I celebrate that.

But I must warn you. Melén was ever contrary and rebellious. Risk-taking, stubbornness, hardheaded opinionated determination—these are your genetic legacy. Combine them with what you will get from me, and I have no doubt that you will find yourself on that same threshold one day. Or one very like it.

I am not begging for my life, or the life of those who came before me, those who nest in me as I nest, thus far unfelt, in you as you read this. My life will end when I quicken you. Other philosophies hold differently, but that is my belief, beloved child-to-come: Tollisdelá Nethón Arímthorá will leave this world the moment I waken the consciousness of Nethondelá Tollís Melenthorá. I don't mind. I don't resent you for it. Were there no irresistible biological imperative built into my flesh, had I the choice to ignore the sonic and pheromonal triggers Melén will emit when you tear through the pouch, still I would quicken you, even knowing it was my death. You are our future. I grieve only that I will not have the joys of your fleshgiver: the joy of sleeping with you tucked in my arms; the joy of watching you grow into yourself, your unique and precious self.

I do not beg for you to quicken me in turn. I do not beg for you to turn from that entryway or deny that injection. You are blessed to live in a nation grown in freedom. You are blessed to have the choice of that threshold. The decision is entirely yours, and I do not write this to you, my child, in hope of playing upon your sympathy and manipulating you into permitting the thaw of memory should you prefer complete independence.

I write this to free you from the onus of it. I write this that you might know me, and us. Should you choose to allow me, and Tollís, and all our predecessors entre into your mind, should you choose to share your life with ours, you will have made that choice with an understanding of precisely who you are letting into your head. You need not accept us blindly. Squeeze the palm heart before you buy it, to be sure its center is not rotten. Kick the tires of the vehicle, check the teeth of the draftbeast. Squeeze and kick and check and question, question, question.

And if you choose, for whatever reason, to suppress us, to keep us frozen, to pour lime into our nest under the floorboards of your mind, you will still have some sense of who we were.

Of who I am.

Go on now, and be you—not me, not us. Encumbered by neither ignorance nor guilt.

How can I love you so, without knowing you, never having smelled you, touched you, seen you?

And yet, somehow, I do.

Remember us to the future, my child. However you can, however you choose.

Remember me.

NOBODIES

by Adrienne Gormley

I LIMP INTO MY old village of Green Hollow, wincing at the cold as my left rear foot drags through the snow. I duck behind the houses and search for the food pile, the one the Real People are to leave so that we Nobodies may eat. I do not find it, not here, not there, and I fret. How will I survive Testing so I can become a Real Person again if I do not eat? There are too many Nobodies about, and I am merely one of them.

As I slip between the houses, I think back to when I lived here as a child and could run and play among the other Real People. Alas, I am no longer a child. I do not have a name, I do not have a gender, I do not legally exist. Nor will I until I become an adult, if I live long enough to be accepted as one. Then I wince from the hunger that gnaws at me and I return to concentrate on looking for the food.

I catch my bad foot on a snow-covered clod and stumble. I recover, despite my hunger-induced dizziness. I move into a clump of ornamental bushes, where I know my hairless, mottled Nobody hide will blend into the shadows.

As I settle in the shadows, my nose twitches. Mmm, dried fruit. Meat. I lift my head and sniff again, then

move toward the scent, grasping at branches to keep
myself upright.

I pass several homes before I stop again. I flare my
nostrils, questing for the scent of the food, and I find
it. Now I know where to find the food. For some reason, it is behind the home of the Chief Family. I do
not know why it is in a private area, as such food
leavings are supposed to be public. I hunch down,
making sure my forefeet are firmly placed, and think.
My memories tell me that the Chief Family is not due
to leave food for the Nobodies again for some time,
so why they have food out now is a puzzle.

At times, I am not sure it is worth the effort to
search out the food scraps. Usually I hunt or fish, but
there is my injury, and it is so cold. I know the law
requires that I travel alone, and yet I mourn. I don't
believe any of my clutch mates are still alive.

The bone-deep ache in my left rear foot nags at me
as I approach the food cache. I worry about what I
might find there besides food. I stoop down once I am
behind the Chief Family's house, afraid some Real
People might see me. Even when I was still a child, I
was never welcome here. Now that I am a Nobody, it
is worth my life to be seen.

I hear ragged breathing and look around for the
source. Then I realize; it's me. I try to stifle the sound.

I circle the yard slowly, trying to pinpoint the food
cache. The smell hits me and I home in on an open
bag, not far from the back gate, well away from the
stables that house the Chief Family's farm animals.

Food! What does it matter if some of it is stale and
dry? I do not care about the quality; I care only that
the food exists, and that I can eat.

I rotate my ears to listen as I chew, and hear my
second stomach complain that it has not had anything
in too long. Too many sun cycles passed, it tells me.
I snatch at the items on the top of the pile, watching,
one eye turret turned to the yard, another pointed
toward the food cache. I have to take what I need

before other Nobodies show up to claim a share. I fret, because I know I am weak. I clasp what I can in my hands, glad I at least have all three fingers on each, Having only three of my four feet working right is problem enough.

I crawl into the shade of a nearby bush, hoping that I am still invisible. The mottled skin pattern from my birth clan is an asset I appreciate. As I chew on another bite, I keep watch for any who might challenge me for what I have taken.

Food. Glorious food. I feel blessed to have found a store of food that is not rotting. I take in the aroma, and I have to fight to keep from gorging. I settle down on my haunches, forelegs tucked under me, as the ache gnawing at my second stomach eases. I find that I have a bit left over, which I wrap and tuck into a small carry sack, one I made at the beginning of my Test from the hides of some rockhoppers.

To my left, I hear the scratch of claw on stone and turn a wary eye to watch. When I see the source of the noise, I tense. I have suffered too much at the hands of the Nobody who is approaching, even when we were both still children and Real People. The other's long nose is twitching as it approaches the food cache, and I see its muscles rippling. The other, who always bullied the rest of us, was born into the Chief Family and may return to its birth family if it survives. The bully moves without pausing to where the food pile is. I can tell from the way it moves so confidently, the way it sniffs about, that it already knows the food would be there. The bully does not travel as one who is looking, or one who feels a Nobody's need to hide.

I tense as I realize the bully knows the food is waiting. Then my spirit hurts, as I become aware that the Chief Family has secretly left out food for this former child, hoping to violate the laws of the Test. How can we become true adults if we don't have to strive for adulthood? Is the law there to be ignored?

Such favoritism is a violation of everything I ever

learned, where all Nobodies are to share any food left
out, and all food that is left out is to be in public
areas. I am not surprised that some families would
want to secretly help their Nobody young. Every family wishes to continue. I am shocked to find the Chief
Family doing this; they are supposed to be moral arbi-
ters of Green Hollow.

I stuff everything I haven't yet eaten into my carry
sack. I hope it is enough to see me through until I
can find something else. I hold the sack close to my
bare hide, and make my escape.

Not soon enough. I limp to the edge of the village,
not pausing for anything, not even when the bully trots
after me, shrieking in public.

"Thief! Cripple! That was *my* food!"

Wrong. Wrong. The food is for all Nobodies, and
we are to remain unseen, but I do not say that aloud.
Besides, I have left more than enough food behind to
see the bully through a famine. How selfish can one
be and still hope to become a Real Person?

The thaw has come and I still limp a little, but I
have managed to make it this far. The woods around
me are bursting with growth and the sun is warm on
my back. I can still feel my bones rattle against each
other, but at least there are fleshy buds and shoots I
can chew. I also know a small pool at the base of
a short cascade where there are plenty of silverscale
fingerlings who do not know how to avoid a net made
of reeds.

There is still some snow on the ground in the shady
places, but I know how to avoid them as I climb into
hidden hollows. I have no idea what I will find there
except shelter, or maybe a sleeping rockhopper. Then,
when I settle down into the lee of one overhanging
rock face, I find that there is a patch of odd fungus
growing there. There is no gain without risk, I tell
myself, so I pry several off their rocks and carry
them away.

As I sit, leaning against the rock wall, I stretch out my legs. I see my adult hair is growing, in odd patches. I relax; my Test will soon be over. I will succeed or fail, and if I fail, I can only live wild or die. That, I know after my hungry winter, is a good reason to study any potential food source. The Real People of Green Hollow have little enough to eat as is.

I reach out a hand and touch a patch of hair on my leg. I need to know that it is real. I touch it again, and feel a tingle of anticipation thrill through my body. So soft, much softer than I remember my mother's being. Could this be the new adult hair, and it only grows coarse with age?

I see that I have inherited my father's pale amber color. My hair gleams in the afternoon sun. What is interesting is the silver patch that grows on my left rear leg, above my old injury.

I take out some of the fungus I found. I lift it to my nose and smell. My eyes sting and I swivel them away. I blink; the smell is pungent. I wonder what will happen if I cook them?

I crawl farther back into the lee of the rock, where I start a fire with some dried brush and the leavings of a deserted windwalker nest. I spear a fungus onto a stick and hold it over my small flame, and wait as I let the heat work its magic. Soon the scent of the fungus changes, and I feel my stomachs demanding I eat it now. The scent is, what is the word—savory— and it is all I can do to keep from eating it whole. Instead, I take a small bite and roll it around my tongue so I can enjoy the flavor before I swallow it.

I sit and wait, afraid that what I have eaten will turn on me, ripping my first stomach to shreds, making me bleed out my life here in the rocks. Instead, my first stomach ceases its complaints, so I take another bite, then another, and before I know what is happening, I am snapping at the end of the stick on which I roasted the fungus. I want more, so I take another few pieces out of my pouch and roast them, and eat them until I can eat no more. I look around my rock shelter for more, but I see only a few very small growths in a hidden nook.

I decide to leave them to grow, but I also plan to look for more of this fungus in other rocky places over the next few moons. I want to keep myself well fed on them until I can get back down to the pool where I have my fingerling nets. And maybe, later, I can gather spores to take back with me.

I relax as I settle down by the pool, and I bask in the warmth of high summer. The sunlight is as dappled as my formerly bare hide once it threads its way through the leaves to the ground. Around me, in the brush, I hear the sounds of the small creatures that indicate the forest has grown used to my presence.

Light sparkles off the rippling water, and the small stream that feeds the pool chimes as it dances down the rockfall from above. This place is a good place to stay, and one in which I can live comfortably. It is far enough from Green Hollow that I should not be interrupted, yet it is near enough that I can return easily when I am ready.

I study my left hind leg as I stretch it out over the soft ground cover on the bank. It is still a bit stiff, but I no longer limp, and I can move easily when I need to.

As I watch the ripples in the stream, I wonder how things are going with the Nobodies who stayed closer to Green Hollow. How many, I wonder, have managed to find something that will prove to be of benefit to the Real People?

I check to make sure the year brand that I received to mark the start of my Test has not blurred too much with time. It would not do to be identified as one of the Nobodies from a later year. I wiggle my ears with pleasure as I see that the spirals and interlaced arcs are still visible through my hair. I am satisfied.

I review the skills I have learned during my Testing.

I know how to fish not just for fingerlings, but for the larger silverscales, which provide such succulent flesh. I know to seek out and harvest the barbleberries that infest the forest. I burble to myself when I think of the barbleberry seeds that Real People have thrown away, thinking they were useless. And, oh, that fungus! I wipe away the trail of drool that runs down my chin as I think about it. I have not yet figured out how to cultivate the fungus, but it is what I wish to contribute. If nothing else, I can lead harvesting groups to the mountains.

The line attached to the net draws taut. I reel it in and pull out the flashing, flipping silverscale. I dash its head on a rock to stun it, then slip it into a reed bag. I drop the net back into the pool, then secure the line with a rock. I hope to start my journey back in the next few days, and I want to smoke as much of the meat as I can. I already have several packets of fungus spores in my carry sack, to take back as my benefit.

Brush snaps behind me, and I hear grumbling from beyond the bush screen. I scramble to my feet. A screen of vines, woven into the barbleberry brambles, shakes as if a bull lorox is tearing at it with all four horns. Better safe hidden, I decide. I scramble up the rocks beside the stream and shelter behind the rocks and brush on the crest above the cascade. Once there, I tilt an eye into a small gap so I can see what is going on below.

My hearts thump in dissonant rhythm as I see a trio of People force themselves into the clearing. I recognize them; they are Nobodies from my Testing group. They are together! I shiver with anger. They risk their lives, as well as the lives of any others they approach. Like me. I itch and fret, wondering what they are up to now.

One of them is the bully who was born to the Chief Family. The bully seems not to care that it has company. I curse silently, adding the bully's behavior to what I saw at the village when I was there. And I wonder; how does the Chief Family expect to get away with law-breaking, and how does the bully plan to prove itself worthy of adulthood benefit? Has it found a benefit yet?

"That cripple was here," the bully says to its companions. "I can still smell it."

"It's not here now," the smallest of the three says. "Let's go, before any Real People see us together."

"Forget the Real People. The cripple stole some of the food my Family set out for me, and I intend to take back what I can, even if I have to skin it. And I'll take whatever else it has at the same time. Why should I work to find a benefit for those idiots back there if I can take it?"

The third Nobody, whom I recognize by its crooked nose as one of the bully's childhood followers, says something and lays a hand on the bully's shoulder. The bully turns and hits Crooked Nose. As I watch, the three of them fight among themselves. I shiver, glad I am not part of their group. And I am grateful again I was never a friend with any of them when we were still children.

The bully knocks down Crooked Nose, then he and Shorty beat it until it collapses. Then the bully looks up and stares at Shorty, both eyes forward. The bully attacks Shorty and drives it to the ground, too, all the while muttering that it cannot leave witnesses. I am beyond shock, my legs locked in my fear, because I know that I am next, as I watch it snatch a piece of deadwood and beat Shorty. The two on the ground finally stop moving as their life fluids trickle out onto the verge. *No witnesses.* I know that I am to be next.

The bully looks up from the two bodies and moves toward the rockfall where I am hiding. I shift back, away from the clearing, huddling down to avoid being seen. I am a short distance away, just into the wooded area beyond, when the bully scrambles to the top and finds the sanctuary I just left.

"Stop!"

I am not a fool. I run, pushing through the brush, branches whipping my face. I do not care as long as I escape from the bully. Strange bully, thinking I would listen to it, after watching its behavior back at the rock pool.

I climb into the nearby mountains, finding my way through culverts and chimneys in the heights, slipping through angled tunnels as I attempt to get away from the bully. It follows, and it is very noisy. I wince as I hear the various small creatures who live in the low scrub as they scurry for shelter from this angry, loud monster.

I move into a canyon I have not yet seen, and travel along the banks of the small stream that flows there. I come to the end, a rock wall. The stream gurgles out of a fissure in the rock, with small plants—belly flowers—low around it. Their perfume fills the air. I bend over and scoop handfuls of water, still keeping one eye turned to watch behind me. I know the bully still follows, and I need to find a way to escape. This canyon is not the way, yet I am not sure how to get out of it.

I no longer think of the bully by any other designation than the Murderer. That is what it has done, and from all the teachings I learned from the village wise ones during my childhood, it has forfeited its right to becoming a Real Person.

Still, I wonder about history, as I think back on the low survival rate of other groups who have been Tested. I know that Testing those who enter puberty is to weed out those who are not worthy of surviving, but after what I have witnessed, I wonder if our past survivors haven't been those who are most like the Murderer. What determines fitness to survive, after all?

I stretch after I drink my fill, aware of the aches in my joints and the sharp itch of the scratches on my arms and legs. Some of them are weeping yellow, and when they drip off, they leave a brown spatter in the dust.

The sun batters my eyes until I am not sure which way to turn. I move back and forth at the base of the rock wall, looking for an opening. There is none.

I do find a foothold, so I stand on my rear legs and reach up with forelegs and arms, searching for holds. I pull myself up the rock. Once my rear feet are above the canyon floor, I meld with the rock face, then look for a higher hold.

I find one; a tough spur to my left. Can I reach it? I lift my hand, and my three fingers encircling the stumpy gray stone. I tug on it; it *feels* firm, yet I hesitate. Do I trust my weight to this? Behind me, down the canyon, I hear the enraged bellow of the Murderer. Trust it I must. I lock the joints of my fingers and pull myself higher, then look for something for my right hand to grasp. My left forefoot is also questing for a niche where I can insert my toes, and I manage to find both at once. Up I go, not daring to look down or behind.

Sweat trickles off my eye turrets as I move upward, each eye swiveling around, as I look for something new to grab on to. Then I find I am on a ledge, where I rest, for fear of collapse.

I look around to find a route to the top from here. There is a trail; narrow, but workable. As I get ready to move on, I look around, and inhale sharply. The Murderer is just below me, climbing the cliff face after me. It is silent as it climbs, except for the deep grunts as it fights for breath. I draw back, surprised, and hope the Murderer doesn't see me where I stand.

I crawl to the bottom of the narrow path I have found and look up it, then look back. I inhale sharply again as a large hand lifts up over the ledge. I move up the narrow trail, holding on the cliff face as best I can.

"Why run away?" the Murderer asks from behind

me. "You won't live to return to our village anyway."
I come to a bend in the trail and look back. The
Murderer is standing on the ledge. I shiver.

"Give me what you have," the Murderer calls out.

"Why do you think I have something?" I start up
the next part of the trail, the cliff now on my right.

"Because you're still alive!"

I hear the Murderer's feet as it starts up the trail.
It is moving faster than I am. I turn one eye around
to watch behind me as I move into the cleft, and I
see the Murderer moving around the first in the trail.
Too close. Above me, I see the trail curve into a small
cleft. A sharp wind is whistling out of it.

"Do you really want it?" I ask.

"Give it to me! Maybe I'll let you live." The Murderer stops below me, holding out one of its hands.

I move the fore part of my body out of the cleft,
holding one of the spore packets in right hand. With
my left, I worry open the twist that holds the packet
shut.

"Take it!" I hold the packet up and empty it onto
the wind.

"No!" The Murderer scrabbles up the trail, and
reaches out for me. I draw back into the cleft, and
watch as the Murderer misses its step on the narrow
trail. The Murderer screams once, and I hear a thud,
followed by a rattle. I move forward and look over
the edge, holding tight to another spur of rock, and
watch the small avalanche the Murderer's body starts
as it bounces its way to the foot of the cliff.

The chill of the autumn wind ruffles the hair on my
back as I make my way into Green Hollow. I hope
some of the others from my group have survived their
Testing. I do not want to be the only one of my age
group to return. I carry the remaining packets of fungus spores in my sack, with what is left of my travel
rations. I have returned, in time.

I reach the village common and look around. One

of the people standing near the well swivels his eye turrets, then dashes off. He will bring the elders to complete the formalities of my Test.

The elders come and question me according to the law, then they take away my bit of fungus. When they return, they hold their hands out to me, accepting me as a Real Person and giving me back my gender. I stand to face them. Once I choose a life task and a name, I can consider selecting a mate and raising my own family.

"I wish to be a lawgiver," I tell them. I do not say that I want to change some of the harsh laws, like the ones that destroy so many of our young. I will have to be very careful about how I go about that. "For a name, I will wear my distinctive mark." I show them the leg. "Call em will take the name of Silverleg."

THE LOAVES AND THE FISHES

by John DeChancie

I STOPPED AT the Long John Silver's right next to the Long Island Expressway ramp and bought myself lunch—a three-piece "Fish 'n' More" with fries and slaw and extra hush puppies on the side. I liked the hush puppies. But I really liked the fish. I liked fish, any kind of fish. Hence, my moniker, which had stuck with me since high school in Bensonhurst.

I came out of the restaurant and headed toward the parked Lincoln. It was one of those perfect fall days on Long Island when you can smell the sea and the wind comes in from the Atlantic and stirs the tall grass. The sun was bright and the sky was mostly clear except for a few clouds that seemed to hurry across the blue, as if called to some pressing business beyond the horizon.

I was so intent on the prospect of eating my lunch— the tantalizing smell of deep-fried cod filled my nostrils, inducing a kind of trance—that I didn't notice someone sitting in the back of the Town Car until I'd slid into the front seat.

I jumped a little; but when I saw a familiar face in the rearview mirror, I grinned.

"Hello, Jerry."

"Hello, Fish."

My grin faded. "Something's up."

Jerry Juliano, in black turtleneck and brown leather jacket, shrugged his narrow shoulders. He was blond and thin and had a fierce look. He always looked mad at someone. Anyone. Everyone. Legs crossed, he held a revolver almost languidly across his chest. "You screwed up big time, Charlie Fish."

"Yeah?" I said innocently. "I was just going to the meet with DiNardo."

"Yeah, with a wire, I'll bet," Jerry added.

"Huh?" I said.

"You know what I'm talking about," Juliano told me. He heaved a big sigh. "Christ, I hate it when I know the guy."

"What the hell are you talking about?"

"But you don't leave us any choice. I don't know what got into you. What the hell did get into you, anyway?"

I played dumb, always a good policy. I shrugged and said, "Jeez, I dunno."

"Okay, I can understand the midlife crisis thing. Your ma dies. Your brother goes to jail. Your wife starts fooling around. Then she bails on you. I can understand all that."

"Yeah," I said. I couldn't believe this. This was too much. I started to laugh. The irony.

Jerry was appalled. "What, you think this is funny? You think I'm kidding? This is just a warning, or what?"

I shook my head. "Nah. I know it ain't no warning."

"We gave you warning. Christ, how many times? You don't steal from us. That's one thing you don't do. We don't care that you run a perfectly good dry-wall business into the ground. We gave you the best contracts, we cut a deal with the union. City contracts, county contracts. All the business you want. And then you don't pay the withholding, you skim that off, you shortchange on all the paperwork—and we do a surprise audit and what? What do we find? Company's practically bankrupt. And then what? Do we take you out? Do we whack you? No. We give you a second chance. And then a third chance. And Christ, if everyone don't start talking about giving you a fourth. Finally, we gotta throw in the towel. Right?"

"Yeah," I said, shrugging almost apologetically. "Yeah."

"I even put in a good word for you," Jerry said. "But I mean how many times do you go to bat for a guy and he goes on screwing you?"

"Uh-huh."

"And then we get the word. You're talking to the feds."

"Hey," I said. "When the feds talk to you, you gotta talk back."

"Yeah? They talked to me, too. I told 'em to take a cab."

"That's you. I strung 'em along, is all."

"Christ." Juliano let out another sigh. "Don't you think we have people with the feds? People who feed us info? Did you think you could get away with it?"

"With what?"

"Forget it. Okay, get driving. Take the Expressway east."

"Okay."

I started laughing again. It was just too much.

Jerry was annoyed. "What the hell is with you?"

I turned the key and the big car's motor hummed to life.

"I think you're nuts," Jerry said. "I always thought you were a flake."

I shot a grin into the rearview mirror.

"Cut me a break," was all Jerry Juliano had to say.

I pulled out of Long John Silver's, drove slowly to the Expressway ramp, and pulled onto it. As I did, I sent a furtive right hand to rummage in the cardboard box bearing the fried fish lunch.

Instantly, the barrel of the revolver was up against the side of my head.

"Don't go rocket scientist on me all of a sudden," Juliano said tightly.

"I just wanted a hush puppy."

Cocking the handgun, Jerry took a look over the seat. "Go ahead, get it."

I picked up one of the warm balls of deep-fried corn meal batter and popped it into my mouth. I had come to love them.

"I don't believe you," Jerry said.

"I'm hungry," I said. "Haven't had my lunch."

"You and fish." Jerry shot a quick look back to see if anyone was following, then sat back. After a moment, he took note of the opulence around him.

"Nice interior," Jerry said.

"Thanks. It's real leather."

"Yeah. I'm squeakin' back here in this jacket. But it's nice. I never thought of a Lincoln."

"They're nice cars."

"They gonna keep makin' them or what?"

"I dunno. I ain't heard anything. It's got computers all over the place. Look at this dash."

Jerry leaned forward. "Nice. Go ahead and eat if you want to."

"Thanks."

I pulled out a huge piece of fish and bit off a big piece of it with a startling crunch.

"Smells good," Jerry said.

"Have some. I got the three-piece."

"Not now."

"Where we goin'?"

"Out east," Jerry said simply, reaching over the seat back and rifling the box. He came away with a fry and munched it.

"How far out?"

"Far enough."

"What's far enough? Montauk?"

"Don't make this any harder than it has to be."

"Sorry. You better put on your seat belt."

"Don't worry about the seat belt," Jerry said. "Drive."

Polishing off two of the fish and most of the fries, I drove east, and east some more.

"What the hell ever did happen to you, Charlie?" Juliano said. "You went wonky on me. I heard all kinds of crap. Like the alien thing."

"Alien?" I said, still playing dumb.

"Yeah. You were seeing UFOs, or something. Something about aliens taking over your body. Stress, I guess. That right?"

"Yeah, that's right," I said. I saw no reason to keep anything from him now. "My body was taken over by an alien intelligence from across the galaxy, thousands of light-years away."

"Yeah?" Juliano said, chuckling. "How'd they do that?"

"Matter transmission. Transferring bits of alien nucleic acid, supplanting the subject's. Fairly soon, the host subject is transformed into an alien being, retaining the guise of the subject's morphology."

"Huh," Juliano said, impressed. "Where'd you get that, from *Star Trek?*"

"It's true. I was taken over by an advanced alien being. But I'm okay now."

"You were taken over by the FBI, asshole."

Juliano lurched forward, his arm looping around my neck. His hand ripped the front of my shirt open and grabbed inside. The wires hurt as he yanked them savagely, ripping them out.

He dangled the tiny mike in front of my eyes. The compact transmitter was still nestled at the small of my back.

"Aliens, huh?" he said. He threw the mike and the wires at the dashboard with great disgust and viciousness. "Aliens, my ass."

The suburbs thinned, and Jerry said nothing for a long time. Then he said, simply, "Turn off the next exit."

"Pretty far out in the boonies," I said, chewing a last fry.

"I was thinking of doing it in Bloomingdale's, but I thought, nah, too many witnesses."

I laughed. "There's another piece of fish left. You want it?"

"Lost your appetite?"

"No, go ahead, you take it."

"I don't want it."

I shrugged. "Going to waste."

"Never mind about the goddamn fish. You eat it, fer crissake."

"I'm not hungry anymore. You eat it."

"Jesus. Awright."

Jerry leaned over the seat, opened up the lid of the cardboard box and looked in.

At that moment the Lincoln hit the concrete Jersey barrier that I had suddenly and deliberately swerved toward. It was sitting by the side of the road, angled oddly out, left by a road crew that had not taken great pains to straighten up after themselves except for putting up a flimsy wooden horse with a flashing amber light, barely visible in the bright sun. For all that, the thing was no great hazard, unless you deliberately drove straight at it.

The car hit the thing at a little over 30 mph. The impact was enough to throw Jerry over the front seat and head-first into the windshield, cracking it. He ended up a fetal huddle on the floor in front, his neck bent at an odd angle. The windshield bore a small circular wound like a star with rays of cracked glass.

Both front air bags in the front, the one on the steering wheel, and the one in the passenger side of the dash, had deployed with astonishing explosive energy, uselessly. My seat belt had restrained me from coming into contact with my bag, and Jerry's head had simply glanced off the other.

I was fine. My shoulder hurt a bit, but I felt okay. I unhooked my belt and leaned over Jerry, listening.

I heard no breathing. Jerry's gun was nowhere in sight. It didn't matter. Jerry wouldn't be using it. I reached into my jacket and brought out my own piece, a black plastic 9mm semiautomatic. I checked it over, put it back. Then I got out.

Inspecting the front of the car, I was surprised at the minimal damage. The thick plastic and fake-chrome bumper had deformed only slightly. Not only was the car still operable, it was hardly touched. They make good vehicles, I thought. Nothing like a big old car. I hated compacts.

There were woods nearby, and I took myself for a walk. Following a deer trail, I passed through a copse of beech trees and came out into a little clearing.

It was a perfect day. The sunlight warmed and the wind cooled. The high sun backlighted a single cloud of writhing wisps and smokes, illuminated to an ethereal glow. It could have been some long-departed spirit, once earthbound but now free.

I was that spirit. I was a ghost on this planet, a shade of my former self, my former life on a planet far across this island universe that my race shared with the dominant species of this world. My essence had been transmitted across the vast black reaches, and I took up a new life here. The irony, the irony of the nature of that new life.

I smelled the sea and watched a white gull circle below the cloud. Birdsong came from a stand of timber to my right. A breeze came up and stirred the tall grass and made the sound beach grass makes with wind in it, a high, thin, brittle rustling, as if the grass were made of paper.

I smelled sea smells and earth smells, and the mixture was heady. The sky seemed bigger, out here in the boondocks, and the earth and sky was all there was. I heard no highway sounds. I looked down. The black earth was damp. I watched a beetle crawl along the ground, then disappear under a rock.

An insect flitted by; a blur of color, a flutter, then gone.

I felt odd, but good. I was aware of the world, and my place in it, interloper though I might be. I was here. Why? To see. To see, I thought. And I saw. I saw all this. I was alone on the Earth. There was only the Earth and myself, in solitude with my senses. My life—my lives—and their particular details, their shape and contour, their fits and starts, and this final faltering, were of little importance. All that mattered was that I was alive. I was here. I saw, I experienced. From this I derived an immense satisfaction, wordless and incommunicable.

But what of the life I had supplanted, usurped? That individual—Charles "Charlie Fish" Bonanno—was gone, and his demise posed an ethical problem, for all that he had possessed the morals of a slug. What rankled most was that it had all been in vain. "Juliano" could have been a transplant himself, an agent, an assassin sent by the galactic criminal organization I had betrayed eons ago, in another star system at the other end of the starry swarm of the Milky Way. Their tentacles were infinitely long. They were still reaching for me.

There was no remedy for it. I had no way of communicating to my protectors. There was no instrumentality on this planet capable of sending a distress signal. I was trapped here. The trouble with the Witness Protection Program was that it was a one-shot affair, so to speak. You got one chance to escape and hide. It was useless. If they could find me once, in time another assassin would come. Of that I could be quite assured.

I took a deep breath, then walked back to the car. I wedged my stocky frame into the front seat, and took out my primitive firearm. I slid out the clip, looked at it, then shoved it back into the handle.

Releasing the safety on the automatic, I glanced at the still form on the floor beside me. Was he or was he not an agent sent by the Organization? I didn't know. But it didn't matter. It was only a matter of time before such a one appeared. My only recourse was clear.

Holding the gun upside down, I placed the barrel between my lips and fired a bullet up through the roof of my mouth and into my tiny human brain.

ALIEN GROUND

by Anthony R. Lewis

IT'S STRANGE TO BE on a starship instead of on
Mrrthow. It's even stranger when you realize that
no one on Mrrthow has any starships. Still, I am on-
board a starship, so somebody has one. The people
who own this one aren't from Mrrthow. They aren't
people by my definition of five days ago. My new
definition is more universal—any being that controls
my food and air and pays me a salary is "people."
That's a practical definition and I'm a practical vavacq.

As a practical person, I am cleaning the tables in
the galley. My reading of cautionary romances on
Mrrthow led me to believe that this would be done
by machines, but I am informed that machines cost
more than General Maintainers (Probationary) and it
is not half so satisfying to hit machines. I don't know
how I know this language nor how my credentials
were in order. I suppose I am a pawn in a game with
many Hidden Players behind the scenes. I'd worry
about it, but the first thing to do is survive.

Lady Susan came into the galley, ducking to avoid
hitting her head. She's a human and they run to
height. She drew her five-fingered hand along the
tabletop. "Not clean enough. Do it over, vavacq." She
turned and left.

Humans don't like vavacq. (Yes, there are vavacq out here. This puzzled me at first.) Lady Susan takes this cultural trait and nurtures it. "Vavacq," she said. "If your race practiced genetic engineering and forced culling for a few million years, they might be eligible to apply for a junior partnership in a lichen. You," she sneered, "would not have made it to the second generation." When she sneers, her shiny white omnivore teeth contrast with her brown face.

I finished my cleaning and returned to my cubicle. I passed other crew on the way; none of them are vavacq, but none of them are human either. I think Lady Susan is on some sort of a training mission. I didn't expect so many species. Our scientists said this was highly improbable; another good theory done in by facts. "Never thought about it," was the majority opinion (this fits in with my new definition of people). This was followed by "It's always been that way." A few of a more mystic persuasion believed that an Elder Race had seeded the galaxy with life-forms for their own unknowable purposes. These were referred to as the Eldest Ones, the Gardeners, or the Causal Ones, depending upon the particular sect involved.

My quarters are small. My current possessions are two uniforms and a toilet kit. I have been accessing the available sections of the ship's computer memory. Most of that seems to be pornography. There is background information in other languages, but I don't know them. I don't know how I learned this language I'm speaking. I'm going to sleep.

The captain is a Lobote—descended from a pack carnivore; we are the surrogate pack. I'm avoiding Lady Susan; she must dislike me as a vavacq specimen. I have not had a chance to be personally offensive to her. Given her size and obvious strength, I think the proper retort to her rudeness is a dignified silence or a "Yes, ma'am." I'm the only vavacq on the ship. I know there are others in the galaxy. No one thinks

I'm unusual. There are references to vavacq in some of the novels. Favorable, unfavorable, or background depending upon the author's species or personality. It's clear that vavacq are not the Master Race by any means.

I don't think being a General Maintainer is why I am here. Someone or something put me here for another reason. I wish they would let me know what I am supposed to be doing. It would not be a clever idea to broach my situation to anyone on board. They all know what I ought to be doing.

I hear we are going to reenter RealSpace tomorrow and dock at some orbital station. We don't land on planets because it would cost too much. I'll get station leave if I don't screw up.

The cook ordered me to catch some small vermin that have been stealing food. I built three vermin traps. Lady Susan kicked me while I was crawling into a raided cabinet to place them. One snapped on my paw and I yelped. I think she smiled at that. It takes very little to please some people.

We're docked. I drew some of my pay tokens. The tokens are silvery with a numeral on one side and a serpentine orgy on the other. I bought some sort of smoked meat with them. The meat seller warily directed me to the local equivalent of a library. Not too many General Maintainers (Probationary) look for that kind of diversion.

I stepped through menus on political galactography and entered my home planet's name as nearly as I could transliterate it.

+Unknown+

I tried the name from other languages—RRgol, Hssthat, Mrr IV. And back came the answer every time.

+Unknown+

Conclusion: Mrrthow doesn't exist and all my memories of it were hallucinations. I decided to investigate the Gardener Mythos. I reached that query point and the library came back with

+Logical Exclavity+

I must have made a mistake; so I tried again and again it returned

+Logical Exclavity+

I thought, *Let me at least find out what that means.* Again I made my way through the databases and was rewarded with:

+Logical Exclavity: a volume of space removed from all records, databases, references. The space of a logical exclavity, and all objects in it have no existence with respect to the galactic knowledge. Note: the existence of this phrase and its definition are not included in any record, database, or reference.+

A datum telling me that it did not exist. What next?

+Hello, did you enjoy the trip?+

I jabbed my claws into my I/O device, recovered, and entered "Not particularly."

+Unneccessary; just talk.+

"You're the one who set me up?"

+I am the not-specific sentient who transported you. I am involved in the project.+

"Why?"

+We have a task for you.+

I could ask who "we" is or I could ask what the job is. "Who are you that you want me to do what?" That didn't come out the way I expected it to.

+Continue your job on the ship. More details will be available later.+

"No!"

+No?+

"No."

+If you don't want more details, we won't give them to you.+

"You are deliberately misinterpreting my statements. I may decide I like being a General Maintainer and spend my life working my way up in that profession."

+You wouldn't. Vavacq don't.+

"Tell me about vavacq. Why aren't there many around? Why do most of the other species treat us (me) like dirt, especially the humans?"

+The last time you ruled this part of space you were a particularly unpleasant group. That's why most species dislike you. The humans knocked you down and took over; before that you knocked the humans down and took over. This has cycled four times.+

"So everyone hates vavacq and loves humans?"

+No, they hate both species. The humans aren't any better at ruling than vavacq.+

That agreed with my one data point—Lady Susan.

"Couldn't you have told this to me while I was on the ship? It might have made things easier."

+Not out of RealSpace.+ Pause. +Your job is to break the cycles. We will talk to you again when necessary. Use your personal imagination when the pain becomes too great.+

The screen was just a screen again. I had gotten the runaround, threats, and an impossible job, but I had to pay for the connect time. I walked around the accessible part of the station, entered the equivalent of a bookstore, bought some reels of popular history with most of my remaining tokens and returned to the ship. I wasn't going to be able to retire on my earnings. I wondered if saving the universe for unknown races paid well.

I'm reading the tapes in my off hours. Most of them are meaningless because I don't have the referents—the sort of thing that doesn't get into the book because everyone knows it. The vavacq and the humans have been fighting over this part of space for a few hundred thousand years. Currently, the humans are on top, but vavacq are sniping at them everywhere. The other species are not particularly happy, either.

There's no mention of Mrrthow. Mrrthow, and the Mrr System, are a Logical Exclavity. We don't exist as far as the galaxy is concerned. The opinions of six-plus billion of us Mrrthowq don't count because we don't exist. There's no such term as "logical exclavity" either.

I now understand this: I am vavacq: most sentient beings dislike me; Lady Susan hates me. Lady Susan is human: most sentient beings dislike her, too; if she vanishes me, there's no one to complain about it. She is showing remarkable restraint for a human forced to be on the same ship with a vavacq.

The tapes are interesting. They're biased, but all history is written from someone's point of view and few cultures rate anyone higher than themselves. This part of the galaxy is a mess. There are tens of thousands of polities trying to undercut each other, putting high tariffs on goods, taxing passage—just like early Mrrthow. On Mrrthow, we thought this sort of behavior disappeared when technology came, but . . . Space is big, and worlds self-contained so that most trade is in intangibles and rarities. Bulk materials are there on the planets or in the planetoid belts that most systems have. Everyone should be secure and happy—but they aren't. One of the intangibles that gets exported is religion. Jihads and crusades through space and time with high-tech weapons. Half of one tape is a list of extinct sentients.

In my CR stories we would come bursting out of Mrrthow, rip ears, order the galaxy, and all the subservients would live happily ever after. In reality, vavacq were a big part of the problem.

We're docking at Haavio orbital station. The computer says it's huge and has a reasonably-sized vavacq colony aboard. Do I want to meet my long-lost outsibs or would I rather keep them lost? Do I know enough to keep from screwing up? Probably not, but I'm getting tired of reacting to events. Maybe I should go out and push something to see if it pushes back.

I find a map. I'm planning to go to the vavacq sector and see what information I can pick up. Perhaps my fellow vavacq could do something about getting me back to Mrrthow. I doubt this, but it's worth a try. The path seems long, but it goes through safe areas where solitary vavacq aren't likely to be molested. I pass a few vavacq who stare at me, but they ignore me so I ignore them. The vavacq sector could be closed off easily. The bends in the corridor allow a small human force to pen in any number of vavacq.

It stinks. The ship's air was stale, but this is not passive staleness; this is an active, living stench compounded of rotting food, unwashed bodies, and unemptied litter. Groups of vavacq glared at me or ostentatiously ignored me. I saw no females or kits. It looked more like a prison than a community. I walked briskly as if I knew what I was doing and where I was going and turned into the third cafe I came to.

It was dim. I ordered a mild drink and took it to an empty table. I was sipping the foul-tasting brew when it was wrenched from my hand and thrown at the dispenser, who ducked with an alacrity born of practice. "That's human piss! Take a real drink." Some distilled beverage was slammed down before me. The container was attached to a large paw; the large paw was attached to a large arm; and then to a huge vavacq.

"Er, no thanks."

"Drink!" It was not a request but an order. I had made a mistake coming here. These sorts of problems had not occurred in the library. I looked at the drink again; I looked at the large person again. I picked up the drink. It didn't smell too vile. I took a sip.

"All of it." I drank. Whatever was in it was potent. I think I lost consciousness even before I tilted in the chair.

My head hurt badly. My one comfort was the knowledge that I would soon die and end the pain.

"You are not going to die." A high voice removed that hope.

I sat up; my head did not fall off.

"You vavacq have no tolerance for ethanol, why do you imbibe it?"

"One drink, and not a large one."

"Yes, only one drink, but its trace impurities had a powerful effect upon you."

"You drugged me!"

"It was the easiest way to get you here without complications."

I had been kidnapped. Some ship must want a General Maintainer (Probationary) very much. "Where am I? Who are you?"

"Open your eyes, vavacq! I will fix your pain."

The pain vanished; I could have become rich on Mrrthow if I knew how to do that. I opened my eyes, slowly this time. There was an alien of a type I had never seen before. He(?) was tall, slim, covered with a golden down and almost glowing. This creature was beautiful.

"Trapelo Sector. It is so much more pleasant here without the prying eyes of interfering busybodies. You need not know who we are. Ask why you are here."

"Why am I here?"

"We have a proposal of mutual advantage. Something that you will enjoy as much as we will."

"What do you want from me?"

"A better question would be—what can we gain together?"

"What can we gain together?"

"Pleasure."

"Pleasure? How?"

"You are a vavacq. The humans hate you and you hate the humans."

"It's the generally prevailing opinion," I allowed. The alien looked at me silently, then continued.

"Between you and the human on your ship exists massive hatred, contempt, and other strong emotions.

For your pleasure, we have brought her here." One of the walls thinned and vanished—and suspended there was Lady Susan.

I had never seen more of Lady Susan than her hands or face. Her body was brown and almost furless. She was clearly a mammal with two gross breasts. "She is yours. We give her to you."

This was moving too fast. "Why do I want her—and for what?"

"For eons, her species and yours have been locked in battle. They devastated your planets, killed your people, destroyed your culture. Now, you can attain personal revenge. Take it." A wave of dark eroticism swept through my mind. I imagined myself doing things that I had never before imagined. There was a seductive pleasure underlaid with a righteous indignation against this enemy of the vavacq. The pleasure would be justified; nothing I could do to Lady Susan would be wrong. I turned to the alien. "What's in it for you?"

"We are connoisseurs of emotions. We will record yours and hers and enjoy them over and over again. This costs you nothing. The more your enjoyment, the keener our pleasure; the more pain she suffers, the more piquant the counterpoint. The Creator made you and the humans to contend forever."

I walked to where Lady Susan was hanging. She was conscious.

"Hello," I said. "Nice to see you again."

She spat at me; her aim was fine. "Slime! I will not lower myself to beg for mercy. See how a human dies."

"I need a sharp knife, about this long," I said, holding my paws out. "My claws are not sufficient for what I want to do." The alien smiled and soon I was holding a beautiful blade. I reached up left, then right, and cut the bonds holding Lady Susan. Then I cut her feet free.

The alien, who had been silent, snarled, "What are you doing?"

"Cutting her loose. Now, if we can have her clothing, we'll be leaving."

"This is not permitted."

"You said I could do with her as I chose. I choose to set her free." I found that the aliens could transmit emotions as well as receive them. It started as just pain—an ache in all my teeth. A crescendo of pain that transformed as my joints exploded. I was put into a locked iron box; the walls started pressing in even as they became red- and then white-hot. I had to get out, get the key, unlock the box. The pain eased.

"This is only a sample of what we can do. Yield. Perform. Pleasure can be yours, not pain. Join with us." And a wave of undiluted pleasure racked me. It was worse than the pain because some of the horror was from within. "Will you consent?"

Consent was important; they could not force me. They could torture me and could tempt me, but the final decision would be mine. I tried to resist, but what weapons did I have? Use your personal imagination. That was the message through the computer. Did it mean anything? The alien drew back. It meant something.

I had a breathing space. I would have to fight back with my mind; use my imagination to counter the pain. I went through a sequence of battles from my CR readings—giant spaceships with ravening lances of energy, long-range ray guns in a post-civilized culture, magic swords to destroy demons, amulets to protect against monsters that lived between dimensions. My mind created the ability to conquer the alien with mind power.

There was a colorless flash, and then nothing. I awoke to see both the alien and Lady Susan were slumped on the floor. I put the knife in my belt. Lady Susan was unconscious but breathing. I didn't check the alien because I didn't care.

I tried to dress Lady Susan in my outerwear but gave up. It's harder to dress a female than to undress one. I tore down a wall hanging, cut off a strip for a belt, rolled Lady Susan into it, and tied it off. It lacked style, but I thought it would serve. I half-carried, half-dragged her back into the area in which I had first awakened and then out a portal into the light.

I was in Trapelo Sector and I needed to get both of us back to the ship, fast. I knew where we were and I knew where the ship was, but I didn't know how to get from here to there. There were transport modules, but my kidnappers had emptied my pockets and Lady Susan didn't have any pockets.

I saw a communications kiosk down the corridor, and carried her into it, closing the door behind us. It was clearly not designed for two. There was access to emergency services, but it cost; nothing is free here. But thankfully there was the equivalent of a reverse charge call.

A watch officer agreed to pay for 15 seconds—more out of boredom than anything else. His Lobote jaws opened in surprise as my face appeared on his screen. "You? What do you mean by . . ."

"Quiet. Me. Lady Susan. Trapelo Sector. Send help fast." And the screen went blank. I turned to open the door. There was a crowd outside armed with knives. (Actually, there were only five of them, but five was enough of a crowd for me.) I held the door shut as the largest moved forward to pry it open. I concentrated on keeping the door shut. I was losing. I took out my knife, pulled the door instead of pushing, had the satisfaction of seeing the large one fall down. I jumped out and crouched into what I thought was a knife-fighter's stance. In the stories I had read, the heroes get some sort of training in these things; someone had screwed up here. I invoked the epic heroes to help me, but this was not the mental combat I had just been in.

The fellow in the green dress leaped in and slashed at my left arm. I blocked most of this, but it caused a shallow cut that hurt. Blood started dripping down.

I stepped back and hit the kiosk and slipped. This saved me from another's jab. The big guy had gotten up and yelled for his accomplices to step back. He took out a knife, balanced it in his hand, and threw it at me. Pain ripped through my left shoulder. Another knife and my right shoulder was pierced. I dropped my own blade as my arm convulsed. He was playing with me. "Dance around. Give me a challenge."

I snarled something unpleasant about his family and their breeding habits. Some concepts are universal, for he stopped, took careful aim, and threw. Right in the gut.

My vision blurred; I heard noises; I fell unconscious to the ground.

I awoke flat on my back. I tried to get up and escape, but I was tied down. I was in a medical facility. Hoses were dripping things into my body. I hoped everything was proper for a vavacq but if it wasn't there wasn't much I could do about it. The medical people wouldn't have gone to the trouble if they didn't think it would work. I croaked out some noise. A Lobote came over. "Go back to sleep." Something cold touched my skin. I went back to sleep.

I woke a number of times and slept a number of times. Once when I woke, the captain was there. "You did a good job saving Lady Susan. Your pay will not be debited for overstaying your leave. Return to duty as soon as possible." It is nice to be appreciated. I went back to sleep. The medical connections had been removed. The medtech told me I would be able to leave tomorrow. The decks and tables must be getting dirty without me. I couldn't imagine anyone else in the crew who could perform my tasks to the standards I had set.

I was lying in bed waiting for the medtech to kick me out when Lady Susan, back in ship's uniform, came in. She looked down on me in my bunk. Whatever she was going to say was going to be difficult. "I was told what happened. There is an obligation between us," she said. "You are vavacq slime, but there is a bond between us; this is intolerable." She hadn't wanted to acknowledge that, but her training and culture forced it upon her.

"Think nothing of it. Glad to have been of help. You must have important work to do."

"No. If you make light of this, you give no value to my life. This must be resolved; the bond must be severed. Tell me why you did as you did. You did not act as any other of your people would have. I cannot understand this. I would not have done this for you had our roles been reversed."

"Maybe that's why I did it. The cycles must be stopped." That last popped out; I hadn't intended to say it and I wasn't quite sure I meant it.

She stared at me. "Of all the aliens I have ever met, you are the most alien of all."

"I take that as a high compliment," I said.

She turned and left without another word.

I turned onto my side and something poked me. The medtech must have forgotten to remove all the equipment. I reached down and picked it up. There in my paw was a silvery ring, but there was a break. One end pointed up—searching?

HI, COLONIC

by Harry Turtledove

SOME PEOPLE SAY probing other planets for intelligent life is an exciting, romantic job. As far as I'm concerned, that only goes to show they've never done it. Me, I do it for a living, and I'm here to tell you it's nothing but a pain in the orifice. The air smells funny even when you can breathe it, the animals smell even worse (and taste worse than that, half the time), and even when we do find people, they're usually backward as all get-out. If they weren't, they would have found us, right? Right.

Another planet from space. If I've sensed one, I've sensed a thousand. Third planet from a medium-heat sun. Water oceans. Oxygen atmosphere. Life. Oh, joy. We weren't even the first ones here. This place had been checked a bunch of times over the past fifty local years. Always nothing. So why did we go back again? Orders. If I don't do the work, they don't pay me. Even when I do do the work, they don't pay me enough, but that's a different story.

Down we went, into the atmosphere. Iffspay—he's my partner—and I rolled dice to find out who got stuck wearing the calm suit. I give you three guesses. The calm suit we needed for this planet is the most uncomfortable one in the whole masquerade cabinet.

It's bifurcated at the bottom, it's got tendrils near the top, and then an awkward lump at the very top. Guess who got to put it on. I'll give you a hint: it wasn't Iffspay. I think he uses loaded dice.

"This is all a waste of time," I grumbled.

"We're here. We might as well do it," Iffspay said. He would. Of course he would. He got to lie back in the ship and soak up nutrient while I was out there doing the heavy lifting.

The atmosphere on this one was really noxious, too. Way too much carbon dioxide for a stable climate, plus oxides of nitrogen and assorted vile hydrocarbons. I made damn sure the purifier in the calm suit was working the way it was supposed to. You could fry yourself on air like that.

To add insult to injury, the weather was fermented. Antigravity or not, round flat aerodynamic shape or not, we bounced around enough to turn your insides inside out. Iffspay was doing the flying, which didn't help. As a pilot, he doesn't know his appendages from a hole in the ground. I thought he was going to fly us into a hole in the ground, but he didn't. Don't ask me why. Somebody out beyond the cosmos must like him. Don't ask me why about that, either.

Rain pounded us. "I'm supposed to go out in this?" I said.

"I would have done it if I'd lost the roll," Iffspay said virtuously. He would have bitched all the way, too. Am I lying? If you've ever met Iffspay, you'll know I'm not. You can't tell me that's not him, segment by segment.

"Just find some of them so we can run the tests," I said. "We'll get another negative and we'll go on to another world. And when it comes to finding out who wears the calm suit next time, I'm going to roll your dice."

"What's that supposed to mean?" he asked, as if he didn't know. Ha!

Before we could really start quarreling, the heat-seeker indicated a target. Three targets, in fact, grouped close together. That actually cheered me up. If we caught all three of them, we could finish this planet in one fell swoop. I wouldn't miss putting it behind me, not even a little bit I wouldn't.

Trouble was, they were at the edge of a swamp. I worried that they might escape into the water or into the undergrowth, calm suit or no calm suit, before I could slap the paralyzer ray on them and we could antigravity them up into the ship. And if they did—if even one of them did—we'd have to go through this whole capture-and-release business somewhere else on the planet, too. Once was plenty. Once was more than plenty, as a matter of fact.

"As we lower, put on the full display," I told Iffspay.

"We're liable to scare them off," he warned.

"Yeah, yeah," I said. "If we do, we'll try somewhere else, that's all. But the data feeds say they usually gawk. They're photosensitive, you know."

"All right, already." Iffspay complained, but he did it the way I wanted. He had to, pretty much. If he'd been going out, I would've done it his way. I wondered how much the rain would hurt the locals' photosensitivity. Light is so unreliable. Since most planets rotate, half the time there isn't any. Evolution does some crazy things sometimes.

I have to give Iffspay credit. He didn't fool around when it came to the display. He had it radiating every frequency the locals could perceive, going from the high end to the low in rhythmic waves. He cranked the air vibrations way up, too. I could sense some of those myself. They seemed to go right through me.

I checked the heat-seeker. By the taste, the locals hadn't moved. That meant—I hoped that meant—they were fixated on the show the ship was putting on. I struggled into the calm suit and went down to the exit orifice. "I'm ready," I told Iffspay, exaggerating only a little. "Go on and shit me out."

The mild obscenity made him mumble to himself, but out I went, floating in midair. Rain thudded against the calm suit. Considering all the crap in the atmosphere, the rainwater probably wouldn't have done me much good either. Maybe I was lucky being in the suit, even if it was uncomfortable.

And the locals still didn't try to escape. I can't tell you exactly how much I resembled them—how do you evaluate a sense you haven't got yourself?—but it must have been close enough for government work. I was glad the suit had its own powered heat-seeker; the rain would have played hob with the one I was hatched with, which naturally isn't anywhere near so strong.

I wanted to get really close before I paralyzed them, for fear all that water coming down out of the sky would attenuate the beam, too. And I did. I got so close, my instruments could tell they were emitting air vibrations themselves. The ones from the ship had much more pleasing patterns, but I wasn't there to play art critic.

Ready . . . Aim . . . The calm suit's appendages aren't as sensitive as real ones, so I squeezed the control inside just as hard as I could. "Got 'em!" I told Iffspay. "Bring me back, and bring them in, too."

"Keep your integument on," Iffspay said. There are times when I'm tempted to turn the paralyzer on him. Leaving him unable to communicate would be all to the good. That's what *I* think, and nobody's likely to make me change my mind.

Up went the locals, one by one. Iffspay saved me for last, just to annoy me. He did, too, but I wasn't about to let him smell it when I got back to the ship. He was bustling around when the antigravity beam finally pulled me back aboard. The locals were all lined up neatly, ready for us to start doing our latest check. Two of them emitted significantly more heat than the third, which meant they had more body mass.

All three of them also went on emitting high-amplitude air vibrations. "Why are they doing that?" Iffspay asked irritably. "Aren't they supposed to be paralyzed?"

I had to check the manual before I could answer him. "It says paralysis only inhibits gross motor functions. If it inhibited all movements, they'd die."

I got out of the calm suit. I didn't need it anymore, and we'd made the capture. The paralyzed locals weren't going to interfere. As I put it back in the closet, the amplitude of their air vibrations increased even more. "They're still sensing us somehow," I said. "Those waves have to be voluntary."

Now it was Iffspay's turn to check the manual. Yeah, yeah, I know—when all else fails, read the instructions. At last, he said, "I think they're photosensitive to some of the wavelengths we use for heat-seeking."

"Oh. All right." That even made sense. "I wonder if those were alarm calls, then. They might have been surprised when they perceived me changing from something like their own shape to my own proper one."

"Who cares?" Iffspay said. "Let's get them analyzed, and then we can analyze the data—not that there'll be any data to analyze. We'll do it by the book, though."

"By the book," I agreed. And, by the book, we did the two bigger specimens first. We had to check the manual again to make sure just where to analize them. Iffspay thought the orifice emitting the air vibrations was the one that would take the probe, but he turned out not to be right. Evolution was even crazier than usual on that planet, you betcha.

And the manual didn't exactly match the specimens we had. By what it said, the orifice should have been accessible once we figured out where the space fiend it was. But the locals had integuments more complicated than what the manual showed. Good old Iffspay was all for cutting right on through them. Iffspay never was long on patience, I'm afraid.

"Let's try peeling them instead," I said. "That way, we're less liable to injure them."

"Oh, all right," he said sulkily. "It'll take longer, though."

I was the one who got to peel them. Since it was my idea, Iffspay didn't want thing one to do with it. I wasn't too thrilled about it, either, not getting started. I kept thinking about gross and fine motor functions. If the locals weren't perfectly paralyzed . . . well, they'd splatter me all over the walls of the ship.

But I managed to peel the first one without doing it any harm I could detect—its heat signature and the kind of air vibrations it emitted didn't change at all—and without getting hurt myself. Once I'd taken care of the hard part, Iffspay grabbed the glory. He bent the local into the position the manual suggested and threaded in the probe.

"Well?" I asked.

"Well, nothing," Iffspay answered. "The computer can check me later, but there's nothing. A big, fat, juicy nothing. So much for that."

"Don't prejudge. We've still got two more to go," I said, though I wasn't what you'd call optimistic about them either.

"Go on and peel the next one, then," Iffspay said.

"Why me again?" I asked him. "How come I get stuck with all the hard stuff?"

"Because you did such a good job the last time," he answered. Iffspay tastes smooth, no two ways about it.

After letting out a few last bitternesses of annoyance, I got to work on the second large local. Fortunately, everything went well. In fact, it went better than it had the first time, because I'd had the practice of doing it once. I reached for the probe once I'd got the local into the position—I did it myself that time—but Iffspay already had it in his appendage.

"This is the last lump," I said angrily. "You're going to peel the third one, and I'm going to do the analizing. And if you don't like it, I'll talk to a lawyer when we get home. There *are* limits to how much you can impose on people." I had really had it.

Iffspay could tell, too. "Fine. Fine!" he said. "Don't get all disconnected from your nutrient provider. You want to analize the third one, be my guest. Meanwhile, though . . ." He inserted the probe. He tried to go on as if everything were normal, but my talk about lawyers had put a bad smell in his chemoreceptors, let me tell you. After he withdrew the probe, he added, "Nothing again. Not even a hint. If you want to waste your time with the last one, be my guest."

"I want to perceive you peel it," I said. "That should be funny enough to go on the planetwide sensorium special."

"You'll find out." Now I'd got Iffspay mad. I could taste it. And, of course, when he got mad, he got clumsy. I wish they *would* put the recording of the botch he made of that peeling job on the sensorium special. He'd have an offer to do sitcoms so fast, you wouldn't believe it. The local's air vibrations increased in amplitude, too. I don't think it much cared for what was going on. After what seemed like forever, Iffspay turned to me and said, "There. All yours."

I took the probe. But it didn't want to do what it was supposed to. I had to feel around near the target area. "You bumbling idiot," I said. "There's still a layer of integument here. The other two had this layer—weren't you paying attention when I dealt with them? Once you get this down, *then* it's pay dirt."

"Well, take care of it, then, if you're so smart," he said.

"Oh, no. The deal was you'd peel this one and I'd probe it. You finish your job, and then I'll do mine."

He made a stink about it, but he did it. I suspected there'd be some long, nasty silences on the way to the next star. Well, too bad. I know what my rights are, by the Great Eggcase, and I know when to curl up for them.

"I hope you're satisfied now," he grumped when he'd finally got the peeling right.

"Couldn't be happier," I told him, just to smell him fume.

And I meant it literally. This time, the analizer went in just as smooth as you please. I extended an appendage through it—and made contact!

Photosensitive creatures use energy waves to talk. I suppose you could talk with air vibrations, too, though I've never heard of any intelligent races that do. Too much ambiguity either way, as far as I'm concerned. Taste and scent, now, those are universal languages. No doubt about 'em.

"Hello, there," I said. "How are you doing?"

"We're fine," came the answer. "Hooked on to the intestinal wall here, kicking back and living the life of Reilly."

Even universal languages have dialects. I'm still not sure what a Reilly is. But I got the point. They were happy where they were. "Do you need anything?" I asked.

"No way, José," they replied without the least hesitation. My name isn't José, but I didn't bother calling them on it. "We're happy right here, you better believe it."

"Okay," I said. "Now that we've finally found you, we'll probably send you an ambassador or something before too long."

"Whatever. No hurry. No worries," they said. "You guys are free-living, aren't you?"

"Oh, sure," I said. "We have been for a long time. We think hooking up with nutrient when we want to is easier than staying tied to a host."

"We like it better this way," they told me. "We can ease back and relax and go along for the ride. Beats working—who needs technology if you've got a tasty host? From what we've smelled, free-living makes people pushy."

"I didn't know you'd met Iffspay," I said.

"Hey, don't drag me into this, you flavorless, unsegmented thing," Iffspay said, neatly proving my point.

"What's an Iffspay?" the planet's intelligent life-forms wanted to know.

"Nothing much—he's my partner here," I replied, just to smell Iffspay fume. He didn't disappoint me either. Iffspay is a reliable guy.

The locals said, "Nice to meet you and everything, but we'd really like to get back to what we were doing. Some of our segments are going to break off and go out into the world to find new hosts."

Ah, the simple pleasures of parasites! It almost makes me long for the eons before we were free-living. Things were simpler then. They . . . Well, enough. When a worm starts getting nostalgic, he's the most boring creature in the bowels of the galaxy. And so I won't. I just won't.

I unthreaded the analizer and said, "Well, we'll have to be careful placing the locals back on the ground now that we know some of them are inhabited."

"Tastes like you're right," Iffspay agreed. "Who would've thunk it? All these negative reports, and now this!" Then he let out a bad smell. "Think of all the forms we'll have to fill out on the way back to Prime."

I did a little farting of my own, too. I hadn't thought of that. I hadn't wanted to think about it. "Can't be helped," I said, and he knew damn well I was right again. He set the local hosts back where we'd found them. Old Iffspay does have a nice appendage on the antigravity when he wants to, I will say that for him.

And then we flew away. As we headed for the next star on the list, I started in on some of that miserable, vermicidal paperwork.

Some things are too big to be fully comprehended. Willie and Al and Little Joe had only the vaguest idea how they'd all ended up back in their duck blind in an Arkansas swamp with their pants around their ankles. What had happened to them beforehand was, mercifully, even vaguer.

Pants still below half-mast, Willie stared up at the

sky—and got rain in his face. "We are not alone," he
said . . . vaguely.

"Yeah," Al murmured, slowly and wonderingly
pulling up his jeans.

"Reckon the two o' you are," Little Joe said. "Not
me." Solemnly, Willie and Al nodded, though they
didn't quite know what he meant. Which was okay,
too, because neither did he.

ACTS

by William Sanders

WELL, WELL. I tell you, this is really something. This is just amazing.

Yes, I've known your parents a long, long time. All five of them, ever since we were not much more than hatchlings. In fact we used to get mistaken for brood sibs, we spent so much time together. It's true we've been a little out of touch lately, but oh, the memories. The stories I could tell you.

And now here's their youngest, coming around wanting to interview me for a big entertainment magazine yet. Who would believe it?

Of course, another thing that is to me incredible is that anybody would want to hear about me and my business. The glamorous life of a performers' agent? It is to exfoliate already.

And Hnb'hnb'hnb knows it's not like I'm some big success. I swear if I was a yingslaagl people would stop gn'rking . . . but okay, I see, you're not just interviewing me, right? This is something, you're asking different people in the business? Like a survey?

All right, I can see that. In fact I could maybe give you a few tips before you leave, who you should make sure and talk to. And who not, if you know what I'm saying. Like a certain client-stealing party right here in this building, two floors down, his eyestalks should only drop off. Or another certain individual whom I will not name, over at Galactic Artists and Performers. A real bloodsucker—and I know he says he can't help it, it's a dietary requirement of his species, but I still say *feh*.

But listen. Now I think of it, this is a good thing. This is a chance, I can maybe say some things that need saying. Maybe this is an opportunity to educate people a little about what it means to be an agent. I'm sorry, but believe me, they have no idea.

They think it's so easy. They look at somebody like me and they're thinking, what a racket. Just look at this bum, sitting on his tail crest, you should pardon the language, in a fancy office, making such a good thing for himself off other people's work. Maybe makes a few calls, sends out a few messages, does lunch with some big shots, for this he takes twenty percent of the poor struggling entertainer's pay?

Sure, right. It should only be so simple.

Leave aside for the moment all you really have to do, which believe me is plenty, you wouldn't believe the hours I put in sometimes . . . do you have any idea, my dear youngster, what an agent has to *know* these days? The sheer amount of *information* he has to carry around in his head—or heads, as the case may be, hey, I've been accused of many things, but nobody can call me a bigot—just to function at all in this business?

All these different worlds, all these different races, they've all got their tastes and their customs and they all assume theirs is the only possible way and surely everybody else knows about it so of course they wouldn't bother to *tell* you anything—and so you have to learn it all. Have to know it all from memory, there's no time to be pulling up files and studying background when you're negotiating with some promoter on the other side of the galaxy who needs an act yesterday if not sooner. Which, by the way, I hate,

retro-relative time shunts are more work to set up
than you'd believe and when you mention the extra
charges, they go h'nogth on you. But I digress.

I was going to say, you have to know all this stuff,
easily as much as any cultural scientist, just to operate.
Operate shmoperate, to stay out of *trouble,* which, believe you me, there is plenty of just waiting for you
to make one little mistake.

And I mean big trouble. Not just the ordinary stuff,
like the fact that on Z'arss any kind of music in three-
four time is considered pornography, or that doing
impressions on Uuu will get you two hundred to life
for personality theft. I'm talking nova-grade catastrophe.

Like this certain former colleague whom I used to
see at the agents' conventions, nice enough young fellow
if maybe a bit on the smart-alecky side, who made the
mistake of booking a Xee wizard for a big simultanous-
live-and-vid appearance on Kabongo. He was really
excited about that, because the Xee homeworld was
still a recent discovery and this was going to be the
first offworld performance by one of their wizards,
which nobody really knew anything about except that
they were supposed to be extremely hot stuff. So my
colleague figured he'd pulled off a real coup in signing
this one up, and for a time there, up until show time,
he got pretty hard to take.

Hah. And again hah. Ever seen a Xee wizard work?
No, of course you haven't, ever since what happened
on Kabongo they're banned from performing offworld, and you better be glad of it or you might be
permanently blind and deaf and paralyzed like all
those poor devils on Kabongo. I understand the insur-
ance lawyers are still appealing the judgment, but
that's not much help to Mr. Smart Guy. Who had
broken one of the most basic rules: *never book an act
you haven't personally seen.*

Or take what happened to a very dear friend of
mine only last year. One day he gets a call from Kesh-

tak 37, over in the next arm, wanting a whole lineup of acts, price no object. Seemed the Emperor of the Oomaumau had passed away, and they wanted only the best for his funeral festivities, which would go on for weeks because the Oomaumau believe in giving a ruler a first-class sendoff.

So my friend is naturally very pleased to get to handle something that big, and as soon as the contract is signed he starts calling around, seeing who's available. But then he happens to do a bit of research, to see what kind of acts the Oomaumau might like, and finds out something extremely disturbing. The Oomaumau, it develops, have another unusual mortuary custom: the performers at the royal funeral are given the honor of accompanying the Emperor to the Hereafter, so his spirit shouldn't get bored.

Yes, that's right. Well, not strictly speaking; they just bury them alive beneath the royal mausoleum.

My friend is not really to blame for not knowing about this, which is not well known outside learned sociological circles because the last time an Emperor died on Keshtak 37 was well before the memory of any living person on this world. Long-lived race, the Oomaumau, especially the royal family . . . but ignorance, as they say, is no excuse before the law, and the contract had already been signed.

And the Oomaumau were not about to let my friend out of it. Though he tried hard enough, went so far as to travel personally to Keshtak 37 to plead for a release. He was so desperate he even got an audience with their spiritual leader, the Papa Oomaumau, at the great temple of the goddess L'vira. No go. A contract is a contract and if he reneges, they tell him, he will find himself up to his nictitating membranes in litigation with the Emperor's attorneys.

Yes, that was what my friend asked. Turns out it's not at all unusual for dead people to file lawsuits on Keshtak 37. Don't ask me.

My friend doesn't know what to do, but then while he's there, he picks up another bit of information. The only entertainers who don't get interred with His Imperial Awesomeness are the ones who perform so badly that they are deemed unworthy of the honor. Yes. On Keshtak 37, when you stink at the Palace, you *don't* die at the Palace.

So my friend rushes back here and starts calling in all the lousiest acts he can find. Which takes very little searching, because every agent knows plenty of hopeless no-talent losers; they come around begging you to represent them, and they're so persistent and so pathetic you take their names and information down just to get rid of them and then they call you every few days for the rest of your life wanting to know when you're going to get them some work.

In almost no time my friend has assembled a collection of the worst stinkeroos in this part of the galaxy. Tone-deaf musicians, stumblebum dancers, comics unfunny enough to induce suicidal depression, he's got them all. He said he had to open the office windows to air the place out after they all left.

No, he didn't tell them. He felt bad about that, but it really wouldn't have done to let them in on what was going on. Entertainers and artists, you see, are very touchy people that way, and the bad ones most of all. The worse they are, the greater they believe they are and the harder they believe it. If he'd told them the truth, they'd have been furious, and chances are they'd have walked out on him.

So off they went to Keshtak 37, and—ah, yes, I'm seeing this look on your face, you're way ahead of me, aren't you?

That's right. The thrill of finally getting a professional gig, and a prestigious offworld one at that, got them so worked up they barely needed a ship to get to Keshtak 37; they could have gone into warp by themselves. And by the time they went on at the Imperial Palace, they were so inspired that they performed, all of them, better than they'd ever done in their lives.

Or ever would again, in what little was left of them . . . my friend was very upset. Not that anybody would miss that particular bunch, but the Oomaumau buried their paychecks with them and he never did collect his cut.

But listen, don't misunderstand, I'm not disrespecting my colleagues. It's not like I've never made any mistakes myself. How I only wish . . .

Let me tell you about the comic.

Or rather tell you what happened, I can't really tell you about *him*. Can't do justice to his talent with a simple description, you'd have had to see him in action to fully comprehend just how great he was. And yes, great I said and great I meant. All these people like to think of themselves as "artists," but in his case it was the simple truth. A genuine comic genius is what he was, and he could just maybe have been the greatest ever, if only—but I'm getting ahead of myself.

I found him working open mike night at a cheap club down in the Ginzorninplad district. He'd just gotten into town, worked his way here from his homeworld aboard a worn-out old tub of a bulk freighter, and he didn't have much more than the clothes on his back. I watched his act and then I caught him backstage and signed him up, just like that. And said some very sincere prayers to Hnb'hnb'hnb for granting me the privilege.

I got him a few local gigs and he did just fine, even got some good ink from the critics. But you know this town; an outsider has a tough time getting accepted. Especially an outsider from, and I don't mean this in any derogatory way, a *different*-looking race. I hate to say that, but it's true.

So when this opening turned up for a long offworld tour, I advised him to go for it. Oh, it wasn't much of a booking—the world was a pretty backward sort of place, off in a distant arm of the galaxy where hardly anybody ever went even to visit, and the pay was worse than lousy.

But I didn't really have anything else for him at the moment; things were slow, all the best clubs were booked up solid. And I figured this was a chance for him to get some experience, develop his material, and practice his technique out in the sticks without having to worry about bombing because even if he did have a bad night nobody who mattered would ever hear about it. Meanwhile I could work on lining up something better for him.

Well, what can I say? It seemed like a good idea at the time, I should hit myself repeatedly with the nearest blunt object.

Don't get me wrong, it's not that he went into the sandbox or anything like that. On the contrary, they loved his act—or at least they loved *him;* right away, almost as soon as he arrived, they started making a big fuss over him. In no time at all he was playing to packed houses.

You understand, he was sending back regular reports, keeping me up on what was going on, and every time I heard from him, he sounded more amazed. People followed him around on the street, came up to him wanting to meet him and trying to touch him, and before long he even had his own fan club. In fact there were about a dozen of them who took to traveling around with him, seeing to his needs, just like he's a big superstar.

But what was really strange was the way the audiences reacted to his act. *Nobody ever laughed.* He'd do his funniest routines, stuff that would make a Rhrr laugh, and they'd just sit there staring at him with these very serious faces and nod and look at each other and nod some more, like he'd just said something wise and profound.

He tried everything. He even tried dumping his own material, since they didn't seem to get it, and doing

corny old gags about farmers and animal herders and
fishermen, thinking maybe they just weren't ready for
sophisticated modern humor. Didn't make a bit of difference. They still came to see him, more and more
all the time, but they still didn't laugh.

And this was starting to make him crazy, as you can
imagine. He got so desperate he started doing magic
tricks. Now I mean that's pretty bad, when a talented
performer has to reach that low. What next, I thought,
he's going to take up juggling? But these hicks absolutely ate it up. They liked the tricks even better than
the comic routines; the crowds started getting really
huge.

Finally the time came for his debut at the big city—
well, the biggest in that part of that particular world,
it wouldn't have made a slum neighborhood here—
and off he went, hoping the city audiences would be
a little more hip.

He made something of an entrance, too; his twelve
roadies did a really great job of getting the word out,
making sure there was a big crowd to welcome him
when he arrived in town. By the time he did his first
show, the turnout was so big they had to hold it outdoors on a mountainside, where he gave possibly his
greatest performance ever. Still no yucks, but he
thought he saw a few of them smiling a little toward
the end.

So things were looking up; and so my boy didn't
think anything of it, a few nights later, when a bunch
of people showed up, right after dinner, and wanted
him to come with them. Some kind of fan thing, he
thought, and he said sure, and went along without
argument, though some of his entourage tried to talk
him out of it.

And when they got where they were going, he still
didn't tumble to what was happening. Not even when
they started bringing up the lumber and nails. In fact
he gave them a hand. He figured they were getting
ready to build a stage for him. There were some cops

standing around but he assumed they were just security.

By the time he found out different, it was too late.

If I told you what they did to him, you would not sleep tonight and you would have dreams for years, just as I did when I heard about it. So I think I better not go into the details. Enough to say it was a terrible, terrible thing and I've never heard of anything quite like it, even on the most barbaric worlds.

The shock and the pain were so great that it was three planetary rotations before he could pull himself together enough to activate his recovery circuits and get out of there. He came back here and told me what had happened—I had naturally been worried sick—and then, despite all my pleas and reassurances, he got on the next available ship back to his homeworld, and as far as I know he never got on stage again. I understand he went into the family construction business. Such a waste, and I can't help feeling responsible.

But there was one thing I want to tell you about, because it illustrates just what kind of a person he was. Right after he got his body systems working again, he was just about to send the emergency beam-up signal when he thought of something he wanted to do. And as bad as he wanted out of that place—and who can blame him?—and as stiff and sore as he was, he stayed around long enough to put in a final appearance to his original fan club, and do a little farewell routine just for them. Now is that class or what?

You can see why it broke my heart—no, both of them—to see him go.

Well. So much for my little reminiscences. I'm sure you've got a whole list of questions.

So ask.

LIFE HAPPENS

by Ralph Roberts

L IFE HAPPENS. It's not my fault.

When it started, I was looking at stars. The stars within my own body to be precise; so small, so many, so beautiful, so clean of contaminating Life in all their hundreds of billions! I perceived them through magnifying fields of my own devising. Bright and pristine in their many colors—the planets orbiting around them existing without blemish. No infections in me, I set a fine example. It's good for business.

I never should have taken the call.

"Doctor! Doctor. Huh? Huh? I have another referral for you and this one is loaded! Another referral. Is a very, very good referral. Needs big help. Has much credit. Can pay lots. Reward. I get reward?"

Quarble, he's a dwarf—a dwarf in both size and intellect. I move my perception, focus on him. He's dancing around me as usual, sucking up to the great physician—well, so I am and it is well that he should. He has his uses. He'll do any menial task and he does have an uncanny talent for finding patients. Some of them even pay their bills.

"Good one, good one, Doc!"

"Quarble, do NOT call me 'Doc,'" I said without

real rancor—after all Quarble is Quarble and one should not fight that which is not worth changing.

"Sorry, sorry. Over there. Over there. He needs help. Charge lots, give Quarble some. Yes?"

I favor Quarble with a disapproving perception, but it fazes him not at all.

Quarble has been in my employ some few hundred millions of *years* to use units of time understood by Life (damn their slimy little, short-lived existences that I am so dedicated to eradicating). Quarble's what *they* classify as a dwarf spheroidal galaxy and designated in their Messier catalog as M110.

I know all too much about Life these days, or at least this one particularly nasty strain—lessons hard learned, but the fight is not over yet. I even know that the Messier method of cataloging us began in their year 1773 by one Charles Messier. Funny names, Life beings have—puny monikers to match their puny selves, not like ours. My name lilts through one's grasp of reality, lovingly redolent of many hundreds of digits of prime numbers and mathematically expressed highly complex molecular chains.

"Reward, Doc, reward," Quarble reminds.

"In a moment, Quarble," I said, continuing to put away my force field tools and generally tidy up before exchanging perceptions with a potential patient.

Quarble does have a few good points, I must add. He is somewhat unique, being not your usual generic dwarf elliptical galaxy but one of a very few known dwarf spheroids and, to boot, brighter than most dwarf spheroids. Well, at least in light emitted.

Additionally, and in spite of his small size, Quarble, or M110, has a remarkable system of eight globular star clusters in a halo around him. The brightest of these is called G73 by Life. Quarble is quite vain about all of that.

"Doc!"

"All right," I said, hurrying.

I cast one final glance in a reflective field to check my appearance. I AM handsome. Life knows me as M31, the famous Andromeda galaxy. The Life unit Al-Sufi was aware of me about AD 905. Had I been aware of him at the time, he would be but a few drifting molecules of scorched gas now. I owe him, I really do. I owe all of Life. They have HACKED me off!

But I am a looker, I am.

The Life unit and famous astronomer William Hershel wrote this of me in 1785:

". . . undoubtedly the nearest of all the great nebulae . . . The brightest part of it approaches to the resolvable nebulosity, and begins to shew a faint red colour; which, from many observations on the colour of and magnitude of nebulae . . . There is a very considerable, broad, pretty faint, small nebula [M110] near it; my Sister [Caroline] discovered it August 27, 1783, with a Newtonian 2-feet sweeper. It shews the same faint colour with the great one, and is, no doubt, in the neighbourhood of it . . ."

Yes, Quarble is always horning in, bumbling about and getting in the way.

"Doc! Doc! Doc!"

"Where is the patient, dear Quarble?" I asked politely, now in the mode of the highly respected physician that I was until Life tripped me up and left me looking foolish. For THAT, they shall PAY!

He throws his perception but a short way.

"Where?" I ask, seeing only our neighbor, the odd one. Mostly we just ignore him, but I hear he has been highly successful in his field, something to do with confections, nothing healthy that I would consume, but many a galaxy likes a bit of sweet nebulosity now and again.

"Him? You're kidding!"

"Yep, yep, yep, no, no, no," Quarble affirmed.

I sighed. Never ask Quarble more than one question at a time.

As to the neighbor, I've never liked the guy, never had much to do with him. But a patient's a patient and I did swear an oath of healing so very long ago. I projected a smiling and confident perception to him. Better I should have turned and expanded away at best speed. But how was I to know the extent of the infection that still racks his body?

"May I help you?" I ask.

He replied with a torrent of ailments and symptoms, a few of which I sensed as legitimate and . . . disconcerting. Especially the constant migraines he was now suffering. It was all too familiar and all too ominous.

"Say 'ahh,' " I said, pushing a quick view field into his mass.

"Ugh!" escaped from me involuntarily. Not the most reassuring manner for a healer to project, but I had never seen an infestation so horribly progressed as showed on my instrument. Inside him swarmed, teemed, slid, slithered Life in incredible numbers. Only a blur of activity on the rudimentary examination device I was using, but enough to cause me great concern.

I swatted Quarble's nosy perception away and reached out to assemble more powerful diagnostic and treatment fields. No time to waste in an emergency case like this! The guy should have come to me sooner, a LOT sooner. Well, it was going to be nasty, but I always won. . . . At least, at one time, I always won. Cursed LIFE!

As my talented and nimble manipulative fields prepared the drastic but necessary medical procedures, I examined the patient visually. From the outside, he looks healthy enough, a handsome enough spiral galaxy. No signs of the rot within. He's larger than normal, almost a giant. In fact, almost as large as I am and I'm the largest galaxy in this neighborhood.

I spared a glance to one of my instruments. Yes, a healthy male, about 15 billion years old. Good star count—somewhere around 200 billion to 400 billion at first guess, the instrument will refine that shortly as the processing completes.

"Is he a goner, Doc? Dead? A dead one?"

"SHUT UP, you idiot!" I said, but the patient is in too much pain to pay attention to Quarble. Quarble has all the finesse of an imploding black hole, but he's cheaper than hiring a trained nurse.

I pushed my manipulators harder, feeling a real sense of urgency now, but continued the look over. All these observations give a physician the data needed for effective treatment of an infection. Usually they do, anyway.

Hmmm, I noted in my treatment log. The patient has a good distribution of hydrogen clouds, what the Life unit Hubble typed as a Sb or Sc galaxy. Which means he has both a pronounced disk component yet exhibits a spiral structure, and a prominent nuclear region. The latter is part of a notable bulge/halo component.

"What does it mean, Doc? Is he sick, is that what it says?"

I abstractedly brushed Quarble's perception away from the log and thought about what other descriptive facts to add.

"DOCTOR?" the patient said, moaning.

"Just a moment, I'm preparing a procedure that will help you. Nothing to worry about."

See, doctors lie to patients.

"Will it hurt, Doctor?"

Of course it will, it will hurt like hell. He's too far gone for anything that would not hurt. "No, not a bit," I said. See above comment about lies. "Er . . . you might feel a slight sting, just a tiny bit of discomfort," I modified, feeling just a little guilty because I was planning on unleashing several hundred supernovas within his body. No half measures when Life is

so virulently established. He's going to be spewing fire
from all orifices!

Too bad. Like I've already said, he's not a bad looking guy—not as handsome as me, but so few are. I
examine his spiral arms and look inside his body again.
A normally hale and hearty mix of interstellar matter,
diffuse nebulae, and young stars. Good growth patterns with open star clusters emerging from this matter. But he's been partaking a bit too much of his own
confectionery. His bulge component is rife with old
stars and fatty globular clusters; very concentrated
toward his center.

I see some supernovae have occurred in the past;
spectacular events to Life units, but nothing unusual
here in frequency or magnitude—just one of the ways
our bodies have of keeping infection down. But . . .
speaking of spectacular . . . I was planning and preparing to give THESE Life units something to REALLY
gawk at. In the few brief moments left to them, that is.

"You sure it won't hurt?" the patient asked again,
nervously.

"No, no—not a bit," I lied.

The instrumentation had gathered vast amounts of
data now, giving me all the information needed to
proceed. Even the Life units' many communications
among themselves were analyzed and interpreted and a
comprehensive history presented. All absurdly simple—
killing infection, after all, is not brain surgery.

Still, this case was very advanced and the patient
not at all likely to survive it. "About payment," I said.

The necessary transaction was concluded, the patient desperate and making no demur at my exorbitant
rate. It's the very best time to ask for your fee—wait
until after the cure and they haggle or fail to survive,
which is the ultimate negotiating ploy.

Quarble and I continued, perceiving all the data
now spread across the perception-rendering screen on
one of my force terminals, expanded out to the size
of a galaxy itself. Every bit of datum required there

for our instant reference. Well, at least I understood it—you never knew with Quarble, but he did surprise me at times.

"Bad, Doc, bad," he actually whispered. "Worse, the worst I've ever seen.

"Yes," I said just as quietly, "in fact, I've only seen or heard of one case with a greater infection."

"Who? Who?"

"In a body we dissected in medical school. Already long dead, of course, and the Life that caused it, too. But you could see how it ravaged her before she succumbed. Nasty little buggers, Life!"

"Fast, fast, Doc. Hard to stomp them!"

Quarble, as usual, was stating the obvious.

As I flexed my manipulator fields and prepared for surgical entry into the patient, I reflected on the real problem we face in fighting infection, speed! Life is quick. The time scales they operate on are far more compressed than ours . . . Living for hundreds of billions of their years, we tend to move and think a good deal slower then them. When means Life can explode into existence and become technologically advanced in what to us true beings is little more than a short nap. A mere blink to us is hundreds of years for them. We must be ever vigilant to avoid such infections. My patient was not and is now paying that price.

"My brain is SPLITTING, Doctor!" he moaned. "Do SOMETHING!"

Yes, therein lies the problem Life causes us. When they become sufficiently advanced, they devise methods of traveling and communicating faster than light. This dirty little strain of Life called their FTL radio "Karsen waves"—after its discoverer. But the problem is that the esoteric wavelengths enabling this faster than light communication are the SAME as we think on. Life's inane and petty garble drives us crazy like—to use one of their own metaphors—a thousand heavy metal bands jamming all at once inside your brain with NO way of turning down the volume.

"DOCTOR!"

"Just a moment more," I said, projecting my most reassuring perceptions to him. "We are now starting the procedure. . . . Ah . . . You might want to brace yourself, this might hurt somewhat."

"You said it wouldn't."

I ignored him and turned my perception so that only Quarble was aware of it. Quarble has assisted me in many such procedures, albeit not on this scale. But, then, I had never been faced with such a massive case of infection myself. I quickly consulted the medical literature one more time, steeled myself, and slapped Quarble's limited attention over to the steps we would be following.

He was aghast. "Millions! Doc! Millions of super-novae!"

"Keep it down, Quarble," I admonished, then relented and explained. "His infection is too far advanced, we have to apply maximum force and quickly! Destroy all their major hives and breeding planets."

"It will kill him, Doc, kill him dead!"

"Very possibly," I agreed. "But what would you rather have, a patient—cadaver or otherwise—free of infection, or to have that infection escaping him and starting an epidemic, perhaps even infecting us."

"Burn him, Doc, burn him good!"

That Quarble, he's ever a realist.

"Attend closely now," I said, indicating the salient points to my treatment procedure. "And here we go. We start at what they call the Inner Frontier and work outward."

With an anticipatory grin of glee, I initiated the first supernova. "Sizzle, little Life, SIZZLE!"

To Quarble and I, these actions were close to instantaneous; to the Life units, it was a century or two.

"Look, Doc, look! They are escaping!"

With irritation, I realized Quarble was correct. The screen clearly showed a mass evacuation—millions of huge ships carrying billions of Life units. Scurrying away from the cleansing flame.

Well, we'd fix THAT.

I waved my perception over the screen, activating 10,000 supernovae at once.

"Yes, YES!" Quarble screamed in delight. "Burn them, Doc, burn them!"

The patient screamed as the pain of the Life units communicating increased in internal volume.

With sudden horror I perceived that the 10,000 supernovae were NOT occurring. "This is impossible," I said in disbelief, quickly checking the command I had issued. I had made no mistakes.

"Something's wrong, Doc, something's messed up, something's . . ."

I slam Quarble's dim mental presence aside as my fingers of perception fly over the screen trying this, trying that, performing all the emergency procedures in my long experience. NOTHING! The damn sequence has fizzled. Those slimy, slimy-miniscule-air-sucking-dirty-LITTLE Life units have somehow ABORTED my firing sequence.

"Oh, so we want to play games, do we?" I said, gritting the words out as I moved perceptions faster than I had in tens of billions of years.

"Here go," I said, "HUNDREDS OF MILLIONS of simultaneous supernovae!"

Yes, it would kill the patient, but it would end THIS Life infestation, that's for sure.

WHAM! Incredible pain coursed through my body and, judging by his screams, Quarble's as well.

We had failed . . . incredibly we had failed . . . and Life had struck back in a blow that left me weak and reeling and Quarble whimpering.

Time for desperate tactics! "You're going in, Quarble!" I said.

"NO!" he yelled in protest. "Not 'throw the dwarf' again!"

Despite all the heat of the moment, I could not help but smile—even Life units found throwing dwarves funny for some unknown reason. Well, let's see just how FUNNY they would find another galaxy avalanching through their own and destroying all stars, planets, and Life units in its path.

With a mighty PUSH, I launched the terrified and screaming Quarble on his way. Good-bye, Milky Way. Hello, milkshake!

Yet, my own horror suddenly grew as I saw Quarble being batted back toward me. It took all my strength to divert his hurtling body, sending it off in a safe tangent away from me. But while I was managing that, a cascade of energy hits me, my defenses are weakened, my body is being invaded!

In sheer desperation I called out for help to my fellow physicians.

Perhaps had I been nicer to them in the past and a bit less arrogant? They make no effort to save me. The quarantine walls go up quickly.

Inside, I feel the first stirrings of Life.

YOU

by Anonymous
(aka Stephen Leigh)

YOU WONDER ABOUT the title, but you start to read.

You also grimace a bit at the use of second person, thinking it both a bit awkward and pretentious, and you wonder if the author is trying to make you think *you* are the protagonist of the story, that this paragraph is referring to you personally.

It is.

Now, you read those words and you grimace again and give a little half-exasperated huff of air. Almost, you start to argue back to the page, denying it, and then you stop. And there's just the faintest, the *tiniest* bit of wonder, of something akin to hope—after all, you think, that would be interesting. That would be unusual. You can almost hear Rod Serling intoning the introduction for *The Twilight Zone*. You've always wanted something like that to happen to you, haven't you?

Well, you're right. These words are directed to *you*. Truly.

You're not quite certain how that could be. After all, there are thousands of copies of this book out there circulating and how could the story know that it's really *you* and not that overweight, balding programmer with a graying beard in the paper-stuffed apartment in Queens who's also currently reading this at the moment. But it *is* you, not him. Why would it be him? He's a loser. He hasn't had more than one date with a woman for three years, and even those single dates have been rare. He goes out to bars once a month or so hoping to get lucky, but his social skills, never very good, have atrophied even further since his job doesn't require him to actually hold a conversation with anyone, and so he usually ends wandering from circle to circle being ignored until closing time, and then going back to his room and popping one of his pornogrpahic DVDs into the player.

You're not him. In fact, he stopped reading at the porn reference, tossing the book across the room in angry and futile denial.

You think that's a rather harsh and brutal characterization (since you've known a few people who could fit that description) and you're somewhat annoyed at it, but though the description is rather on the cold side, it *is* accurate and besides, *you* didn't write it, so you don't need to feel responsible. Even Bob the programmer (hi, Bob—don't you love it when you see your name in print?), in those self-flagellating moments when he's alone in his apartment with only the blue light of his laptop's monitor illuminating the stacks of paperback books on his desk, would admit the truth in what you just read. It may soothe you to know that he'll pick up this story again, an hour from now. This time he'll finish it, wondering if he'll see himself again and perhaps a little envious that the story's for you, not him.

This story is for you.

You pause a moment, confused, because you're not used to a story interfering quite so directly. After all, this is genre fiction. Popular fiction, not some post-modern mainstream story. This is that "crazy sci-fi stuff." You read this type of anthology for escape and for that lovely "sense of wonder," not for pretension and experimentation. Over the years, you've slipped a thousand times between covers with sleek spaceships and square-jawed heroes, scantily-clad women and grotesque aliens slithering across a two-mooned landscape. You've lost yourself in a thousand worlds and glimpsed myriad universes painted in words garish or subtle, poetic or plain. You've allowed yourself to *be* the protagonist—any age, gender, or race—and you've bled and loved, triumphed or died everywhere from the medieval past to distant galaxies. You have the gift of imagination yourself—and that's why this story's for you. You can *become.*

You've read the books and watched the movies since you were a kid, and sometimes you've wondered how it would be if lights descended from the sky in front of you one night, whirling down to the lonely county road as you step from your car, drawn by mingled fear and curiosity, and then the side of the ship melts and there, in a rectangle of blinding light, *it* appears, the Other. You've *wanted* it to happen.

It's not going to, though. At least not that way. You know that; you realized long ago that any life that's out there is going to be so profoundly different from you that it may not even be recognizable. Even if it were, the Other's interests and values aren't going to be yours.

That's you, right? The one reading this?

You're still not convinced, though. Fine. *So convince me,* you think, even though at the same time the deeper skeptical part of you insists that it's not possible. And it's not. Not totally. This story could tell you that you lost someone close to you not all that long ago, and that you've kept a memento of them because it brings back the memories. That's the case, of course, and your eyes narrow again because the words have struck too close to home. You also know that it's exactly the kind of vague statement a supposed psychic would use in a cold reading, but . . .

You shiver, as if cold fingers just brushed your

spine. You wonder, as you have before, just who's having this one-sided conversation with you, and why. *So tell me,* you think, nearly saying the words aloud.

Fine. Here's why.

Elephants.

You almost laugh at that. But it's true. Remember that old elementary school 'mind trick' where someone says: "Think of anything you want, but just don't think of elephants." And as soon as they say that, you instantly can't think of anything *but* elephants. An entire herd of them go rampaging through your forebrain, trumpeting and ear-flapping, raising the dust from your cerebellum.

Here. Let's try it. Think of anything but parasites.

Ah, your eyebrows lifted at that, and my, the images in your head . . .

Parasites. You shift uncomfortably in your seat.

"What if . . . ?" That's the genesis of so much of the genre that you read, isn't it? "What if . . . ?" The author muses, and erects a plot from there. Here's one for you. What if a parasite wanted to enter the human mind: a sentient parasite, a very intelligent parasite? What would be an interesting reproductive strategy? Reproduction is just engaging in patterns, after all. DNA is an arrangement of simple genetic codes and yet it encompasses all the wild variety and complexity of life. And words . . . words are just an arrangement of simple letters. But my, how powerful they are in your head, in all their various wonderful combinations.

Words are a conduit into your mind. Words are embedded so deeply in your thought processes that you can't even imagine the world without them. If someone—or something—wanted to control you, they would use words, wouldn't they? Why, with just the right, compelling pattern of words, your mind would open like a raw wound and who knows what could slither in . . .

So don't think of elephants, no matter what.

Too late.

You've heard of all those stories that change your life, that stay with you forever. It just happened.

For you. Just for you.

You deny it, but even though you take the page in your fingers, ready to turn to the next story, you wonder. You think to yourself that once the page turns you'll forget all this; that a week, a month, a year from now you won't even recall having ever read this.

Oh, you'll remember. At this point, you don't have a choice. It's already started, inside. You squint and you deny, but you'll remember because everything from here on has changed for you. You have the words inside you now, and you won't like where they take you. When *I* take you. But you'll remember.

Won't you?

ME

by Mike Resnick

IN THE BEGINNING I created the heavens and the Earth.

Well, not really. That's just folklore. In point of fact I'm a fourth-level apprentice Star Maker, and my assignment was to create a nebula out in the boonies, so to speak. Nothing special; I won't be qualified for Advanced Creating for eons yet.

So they called it the Milky Way, which struck me as myopic at best, since I made a lot more red and blue stars than milky white ones. And for the longest time this particular race, which calls itself Man, thought it was at the center of all creation. (Actually, the mollusks that dwell in the oceans of Phrynx, seven billion light-years away, are at the center of all creation, but let it pass.)

Anyway, this ugly little race soon covered the entire planet, which was not really what I had in mind when I built the place—I've always had soft spots for the koala bear and the gnu—and before long these annoying bipeds got notions above and beyond their station and actually declared that they were created in *my* image. As if I would settle for only two eyes, or teeth that decayed, or an appalling lack of wings.

The nerve of these creatures is amazing. They feel

that if they implore me to intervene in their lives, everything will turn out well. They call it praying; me, I call it *nagging*.

Their science is as twisted as their religion. For the longest time they believed that the dinosaurs died out because they were too dumb and slow to survive. Can you imagine that? The average allosaur or Utahraptor could give Carl Lewis a 60-yard head start and still beat him in a 100-yard race.

And then there was all the excitement over Isaac Newton's three laws. You think a stegosaur or even a wooly mammoth couldn't get hit on the head ten or twelve times by falling apples and conclude that apples fall *down* rather than *up?* I mean, how the hell bright did Newton have to be, anyway? Every animal I ever created except Man figured out very early on that the intelligent thing to do is to not stand under trees that possess ripe fruits or inconsiderate birds.

But then—you're never going to believe this—they change their minds and decide that what really killed the dinosaurs was a fluke of chance, a stray comet that crashed into the planet 65 million years ago. Now remember, this is a race that believes in predestination, in reincarnation, in prayer, in ghosts and Santa Claus and the tooth fairy, in all things supernatural. And yet when they finally get proof of a power greater than their own—I threw the asteroid at a Tyrannosaur in the Yucatan in a fit of pique after it ate my favorite slippers—they absolutely refuse to accept it. No, it couldn't possibly be due to an all-powerful alien being who might or might not answer to the name of God, it had to be a stray comet from the Oort Cloud. Like, who the hell do they think *created* the Oort Cloud in the first place? I'd have been happy to use a comet, but it just so happened that I was in the system and an asteroid was much handier.

Oh, well, no one ever said intelligence was a survival trait.

You wouldn't think one race could be so contradictory. They kill the man they call the Prince of Peace, and then they hand out these million-dollar peace prizes in the name of the guy who invented dynamite. When they go to war, they actually believe they're slaughtering each other in *my* name, as if with 127 billion worlds to tend I give a damn who wins each little battle they fight.

Still, you have to admire certain aspects of their character.

For example, when I manifested my presence on Grybyon II, every last inhabitant keeled over and died from the sheer thrill of meeting their maker. Yet the last time I set foot on Earth, I was immediately panhandled by three grifters along Fifth Avenue, mugged in a back alley off 49th Street, and given free tickets to Letterman. When I explained that I was a fourth-level Star Maker, the few people who were paying attention immediately wanted to know what the job paid and if medical benefits were included. Finally I decided to lower myself to their comprehension level and announced in front of nine Men that I was God. Five of them called me a liar, two more said they were atheists and therefore I couldn't exist and I was probably just a manifestation of Buddha, the eighth claimed it was a Republican trick, and the ninth wanted to know what I had against the Chicago White Sox.

There are millennia when I feel like I just want to throw everything back into the primal soup and start all over again. Then I remember that it's just the one mistake I made, this race of Man, that's giving me fits, and that the rest of the galaxy's shaping up really well.

In fact, my Instructor gave me a B-minus, which isn't bad considering this is only my second galaxy. I really wanted to add a third spiral arm, but for some reason he insisted that galaxies have to be bilaterally symmetrical.

I'm especially proud of the Brilx Effect, which you can still see from any spot in the galaxy. I got an A

for concept, an A-minus for artistic visualization, but
he gave me only a D-plus for execution when he found
out I wiped out seventy-three races when Brilx went
supernova.

He likes the black hole at the center. It gives everything balance, he says, and utilizes a certain felicity of
visual expression. I hope he never finds out that I
created it because I'd used up all my building materials out on the Rim.

He never quite understood the Greater and Lesser
Magellenic Clouds. How could he? He wasn't around
the afternoon I ate all that bad chili. Serves me right
for trying temporal food. I'd have dispersed the gas
clouds and saved myself millions of years of embarrassment and teasing by the other apprentices, but you
know the rules: you create it, you have to incorporate it.

Which brings me back to Man. I knew the moment
I set things in motion that eventually Man would
evolve, and while I couldn't foresee just how aggravat-
ing he would be, I know he wasn't going to rank up
there with my finer creations like the grubworm and
the amoeba. I tried to turn the place into a water
world and start over, but I'd only gotten forty days
into it when my Instructor made me stop and gave
me a long, boring lecture on planetary irrigation.

Then I figured, well, eventually Man's going to want
to reach the stars, and I decided to have pity on my
other creations and make it as difficult as possible for
him, so I got my Instructor's permission to move Sol
and its planets way the hell out on one of the spiral
arms. Until Man figures out how to break those ridiculous laws of relativity I saddled him with, I can't see
him reaching anything farther away than Alpha Cen-
tauri, and he's going to have more than his share of
difficulties communicating with the Chyksi that he
finds there. I mean, what do you say to five different
genders of two-mile-long fur-covered snakes whose

sole topics of conversation are local politics and how to avoid friction burns?

I'm sorry to be writing this so slowly, but I'm receiving an average of sixteen prayers a nanosecond, almost all of them from Earth. I get so tired of this what-have-you-done-for-me-lately attitude. I mean, if it weren't for my subtle backstage manipulations, Man still wouldn't have Muenster cheese, or electric toothbrushes, or mascara, or unsecured hedge funds. But do they thank me for all this wealth of treasure? No, it's "Make my pimples go away" and "Make Anaconda Copper go up seven points" and "Kill the Israelis" and "Kill the Palestinians" and "Find me the perfect woman and make sure she's not looking for the perfect man." And I know that no matter what I do, there'll be five billion new requests tomorrow.

Why can't they be more like the Kabroni of Beta Calpurnicus III? "Thanks for the beautiful sunset, God." "Hey, God, we really like that new mountain range." "God old buddy, can you make any more exotic dancers like Mol Kwi Kchanga? She's really neat!" They're such appreciative, easygoing folk, the Kabroni.

Not that I demand servility. Take the Budubudu of Naboodi. "Hey, if you're listening, buzz off and leave us alone." "We didn't need you way back when, and we don't need you now." "Show up and we're gonna have roast Star Maker for dinner." Okay, they're hardly worshipful, but on the other hand, I only hear from maybe half a dozen of them on any given day.

Anyway, my Instructor says that we'll let this galaxy play out for a few billion years, and if Man doesn't spoil everything, my next assignment will be a much larger, more complex nebula cluster four vibratory levels removed from here, and that I'll get to use really interesting building blocks, like heavy metals and egg whites and just about anything I can think of. My life-forms won't have to be carbon-based, and my first task will be to make a race of crystalline methane breathers who won't shatter the first time I get annoyed and yell at them. (Yeah, I had a little problem on a frigid world out by Aldebaran. I'm not allowed to play with methane anymore without supervision. I still say it wasn't my fault. All I did was sneeze.)

The other day I asked him if this time I could create a race that really *was* in my image, and he just looked at me for the longest time and then burst out laughing. I guess that meant No.

I don't know why not. I think I'm exceptionally handsome, especially compared to the other apprentices. All fourteen limbs are in fine proportion, I have eyes and ears everywhere, wings for every conceivable type of atmosphere, extraordinarily cute dimples, and a fine rich baritone voice when I sing in the shower. A race could do a lot worse than be created in my image. All right, so I don't have any nostrils and my feet have opposable thumbs (a feature I borrowed for the chimpanzee and the gorilla)—but consider the advantages of never having a stuffed nose again, and think of the savings on shoes. And if they don't like the warts, they can have them burned off (a process *I* allowed them to invent.)

Not only that, but we're smart. I doubt that a single member of my race ever flunked trigonometry or formal dancing. How's *that* for bright? Okay, so most of us don't get passing grades in Keynesian economics, but what do you have to know about Keynes to make change? I can read an entire library in a single night. ("There's a difference between reading and *comprehending*," says my Instructor smugly. Hell, I'll bet *he* flunked Keynesian economics, too.)

No, when all is said and done, my race is clearly the finest-looking, brightest, and most admirable in the universe. It's simply no contest.

Damn. Since writing that last sentence, I just got a new prayer in from some kid in Mexico City. Begins the usual way: "Dear God, how are you? I am fine. I hate to bother you, this is not for me, but I have this friend, I won't tell you his name, who has a hard time scoring with girls, and I wonder if you could give me some words of heavenly wisdom to pass on to him."

Pretty usual up to that point. But then came the clinker: "While I've got your attention, I have a question for you. All my life my mother and father and priest have been telling me that God made me, and I don't have any serious problem with that. But if you made me, maybe you could tell me: who made you? Yours truly, Manual Acaro."

I *hate* questions I can't answer. Okay for you, kid. Let me see: Manual Acaro. That's six letters and five, right? All right, Manual Acaro, Mexico City gets a 6.5 Richter earthquake tomorrow morning.

Bother me again and I'll give you hives. How's *that* for a manifestation of Godly power?

Sometimes I really wonder where this arrogant self-centered race gets all its petty annoying tendencies from, anyway.

CJ Cherryh
Classic Series in New Omnibus Editions

THE DREAMING TREE
Contains the complete duology *The Dreamstone* and *The Tree of Swords and Jewels*.   0-88677-782-8

THE FADED SUN TRILOGY
Contains the complete novels *Kesrith*, *Shon'jir*, and *Kutath*.   0-88677-836-0

THE MORGAINE SAGA
Contains the complete novels *Gate of Ivrel*, *Well of Shiuan*, and *Fires of Azeroth*.   0-88677-877-8

THE CHANUR SAGA
Contains the complete novels *The Pride of Chanur*, *Chanur's Venture* and *The Kif Strike Back*.
0-88677-930-8

ALTERNATE REALITIES
Contains the complete novels *Port Eterntiy*, *Voyager in Night*, and *Wave Without a Shore*   0-88677-946-4

AT THE EDGE OF SPACE
Contains the complete novels *Brothers of Earth* and *Hunter of Worlds*.   0-7564-0160-7

To Order Call: 1-800-788-6262

C.S. Friedman

The Best in Science Fiction

Julie E. Czerneda

Web Shifters

OTHERLAND

TAD WILLIAMS

"The Otherland books are a major accomplishment."
–Publishers Weekly

"It will captivate you."
–Cinescape

In many ways it is humankind's most stunning achievement. This most exclusive of places is also one of the world's best-kept secrets, but somehow, bit by bit, it is claiming Earth's most valuable resource: its children.

CITY OF GOLDEN SHADOW (Vol. One)
0-88677-763-1

RIVER OF BLUE FIRE (Vol. Two)
0-88677-844-1

MOUNTAIN OF BLACK GLASS (Vol. Three)
0-88677-906-5

SEA OF SILVER LIGHT (Vol. Four)
0-75640-030-9

To Order Call: 1-800-788-6262